HOLLYWOODLAND

The anguish in her face even stopped the patrolmen, their clubs dropping harmlessly to their sides, their mouths gaping as she ran between them into the gang of Zoot-suiters . . .

From the forest of the bizarrely dressed gang gunshots rang out, the loud metallic claps reverberating in the intersection. The two men chasing Barbara Carr reeled backward, the impact of bone-smashing bullets knocking them onto hard pavement . . .

Fuss gazed down at one of the bullet-riddled men sprawled at his feet. The man's dark suitcoat flared open at his sides like the spread wings of a dying bird of prey, a coursing red glow of blood soaking around the exposed gold badge pinned to the rayon lining of the coat. Three letters on the badge's elaborate engraving could barely be made out in the swirl of the neon-bright night: FBI.

Thomas Sanchez

Hollywoodland

MAGNUM BOOKS
Methuen Paperbacks Ltd

A Magnum Book

HOLLYWOODLAND

ISBN 0 417 05350 9

First published in the United States 1978
by E. P. Dutton Inc., under the title *Zoot-Suit
Murders*
Magnum edition published 1981

Copyright © 1978 by Thomas Sanchez

Magnum Books are published by
Methuen Paperbacks Ltd
11 New Fetter Lane, London EC4P 4EE

Made and printed in Great Britain by
Richard Clay (The Chaucer Press) Ltd,
Bungay, Suffolk

1

he Zona Roja was blacked out. The hysterical pitch of an air-raid siren wailed down the crowded street. Neon signs above stores and clubs went dead. Oscar Fuss tried to keep his team of teenage boys together on the sidewalk, screaming commands in the hot night air as he pushed them against the wall of Club Bongo, trying to keep them from being knocked to the pavement by running sailors. Fuss knew he had made a mistake, but he couldn't disappoint the boys. He had promised them Cokes if they won the ball game against Pico Rivera. He didn't plan on the game going till dark, having to herd his victorious team through a blackout just to get to the soda fountain at Ortega's White Owl Drugstore. In the street, cars with headlights blinded by black tape honked furiously at people trying to dodge between them. Only the forms of thick-waisted women did not move, their shadows lounging against open doorways. Fuss looked anxiously to the cloudless sky. In the sudden darkness distant stars glittered in his strained gaze like a million bomber planes invading Los Angeles from infinity. "Cruz!" Fuss lunged for one of his boys slammed to the pavement by a sailor. The boy was scrambling to his feet, trying to grab the fleeing sailor's pants leg. Fuss pulled Cruz up, pinning his struggling body to a wall, yelling into his face above the sound of the siren, "Don't bitch it up! No fights with sailors! You promised!" The hundred-pound weight of Cruz's body strained like one uncontrollable manic muscle beneath Fuss's grip. "Don't bitch it up!" As suddenly as the siren's song of fear had begun, it stopped. The sound of another siren huffed in staccato bursts from the cement needle crown of City Hall blocks away. Fuss anxiously counted his boys along the wall, tapping the baseball cap of each as he ran down the line. All nine were there; his team was intact. The blackout drill was over.

The Zona Roja lit up. Neon lights down the distance of the chaotic street flashed irregularly to life. Electric current flowed in garish colors through letters on pretentious marquees that jutted over cluttered sidewalks, blinking urgent messages:

CLUB COOCH-COOCH CLUB COOCH-COOCH CLUB COOCH-COOCH!
GALS! POOL! POKER! PINBALL! GALS! GALS! GALS!!!
AWOL CLUB AWOL CLUB AWOL CLUB AWOL CLUB AWOL CLUB!

From inside clubs and bars Frank Sinatra's crooning voice, gay strumming of Mexican guitars, and the fierce lament of Benny Goodman's clarinet blared from jukeboxes, competing with the clanging bells of pinball machines. Fuss tried to move his team of boys through the maze of sailors choking all pathways to Ortega's White Owl Drugstore on the distant corner. He didn't want the boys to get caught in the net of drunken sailors jostling them. The thick-waisted women with tight side-buttoned skirts made loud kissing sounds with their bright puckered lips. "Chico, chico, chico!" Fuss pushed the boys away from the laughing women to the edge of the sidewalk, elbowing a path between dark blue forms of several vomiting sailors. Flashing red lights of a Shore Patrol jeep whipped across the faces of Fuss's boys as he herded them to the intersection blocked by two sailors locked in drunken combat, each clutching the brown neck of a beer bottle in one hand and the neck of his partner in the other. The sailors grunted and shoved each other back and forth, banging against honking cars, oblivious to helmeted Shore Patrolmen jumping from the jeep. From both sides of the street, gangs of teenagers screamed encouragement, booing and hissing as the Shore Patrolmen tried to break up the drunken dance, wedging long clubs between the furious-faced brawlers. The shouts and taunts from the two gangs clashed over the heads of the fighting men, just as the Zoot suits they wore clashed in color and cut, broad-shouldered baggy coats of yellow and chartreuse draping below their knees, flared green and purple pants cuffed skin tight around ankles above oversized waxed shoes. Fuss tried to get his boys past one shouting gang that was blocking the entrance to Ortega's Drugstore. A great whoop arose across the street from another gang, standing like an impenetrable forest of outrageously clothed trees around the short fat pumps of the Signal Gasoline Station. The whooping converged from both sides of the street as Shore Patrolmen clubbed the two sailors until they staggered away from one another, stunned and bleeding. Fuss broke his way through the cheering gang before the drugstore, their eyes excited beneath the slouch of wildly colored hats, as Shore Patrolmen pulled the sailors into the glare of red light, handcuffing them together like an improbable pair of doomed lovers. Fuss was astonished at how the young sailors looked exactly like his brother the day he went into the Navy, totally bewildered. He turned back to his team of boys, pushing them through swinging doors into the safety of the drugstore. The Shore Patrolmen were no longer concerned with the subdued sailors. They confronted the two wildly dressed gangs challenging them with angry stabs of Spanish taunts. The patrolmen's clubs swung nervously at their sides as they stalked along the edge of the crowded sidewalks like lion tamers backing off a dangerous beast.

Fuss had pushed the last one of his boys into the drugstore when he heard a new sound that made him shove his way back into the crowd. The scream of a woman was almost lost in the overwhelming blast of car horns. Suddenly the woman appeared, running, dodging between cars. Fuss thought he recognized her, her blond hair twisted and bent in a bizarre ring of curls around her exhausted face, her screams turning to a distinct, terrifying plea. "God's sake! Someone!" Two men zigzagged through the cars behind her, the leather of their shoes slapping against pavement, breath bursting from their lungs in short angry grunts, their bodies heavy and sweating beneath their suitcoats as they closed on her. She ran into the intersection, the horror in her face caught in the whipping red lights of the jeep. The patrolmen turned from the shouting gangs on the sidewalk, trapping the woman in the cleared intersection. She stopped, caught between patrolmen with menacing clubs and the two men about to grab her. "Someone! I'm being kidnapped!" Fuss recognized the theatrical twist of fear in her face. He knew who she was: the movie star Barbara Carr. He tried breaking through the crowd to save her. The intensity of her screams stunned the crowd to immobility. Fuss could not break through. The anguish in her face even stopped the patrolmen, their clubs dropping harmlessly to their sides, their mouths gaping as she ran between them into the gang of Zoot-suiters clustered around the pumps of the gasoline station. From the forest of the bizarrely dressed gang gunshots rang out, the loud metallic claps reverberating in the intersection. The two men chasing Barbara Carr reeled backward, the impact of bone-smashing bullets knocking them onto hard pavement.

The crowd Fuss was pushing against suddenly gave way. Screaming people struggled in wild knots of panic as they tried to run from the scene. Fuss got to Barbara Carr, her hands tearing into her blond curls as she tried to protect herself from the gunshots still thundering in her head. Fuss grabbed her, trying to shelter her from the stampeding crowd. At both ends of the street, paddy wagons of Shotgun Squad cops were unloading. Barbara Carr's terrified eyes stared directly into Fuss's eyes, her fingers flying up, the nails digging into Fuss's cheeks as he screamed at her, "Barbara! You're safe now!" The pain in Fuss's torn face broke his hold on her and she twisted free. A redheaded woman appeared from behind the pumps of the gasoline station and grabbed Barbara Carr, slapping her face until the sobbing turned to whimpering and she collapsed into the safety of the redhead's arms.

Shotgun Squad cops blocked all possible escape from the street, handcuffing Zoot-suiters trapped in the crush of the crowd. Fuss could see his boys inside Ortega's, their shocked faces pressed to the plate-glass window. Between the abandoned gasoline pumps, a lone man knelt, chalking a white circle around a .45 caliber gun lying on the pavement where only minutes before the Zoot-suiters had stood.

Fuss gazed down at one of the bullet-riddled men sprawled at his feet. The man's dark suitcoat flared open at his sides like the spread wings of a dying bird of prey, a coursing red glow of blood soaking around the exposed gold badge pinned to the rayon lining of the coat. Three letters on the badge's elaborate engraving could barely be made out in the swirl of the neon-bright night: FBI.

2

The Hollywood Stars were cold as ice. The afternoon sun was blistering. The field grass was withered yellow. Fuss steamed beneath his shirt and tie. The San Francisco Seals were hot. Fuss was going to lose his bet with Wino Boy. Angel Parra was burnt out. Across the dusty diamond, in the bleachers high above the Seals' dugout behind third base, Fuss saw the man he was waiting for. Fuss did not signal the man; he turned in his hard seat and shouted at the pitcher, "Come on, Angel, throw the Seal a spit! He can't hit! Throw him a spitter!" Angel's pitch went wild and was called ball four. Fuss kept shouting more encouragement at the young pitcher, even though he knew it was hopeless. The Stars were cold as ice and the sun was getting hotter.

The man Fuss was waiting for worked his way around

the stadium through half-empty wooden bleachers; no one paid him any attention. The twelve-year-old peanut vendor spotted the man and ran toward him, but the man brushed the boy aside, walking on, adjusting his dark glasses, pulling the bill of a Hollywood Stars' baseball cap further down over his face, walking blindly to Fuss's box seat.

"What took you so long, Senator?" Fuss asked the question without looking at the man slipping across the paint-peeled bench and sitting so close to him their shirt sleeves almost touched.

From behind thick lenses of dark sunglasses Senator Kinney's eyes were fixed out on the pitcher's mound as Angel threw down his mitt and walked disgustedly off the field toward the dugout. "What's wrong with Angel, Fuss? Something sure is eating him. This just isn't the kind of squared-away team it was last month. No way they can go for the pennant now. The Beavers are sure to murder them next week in Portland."

"His brother was killed, Senator."

Kinney lowered his glasses a crack below his gray eyes; Fuss could see wrinkled lines of disbelief running up from the top of his blunt nose into the sweating forehead.

"Guadalcanal, Senator. His brother was one of the boys killed there. They didn't find his body for four days. Buried in a bomb crater under twelve other marines. Four days to find his body and six months to notify his family."

Kinney shoved the glasses tight against his eyes. "Fucking Nips."

"Fucking war."

Kinney watched Angel walk slowly from the dugout and take up a bat, swinging it viciously at something invisible and menacing in the air. "How can the guy even play?"

"Why did you summon me to testify before a session of the committee next week?"

"Information. We want information."

□ 7

"Everything I can possibly say about the situation is public record. I already told everything I knew at the Zoot-suit preliminary hearing weeks ago, Senator. If you bring me out into daylight like this, it won't be safe for me in the Barrio." Fuss looked over his shoulder to see if anyone had slipped into the empty seat behind him. He lowered his anxious voice. "What new information could I possibly give you in public that would be worth risking the setup we have going? It's crazy, an undercover agent testifying to his own bosses."

"Not you." Kinney watched Angel chop air at a ball high and outside for strike three, throwing the bat against the wire mesh of the backstop to the boos of the crowd. "We want information on the redhead, Kathleen La Rue, the one who was there the night of the FBI killings."

"What could La Rue know?"

"We want her to be there when you testify. With you being called to testify before us, she will never suspect who you work for. We've got an angle on her and want you to investigate."

Fuss slipped a stick of Juicy Fruit gum from his pocket, scraping tinfoil off the wrapper and rolling it into a bright silver ball. He flicked the silver ball angrily onto the playing field as the third Star struck out, the sound of the umpire's voice rising above the hissing crowd, "Steeeeeeriiiiiiike!"

The muscles in Fuss's cheeks coiled nervously from his jaw, working at the stick of gum. "Why didn't you tip me to the situation instead of hitting me cold with a subpoena?"

"We couldn't take a chance on not going through regular channels to subpoena you. We want you normal, above suspicion."

"You don't believe this Mankind Incorporated outfit she's head of in the Barrio is a Sinarquista front? The Sinarquistas are heavy-handed Fascists; they aren't interested in having a white girl who speaks barely passable high school Spanish front for them. They want the Zoot gangs, that's who they're after. The Fascists always develop from the bottom, from the street gangs up."

"We think she's something. FBI ran a report. She's clean. Too clean. Born in San Francisco, a bright girl, only child, went to college at Berkeley, graduated summa cum laude. You tell me why an educated girl from a rich family would join Mankind Incorporated."

"She's probably sexually frustrated. Frustrated females are impossible to figure. La Rue believes this Mankind Incorporated business about a superhuman race of metallic-headed men who will liberate mankind. Let her have her fantasy. Why waste our time?"

"Hey! He struck him out! See that, Angel struck the Seal out!"

Fuss stared blankly at the cursing batter. He tried to control the anger in his voice, irritated he couldn't shout his opinions at Kinney. "The cops shook La Rue down after the FBI shootings. They couldn't pin a thing on her with those murders. Just some dumb woman out to save the world from itself. So what's new?"

"The LA police didn't find any fingerprints on the gun that murdered the two FBI agents in the Zona Roja."

"No fingerprints doesn't prevent the court from trying to pin the murders on twelve Zoots not much older than eighteen. They'll get the electric chair if convicted." Fuss stopped chewing and rammed the wedge of gum up under his top lip. He looked like he had just been slugged in the mouth. "You don't believe La Rue killed those two agents. La Rue couldn't even lift a .45 magnum. I doubt she could punch her way out of a paper bag. If she fired the .45 that night, it would have knocked her off her feet. I saw her at the Zoot-suit hearing; she can't weigh more than a hundred pounds when she's soaking wet."

"Anything's possible in wartime, Fuss. These could be Fascists in Mankind Incorporated we're dealing with."

"Then I'll investigate her, but I don't believe she's a . . ."

"It's not your job to *believe* anything." Kinney's voice rose as he clamped his fist around the rusted iron-bar railing in back of the empty seat before him. He looked nervously over his shoulder to see if anyone had heard his loud words. He lowered his voice to almost a whisper. "I can't sit around and argue the point, Fuss. I've got to get back up to Sacramento for a hearing in the morning on whether or not to lock up Italians living along the coast, same way we did with Jap sympathizers. Any of these foreigners could be a spy. It's okay for America to be a melting pot during peacetime, but right now you can't trust your own mother."

"I just don't believe La Rue's a killer."

"And Chamberlain didn't believe Hitler would invade Poland." Kinney turned the glare of his sunglasses on Fuss, his mouth puckered into an ironic smile. He stood up to the organ music blaring over the loudspeakers for the seventh-inning stretch, his last words barely discernible as he walked quickly away. "There are political enemies in the Barrio, Fuss, and if you don't find them, they'll find you."

3

Fuss couldn't tell if the distant, high-pitched wail outside the closed and locked window was an air-raid siren or a police siren. He turned back from the window, squirming around in his chair to meet the intent gaze of Senator Kinney standing before him in a heavy tweed suit. "My name, Senator? You want my full name?"

Kinney thumbed the lapels of his tweed coat, as if trying to flick off some bugs invisible to everyone but him. "Yes, would you please state to this committee your full name, age, and nationality?"

"Fuss, Oscar James. Thirty-three. American."

"Occupation?"

Fuss glanced down at the worn soles of his beat-up wing-tipped shoes. "Social worker in east Los Angeles."

Kinney walked to the window and turned his back to it, blocking the square of blue sky outside the small room. "If you will be so patriotic as to answer the questions we four gentlemen put to you about the recent murders in east Los Angeles" he nodded to the men seated at the long table before Fuss, "I'm certain you will render your country service beyond simply working with unfortunate Mexican-Americans. You must keep in mind, however, this is a closed-door hearing on un-American activities constituted by the California State Legislature. As long as you answer truthfully about the terrible night in question, you personally have nothing to fear."

Fuss smiled at the silent, stern-faced men rowed before him, unmoving and uncomfortable in hard-backed chairs. "I have a question, gentlemen."

"Yes?" Kinney folded his arms and leaned forward.

"Since this is not a court of law, do you mind if I have a piece of gum? You see, my mouth gets dry when I'm in a nervous situation like this and I . . ."

"Yes, go on, have some." Kinney unconsciously thumbed his lapels again.

"One other thing." Fuss slipped a stick of Juicy Fruit into his mouth and chewed noisily. "What is an un-American activity?"

"An un-American activity, Mr. Fuss," Kinney held the palms of his hands up like he was reading from a book, "is any attack on the constitution of California or the United States."

"Good." Fuss balled the gum wrapper between his fingers. "In that case I will tell you everything you want to know."

"That's patriotic. We are at war both abroad and at home. As you know, murder is not a pretty issue; political murder is the most ugly." Kinney let the smile on his face play itself out into an expression of disgust, then sat down at the long table with the other three men. "Assemblyman Burns, would you like to proceed with the witness?"

Burns's fingers adjusted his bowtie like it was a microphone. His voice boomed in the small room. "Mr. Fuss, do you have a younger brother, Marvin Fuss, a boatswain's mate first class on the U.S. aircraft carrier *Lipscomb Bay?*"

"Yes, sir. Marvin's somewhere near the Philippines now, I think. The government censor always cuts out any direct reference Marvin makes to where he is in his letters."

"Does Marvin know the nature of your occupation?"

"He knows I'm a social worker in the Barrio. He thinks it's a waste of time."

"Do you know the twelve Mexican Zoot-suiter youths who murdered the two FBI agents?"

"Every one, but they aren't Mexican; most were born in Los Angeles. I've worked with their families. They accept me. So far as I know they aren't guilty of murder, only *accused.* I don't know why the press keeps talking about the 'Zoot-Suit' murders."

"We did not call you here to editorialize on the press, Mr. Fuss, just answer the questions. Do you know Kathleen La Rue?"

Fuss turned uneasily in the chair, his shoulders slumping beneath the padded shoulders of his faded sport coat. His embarrassed gaze went to the woman sitting with her lawyer by the door. "Yes, sir, I believe that's Miss La Rue right there."

"And what does Miss La Rue do for a living?"

"She came into the Barrio several months ago. From what I understand she is an apostle of Mankind Incorporated."

"Excellent. Do you know the movie star Barbara Carr?"

"No. Until that night in the Barrio, I knew her only from her films, and from articles I read about her in Hedda Hopper's gossip columns."

"Can you tell us what happened that hot August night in the Barrio? Why you were there, exactly what you witnessed?"

Fuss couldn't take his eyes off Kathleen La Rue. She was such a thin, odd woman, not nervous, but seeming to burn with a strange energy, energy not only fueling her existence but consuming her at the same time. Her face was pale, so ghostly white it made the wild curls of her red hair appear even redder, like the sudden dazzling crimson of ignited road flares in the night. The top three buttons of her flowery cotton dress were left carelessly open, exposing a quick, tapping pulse in the center of her white throat. The heat of the stuffy room brought only the slightest trace of sweat along the soft white down above the lipstick of her upper lip. She looked like she was about to faint.

"Mr. Fuss, are you going to answer this committee's questions?"

"Oh, yes, Assemblyman Burns." Fuss forced his eyes away from Kathleen La Rue. He turned and tried to focus his attention on the Assemblyman. "Yes, sir, I remember that night well. I had just finished over at Lincoln Park with my CYO boys, we were in the summer baseball playoffs against Pico Rivera. We won."

"CYO would be the Catholic Youth Organization?"

"Yes, teenage kids mostly."

"Some of these boys are related to the Zoot-suiters?"

"All of them; no one in the Barrio isn't." Fuss couldn't keep his attention on the Assemblyman. His gaze was pulled back to Kathleen La Rue, as if he had to answer the questions to her satisfaction. "I was walking some of the boys home on Flores Street; it was late, hot. That used to be a good street before the war, a nice neighborhood before it became the Zona Roja. Now it's become dangerous, bars and clubs, young sailors prowling the streets for a good time. Not safe."

"Why would you expose teenage boys to such a scene if it's so dangerous?"

"Because the Barrio was crowded, one of those nights when everybody is out. People sitting on their front porches, men with their shirts off, women fanning themselves with newspapers, kids running everywhere, lots of noise, loud radios. There is always lots of noise in the Barrio, but for some reason that night seemed worse. I had promised the boys some cherry Cokes if we won the game with Pico Rivera. All the soda fountains were closed except the one at Ortega's White Owl on Flores. I couldn't disappoint the boys."

"So you risked their lives in the Zona Roja?"

"I just thought we could get down Flores very fast. How was I to know we'd get caught in an air-raid drill? Maybe I wasn't thinking straight. There was a Santa Ana blowing, you know, the hot wind we get from the Mojave Desert. Everything seemed dusty, hazy sort of. After the blackout we continued to the intersection at Orange Street, where two sailors were fighting. The Zoots were hanging around on their usual street corners enjoying the fight, the two gangs, the Mateo Bombers in front of the Signal Gas Station and the Square Johns in front of Ortega's White Owl Drugstore. They had their Black Widows with them. All of them were shouting encouragement over the tops of cars to the fighting sailors."

"The Black Widows are the, ah, Zoots' women?"

"Yes, their girlfriends. They wear very tight black skirts. They can't walk fast in those skirts; their legs are in black net stockings. They wear all black, blouses, sweaters, everything. Only different color on them is the silver crucifixes hanging from long chains around their necks."

Burns cleared his throat, trying to dispel an image of crucifixes swinging between young breasts. He adjusted his bowtie like it was a knob turning up the volume of authority in his impatient voice. "Did you *see* Miss La Rue at the time?"

"Not then. Not till after."

"What happened next, as you approached the two Zoot gangs?"

"It was confusing, Assemblyman."

"But not so confusing you couldn't witness everything?"

"Everything." Fuss noticed Kathleen La Rue watching him, her eyes wide and brilliant, like she was taking flash pictures of his every expression, recording his every answer.

"Continue, Mr. Fuss. We haven't much time allowed here this afternoon. You are at the corner of Flores and Orange and the sailors are fighting."

"The Shore Patrol broke up the fight. Then I heard a woman screaming."

"You heard screaming before you saw the woman running?"

"I couldn't tell which direction the screams were coming from. There was lots of confusion because horns were honking. Then I saw the horns were honking because she had run into the street between cars trying to get through the intersection."

"Did you recognize the person running as the movie star Barbara Carr?"

"I didn't know who the person was at first, a blond woman running, screaming, two men chasing her. How could I tell who it was? Barbara Carr was the last person I expected to see in the Barrio on a Friday night."

"Could you make out anything she was screaming?"

"She was screaming she was being kidnapped."

Burns leaned quickly forward, as if he could hear screaming in the room. "What did she *exactly* scream?"

"What do you scream when you're being kidnapped?" Fuss felt the heat from Kathleen La Rue's flashing eyes upon him. She was making him feel like he was in a circus spotlight. "Barbara Carr was hysterically shouting for someone to save her."

"Did anyone try to help?"

"It was then I recognized just who she was. I was shocked. I tried to get to her. There wasn't time. It happened too fast. Cars skidding all over the place, people screaming and frightened. The two men were right behind Barbara Carr. She ran straight to the corner where the Mateo Bombers were hanging around the Signal Gas Station. She ran past the pumps for safety. She was only five feet from the Zoots when I heard the shots."

"How many shots?"

"Just the two. Carr stood there before the gang of Zoots, pressing her hands to her head in terror. The two men behind her were both on the ground, shot in their chests."

"Who shot them?"

"From where I was standing, I couldn't tell exactly *who.*"

"You saw the murder weapon?"

"After I ran over. I grabbed Carr. She was frantic, uncontrollable. I had to hold her down. She tore at my face, trying to get away, as if someone was after her. The gun was lying on the pavement by the gas pumps." Fuss stopped talking and stared down at the floor. Sprawled before his feet a man in a dark suitcoat lay dying; blood from a bullet hole in his chest seemed to float his body in a peaceful lake of red.

"At this time you also saw Miss La Rue?"

Fuss jerked up from the nightmare vision on the floor. "Yes, yes, she was right there. She was very courageous, slapping Carr's sobbing face, bringing her out of shock. Miss La Rue put her arms around Carr, stroked her head, comforting her."

"Where had Miss La Rue come from?"

"From behind the gasoline pumps. She's always in the Barrio hanging around the Zoots, trying to get them to come to her Mankind Incorporated meetings."

"Did the Zoots attempt to run away from the scene of the crime?"

"Most of them were as confused as the rest of us, running in circles. I remember seeing the leaders of the Mateo Bombers, Marco Delgado and his cousin Gus Melendez Delgado, trying to get away up Flores Street."

"And did these two Delgados escape?"

"No one got out of there. Within an instant, police cars had both ends of Flores blocked. There was a carload of Shotgun Squad cops. They got everything under control in minutes, holding shotguns on everybody until the homicide detectives arrived. Then I found out, when one of the detectives flipped open the coats of the two dead men. I saw the gold badges."

"What did you find out?"

"The two dead men were FBI agents."

Senator Kinney tipped his chair forward and nervously clicked his ballpoint pen closed. "Thank you, Mr. Fuss, you've been a most cooperative witness."

"One more moment of the witness's time, Senator, if you don't mind?" Burns stopped writing in his notebook and brought his eyes up to Kinney, the irritation in his voice unmistakable. "The purpose of this hearing is to ascertain facts. I have a final important matter."

Kinney leaned back in his chair and looked nervously at Fuss. "Your witness, Assemblyman."

"Mr. Fuss." Burns continued writing in his notebook. "Do you know who the Sinarquistas are?"

Fuss tried to avoid the nervous gaze of Kinney as he answered. "They are a political organization active in the Barrio."

"And what does this word mean, Sinarquistas?"

"Roughly translated, Assemblyman, it means *those without opposition.*"

"And what are the Sinarquistas opposed to?"

Fuss turned away from Kinney's nervous gaze and felt trapped as his eyes met those of La Rue. The blue brilliance of La Rue's open stare seemed to burn a circle around Fuss as he blurted his answer, "I guess the Sinarquistas are opposed to our American way of life."

Burns stopped writing, looked directly at Fuss, and straightened his bowtie. "Excellent."

4

The sun rising was no bigger than a baby's fist in the distance across the concrete Los Angeles horizon. From his window Fuss saw smokestacks of a sprawling tire plant far to the east, where washed-out gray stuccoed tenements on the flatlands blurred into more factories, one after the other, black columns of smoke pricking the blue-bellied morning from a forest of chimneys. He peeled a stick of Juicy Fruit and chewed it slowly, savoring the taste sweetly like it was the last meal of a condemned man. The palm trees swelling up from small squares cut into the cracked concrete sidewalk below always made him laugh. Tall and skinny, bent and bouncing in the wind, higher than the sun-blasted paint of the three-story walkup apartments lining his street. The brief green skirts of palm fronds at the very tops of high smooth trunks made the skinny trees look like swaying one-legged hula girls. The palms stood out almost self-consciously, as if aware they were destined to line some broad boulevard, not a run-down street crowded by ragged children and people unable to conceal desperation in their faces over where the next meal was coming from. Every day Fuss watched the desperation in the faces grow, until he couldn't look in a mirror without seeing the same expression curl down his lips, couldn't hide the glint of fear in his eyes —and he was in the Barrio by choice, not a proud man trapped by fate, like an elegant palm tree growing from a cracked sidewalk. The sound of wind playing through Fuss's dusty venetian blinds was startling, like a monkey rattling his cage for freedom. Fuss carefully unfolded the thin envelope of a red-white-and-blue V-mail letter. For the fourth time, he read the lines that hadn't been blacked out by the censor:

Hi Guy!
How goes it, guy? As you know I can't say where we are, but it's not downtown Tokyo. No action yet, guy. Just maneuvers every day. I still have those night-mares. You know? That the carrier takes a hot one off the port quarter from a Jap Zero and there's fire on the water and we have to jump for it. Terrible. Say, guy, can you send me one of those sexy Esquire Petty girl pictures? Rumor on the tub has it the old man's going to ban all pinups pretty soon. Sure would be a sight for sore eyes to have one of them Petty girls, all that black lace and white skin. I could use a real Betty Grable right now, though. I'd know what to do with her. Everything on this tub is rumor. Like the one Henry Fonda is going to visit the tub. Sure, a big movie star, some luck! Another rumor is there's a Shit-

ter on the tub. It would be just my luck if that rumor turned out to be true. Write to me, guy, I get lonely.

Your brother, Marvin

P.S. Have you started your Victory garden yet? Ha ha!

The long flat streets of the city were filthy. The streets were never really clean, but since Pearl Harbor there were always piles of trash blocking sidewalks, trash for the war effort: black bald automobile tires, mountains of old newspapers, boxes of metal bottle caps, old keys, locks, nylon stockings, everything imaginable that could be reincarnated as a uniform or a weapon. It took Fuss twenty minutes to walk the seventeen blocks downtown from his apartment, past empty padlocked storefronts in what was once Little Tokyo, with *NO JAPS WANTED! NIP LOVER! NISEI TRAITORS!* painted across boarded windows. The sidewalks were so cluttered by the chaos of collectibles to aid the war it was necessary to walk in the street and risk being hit by honking cars, drivers hurrying from the San Fernando Valley neighborhoods to work in war industry factories crowding the eastern flatlands of the city. On the wall of Paco's Supermercado two Civil Defense workers were scraping off words slashed in red paint the night before: *SINARQUISTAS POR LA RAZA!!!* At the corner of Orange and Flores streets a black billboard on top of Ortega's White Owl Drugstore spelled out in bold white relief: *DIALGOD.* Fuss turned the corner at Flores. Morning light threw singular shadows of shaky, drunken men standing idly for block after block in the debris of sidewalks. The forms of men leaning against storefronts gave the illusion that buildings along the entire street were supported by nothing more substantial than wobbling shadows.

"Compadre!"

Fuss shielded his eyes from the sun, trying to pick out

which of the long line of drunks had called his name. He kept walking.

"Compadre, que pasa?"

A short, dark man stumbled out from among the leaning shadows of a building, his worn boot heels catching the edge of the street gutter, pitching him face down on the pavement. No one moved to pick him up. Fuss ran into the street, holding a hand up to stop a car speeding around the blind corner. He pulled the man out of the gutter and supported him against the window of Ixatlan Cantina. A young waitress inside the restaurant ignored the two men as she propped a black slate against the inside of the window advertising the special lunch menudo.

"A case of Gallo! You owe me a case of Gallo Tokay, compadre."

Fuss brushed off the old man's torn jean jacket. "You're right, amigo. I owe you."

The old man's wrinkled hands were shaking; the brown eyes in the weary face seemed to be worn down to their final shine. "Señor Fussy, you owe. Angel was burnt out."

"Damn you, Wino Boy." Fuss shook his head and grinned sarcastically. "You knew his brother had been killed, that's why you laid that heavy bet on me." He reached inside his coat and pulled out a folded five-dollar bill, tucking it into the frayed pocket of Wino Boy's jacket. "I just hope you're sober enough to handle this. You might be so drunk already, you'll stumble into church and donate it to the poor box by mistake."

Wino Boy took Fuss's hand and held it solemnly like he was about to propose marriage. "Compadre, trust me. I know nothing about dead brothers, I just know bazebull." He tossed his head back, banging the windowpane and laughing long enough for Fuss to count the five decayed teeth left in his mouth. The girl inside the restaurant shook her fist.

Like a magician with an endless supply of white rabbits, Fuss slipped a hand inside his coat pocket and produced another neatly folded five-dollar bill.

"Compadre, que es?" Wino Boy stopped laughing. "You buying me *two* cases of the Tokay?"

Fuss glanced suspiciously up and down the street, then hunched his shoulders against the people passing by and spoke softly. "I want information. We speak only in English, otherwise someone might hear."

Wino Boy puffed up his chest. "Only in the English, my friend. There isn't no more than five people on the whole street who can speak it so good."

"What do you hear in the Barrio about Mankind Incorporated?"

"They are coco locos."

"In English, Wino Boy, English!"

"They are crazies in the heads."

"Do many people follow them?"

"Does the dog, she shits in the same hole twice?"

"If not many people follow them, why are they in the Barrio?"

"The same as the Catolicos, because the poor people be in the Barrio. Poor people will always be paying the money for the chance to be no poor people no more."

"Who is the Voice of the Right Idea?"

"He pretend he Cristo. But the people here, they no born stupid, they know better."

"The woman, the thin young one who says she is the head of Mankind Incorporated's Latin Service Bureau, what do you know about her?"

"You meaning the pretty one, the one with much hair the color of fire?"

"Yes."

"You meaning the pretty one with the little," Wino Boy cupped his shaking hands to his chest like he was carefully caressing two nice-sized peaches.

"Yes, I don't need you to go feeling her up. What do you know?"

Wino Boy pursed his lips and leaned against Fuss unexpectedly like he was going to give him a big kiss. "I giving you only the truths."

"Only the truths, or you can give me back the other fiver I gave you as well."

"Nada mas." Wino Boy shook his head slowly, then the worn shine of his eyes brightened. "Wait, I do know something. But how to say in the English. She's a sick one. The ones who cannot always breathe." He pounded his chest and coughed. "The ones not strong in the chest."

"You mean asthma? You mean to say Kathleen La Rue's an asthmatic?"

"Si." Wino Boy laughed mischievously and grabbed the five-dollar bill. "That's all I know!"

"Fat lot of good that kind of information does me. I could go up the street to Esteban's Barbershop and for two bits I could get the same information, plus a haircut, shine, and shave." Fuss turned disgustedly and walked away.

"Momento, compadre!" The urgent tone in Wino Boy's voice stopped Fuss in his tracks.

Fuss turned and walked back, standing close to Wino Boy's wrinkled face as he breathed in the sickly sweet odor of cheap wine. "You have something else?"

"Si, somethings you like knowing." Wino Boy smiled proudly. "I just get the V-mail from my grand-nino at Forts Lee. After cinco months they be promoting him to private. My Alejandro's going to be a *hen-ee-rahl* before Hitler's getting to kiss the Queen in Londres."

"Promoted to *private!*" Fuss shook his head in disbelief at the near toothless smile of the old man. "Jesus, Wino Boy, you're a real pill."

5

he voice was breathless, its soft tones carrying to the ceiling, caressing the gloss of green paint, undulating over long fingers of fluorescent lights spotted with fly specks. The cool flickering light played through the woman's shining red hair; fire-engine red lipstick gave the provocative pout of her mouth an unearthly appearance against the ghost white face. Her mouth seemed to have a life of its own. The woman's tortured breath snaked like smoke from a cave, her hesitating tongue glistened brightly while she struggled to bring her story clearly into the room, so even those in the distant rear could hear her wonders.

From his seat in the back pew of the room, Fuss cocked an ear to Kathleen La Rue's ethereal words, straining his right shoulder forward like a catcher waiting to take a tricky pitch.

He had heard her speak before, during the five-day preliminary hearing of the Zoot-suiters, but he had never really *listened* to her until this moment, never noticed the absolute blue of her eyes, like the dazzling crust of an ice pond reflecting its sheer blue vision of a winter sky. The fifty people crowded into the room seemed suspended on the slippery surface of La Rue's blue gaze, out on the dangerous middle of the ice pond, waiting for the net of her words to save them.

"Swiftly, and without effort, the two men climbed to the top of a mountain towering above the clouds." La Rue's words stopped, her thin chest heaving, as if she herself had just scaled the great heights of the pinnacle. Then her eyes widened in absolute wonder. "There, upon a vast plain far below the men, appeared an awesome sight. Behind a great impregnable wall lay a beautiful city of gracious homes, spacious gardens, schools, churches, shops, factories, stores, everything for happy and contented living. A large luminous sign floated celestially above this marvelous apparition: *THE CITY OF ETERNAL BROTHERHOOD*. Before the wall was a group of International Vigilantes making ready to swing back the great gates of the fabulous city to all humanity's bewildered and suffering masses." La Rue hesitated until the broken breath of her words could catch up with her wondrous vision. Suddenly, without warning, the brightness in her eyes faded, her gaze going to the back of the room, falling upon Fuss, filling with terror as she continued. "Advancing at fearful speed upon the city appeared an awful figure, an awesome Green Monster with blood-drenched hands, large glittering teeth, and terrible eyes breathing withering death and destruction, War. The Monster of War, accompanied by his followers Greed, Fear, Lust, Love of Money, Famine, Pestilence, was driving relentlessly on to keep the people from entering the City of Brotherhood."

Kathleen shifted her gaze from Fuss and looked directly at the old Mexican woman sitting alone in the front pew, her thin voice asking the old woman in horror, "Do you think those people can get the great gates of the city open?"

The old woman shook her head in a hard *no*.

"Who are those people at the great gates, banging desperately on the impregnable wall?" Kathleen's question went to every person in the room. She answered the blank looks. "They are Mr. and Mrs. Average Citizen. They are Mr. and Mrs. General Public, and they cannot open the gates to the City of Brotherhood. But" . . . she allowed the bright red of her lips to smile in recognition, "the people inside the city recognized those at the great gates as something beyond just being Mr. and Mrs. John and Jane Q. Public, for all those at the great gates were International Vigilantes, who wore proudly a badge upon their breast, a beautiful shining emblem that shielded them. It was deep blue with the globe of the world etched in gold; the earthly sphere was upheld by clasped hands of Brotherhood and Sisterhood. In dazzling letters around the gold globe were the words *MANKIND INCORPORATED*. The great gates to the City of Eternal Brotherhood swung open!"

Kathleen's shoulders slumped, the breath from her lungs spent from the intricate weaving of her tale. Exposed in the V of her high-topped dress undone at the neck, her pulse raced wildly, blood pounding like a small fist in the slender cavity beneath her throat.

"Y Jesu?"

Kathleen looked blankly at the old Mexican woman in the front pew, but she did not answer her, the blue of her eyes rolling over pew after pew to the back of the room like sheer blue waves calming after a storm.

"Y Jesu?" the old woman demanded.

Kathleen still did not answer. A man in the pew behind the old woman stood up, rubbing his sweaty palms across the felt crown of the fedora he had absentmindedly crushed between his shaking hands as Kathleen told her awesome story.

"Señorita." The man spoke quietly, glancing away from Kathleen, intimidated by the intense blue in her eyes. "Señorita, what this woman wants to know, she who understands your English but cannot speak it, is what about Jesus Christ?" The man sat down, then nervously asked the question he had been afraid to direct to Kathleen while still standing. "Is He in your beautiful city?"

"What about Jesus Christ Our Savior?" Kathleen repeated the question with delight, her chest heaving with anticipation. "On December twenty-fifth, in the year 1885, a tiny group of generous and deeply sincere men and women, only sixty strong, met for the purpose of dedicating their lives and personal fortunes to the establishment of a worldwide commercial organization that would, by its works as well as its words, fittingly commemorate the birth of mankind's greatly beloved exemplar and Way-Shower, *Jesus Christ Himself.* These sixty men and woman were the Sponsors of mankind's last hope for salvation."

The old Mexican woman in the front pew twisted noisily around to ask the man behind her what a Way-Shower was.

Kathleen waited until the old woman turned with a smile on her lips back to the front of the room, delighted that Jesus was living in the Eternal City of Brotherhood with the rest of history's sainted Way-Showers.

"Are you the Voice of the Right Idea?" a man challenged from the center of the room.

"No." Kathleen blew her answer out from pursed lips, the word floating fragile as a bubble, hovering over the man's head before bursting. "Absolutely not. I am not the Voice of the Right Idea. I am simply captain of the Pacific Coast Latin Service Bureau. There is only one true Voice of the Right Idea, although he has many doubles and can travel to a multitude of places at the same time, speaking in a multitude of tongues. He is the guiding spirit. He is many and all things: division superintendent of our worldwide bureaus, prophet-scientist of our International Institute of Universal Salvation and Administration. He is Mr. Department A, originator of the International Vigilantes, interpreter of the original Sponsors' plan for mankind's last hope. Above all else, he is founder, father, fountainhead of Mankind Incorporated."

6

Fuss picked his way cautiously through noisy people crowding the one short block of Olivera Street, wedged into the cement high rises of downtown Los Angeles like a phony movie set. Between outdoor Mexican restaurants studded with plastic palm trees loud vendors waved tourists into narrow market stalls jammed with cheap Mexican curios. Hundreds of garish peasant puppets dangled from strings beneath shelves overloaded with giant sombreros and big-horned fuzzy pink bullfight toros. Sailors and soldiers on overnight leaves, weekend furloughs, and one-day passes nuzzled their teenage girlfriends. They strolled awkwardly, sides of their thighs pressed together, arms around each other, the men laughing, flushed faces of the self-conscious girls half hidden behind enormous puffed balls of cotton candy, their tongues darting tentatively at sticky pink clouds of spun sugar. Fuss crossed the edge of palm-fringed Olivera Park at the end of the short street, the sharp sound of mariachi guitars pursuing him as he ran across four lanes of honking cars on South Grand Street and up red-tiled steps into the old Spanish church. He shut out the midday sun behind him with towering oak doors, his eyes taking a moment to adjust in the long cool cavities of darkness fingering off into small altars. Far before him, at the end of adobe walls, the ornate main altar appeared on fire from steep banks of penance candles flickering wildly in wine-red glass holders. Fuss knelt in the center of the main aisle and made the Sign of the Cross while his eyes carefully searched out others in the church. He approached the altar quietly, keeping his back to several praying people scattered about in hundreds of pews beneath dark hanging candle chandeliers. He waited by the life-size statue of the Guadalupe Virgin, pushing the sleeve of his coat above his wristwatch. It was exactly two o'clock. He knelt before the Virgin. Behind her the sacristy door swung open; the nylon swish of a priest's black cassock rushed through the hazy air around Fuss. The priest approached the altar, knelt, and continued toward Fuss, carefully placing a silver vase filled with the heady odor of fresh-cut lilies at the feet of the Virgin.

The benign brown of the priest's eyes peered questioningly at Fuss. "You are in need of confession, my son?"

"Yes, padre."

The priest nudged the edge of his cassock above his wrinkled wrist, contemplating the stiff gray hairs standing off around the gold of his watch. He looked solemnly into Fuss's eyes. "It is time."

Fuss rapidly made the Sign of the Cross before the Virgin, then rose, hurriedly walking along the outside aisle to the back of the church and slipping quietly into the dark confessional. He fumbled in the dark for the kneeler, touched its padded leather top, and knelt down. Behind the opaque screen before him was the indistinct shape of a head. A small light clicked on over the head, its soft illumination barely outlining the blunt features of Senator Kinney's face.

"Have you seen the Voice of the Right Idea?"

"No, just La Rue."

"What do you think?"

"She's crazy."

"Can you get to her?"

"I've been to two weeks of those crackpot meetings. She knows I'm there."

"Can you get to La Rue or not, Fuss?"

"Yes, but I don't know what this has to do with gathering intelligence on the Sinarquistas. I play around at those silly Mankind Incorporated meetings much longer and I won't have any credibility left."

"Don't worry about that, it's not your concern now."

"Don't worry about that! There I am, alone out in the Barrio, and all you say is don't *worry.*"

Kinney slid the screen back, showing Fuss a smug smile of confidence. "Don't worry, we've got you covered."

"Swell, just like you had those two FBI agents covered."

"That was unfortunate."

"Unfortunate doesn't make them any less dead. The thing is I'm not even like those two guys. I'm out there alone and unarmed. You're the only one who knows who I really am."

"We'll take care of you, I promise."

"Promises won't protect me from the Sinarquistas. These guys play for keeps. In case you haven't noticed, the Fascists won the war in Spain."

"Then you'll receive a weapon. Now tell me, what do you know about this so-called International Legion of Vigilantes?"

"For the last time, Senator, investigating Mankind Incorporated is a waste of precious time. There are real enemies out there, killers, Fascists. When I hired on after Pearl Harbor to do this job of investigating un-American activities in the

Barrio, it was because you said I'd be doing a service for my country. You said I'd help the war effort more by going underground in east Los Angeles than by fighting Japs and Jerries overseas. If you don't let me dig to the bottom of Sinarquistas activities, and keep me sniffing around the Barrio after a bunch of religious wackos, then I'm trotting to the nearest Marine recruiting center and upping for the rest of this stinking war."

"You're too old. The Marines want young bucks, they would never take you. Now forget all that nonsense and listen to me." Kinney slid the screen closed, flicking off the bulb over his head. Fuss was blinded in the sudden darkness. He could no longer see Kinney's face, but he could hear his words. "Whoever the Voice is, he's dangerous, he might become another demagogue. What this country doesn't need is another Huey Long. People like that always start their recruiting with the poor."

"They have four hundred churches, only half are in this country. What's that compared with the Catholic Church?"

"Too damn many. That's why the Voice is being investigated not only by the FBI here in California, where he started, but also by the Wartime Seditious Acts people. Now get out there like a good soldier and do your job. Don't forget, the life of your young kid brother, and thousands of others like him overseas, depends on all our loyalties here on the home front. We are the first line of defense, Fuss, the *first* line."

i Guy!

Guess what? It really happened. Guess who was on the ship today? A movie star! No kidding, guy. Henry Fonda really showed up. Told some jokes and autographed some photos. Actually, I think I look a little like Fonda. Great guy, really! Shook hands with all the guys, a real thrill for a lot of swab jockies, you can bet. Hey, I never got the Esquire pinups. Maybe the censors got them, but I don't know what the Japs could use them for. Then again, the pinups might help the war effort if they fell into enemy hands by keeping all those slanteyes' fingers busy. Now for the Big Picture. You're not going to believe this, but there really is a Shitter on board this tub. Guy about twelve berths down from me got hit right after chow last night, comes back to his berth and there it is, big as life, a pile of hot shit. A little note is pinned to the stinking stuff, says, "All good luck," signed, "The Shitter." Pretty weird, huh? Some war we're fighting in, huh buddy?

Your brother, Marvin

P.S. Remember, do your part with a vitamins for victory V-garden. Ha ha!

Fuss set the letter down next to a plate of uneaten eggs on the three-legged card table he used as a dining table, pushed up against the wall below the window for balance. The one-legged hula palm girls wiggled their green frond skirts in the soft breeze outside. The way the early light touched the long tapering trunks of the palms, they appeared almost bone white, slender and smooth, sensual. Fuss felt himself straightening beneath his robe, the heat of his stiffening flesh brushing his thigh. He popped a stick of Juicy Fruit in his mouth, figuring the sudden rush of sugar would get his mind off the crazy idea that the palm trunks had become sexy slender legs, female calves turned shining to the morning sun. He spit the gum out the open window and laughed. It wasn't the palms making him hard, it was the night before. He could see it clear as day, La Rue walking up the cement steps of the church, against her back the thin cotton of her dress briefly outlining her body. He glimpsed the hem of the dress rise up from the middle of her calves, brushing the tender flesh behind her knees, then she was in the church. He unwrapped another stick of gum. Why should he feel this way about La Rue? She didn't have the kind of Betty Grable body he liked, no strong gams with lots of meat defining the calves, not the kind of breasts that swelled out of a sweater like two perfect scoops of vanilla ice cream. Matter of fact, La Rue didn't even wear sweaters, and her legs were skinny. If she didn't have such thin ankles, it would look like she didn't have any calves at all. She wasn't his type. Fuss peeled off the paper plug from the mouth of a quart bottle of milk on the table, scooped the cream off the top, and gulped the cold milk straight down, washing away the sweetness of the gum until he felt an icy prick of pain shoot from both his eyes into his brain. He didn't want to think about La Rue's skinny legs on a Sunday morning. He thumbed through the Los Angeles *Daily News*. The sports section headlined the Stars losing a doubleheader to the Oakland Oaks. Angel had been knocked off the mound in the first game, came back in the second game to relieve and gave up four hits in one inning. Fuss didn't want to read about it, it was too depressing. He kept thumbing until he came to the religious section, parading five pages of ads for Catholics, Christian Scientists, Episcopalians, Mormons, Jews, Muslims, Holy Rollers, Jehovah's Witnesses, Lemurians, Rosicrucians, Technocrats, Anglo-Israelites, I AM, New Thought, Unity, Theosophy, Yoga, Hermetics, Mentalphysics, Pyramidology, Spiritualism, Oahspe Bible, and every manner of faith healer, doomsday sayer, layer on of the hands, water dunker, and speaker of tongues who had the price of a two-dollar advertisement. People will believe in anything, grasp at any straw, especially when there is a war going on; in California, even when there isn't a war going on. On the third page of the religious section, outlined with a black border in the upper left-hand corner, was a simple statement:

THE VOICE OF THE RIGHT IDEA WILL SPEAK
AT THE SHRINE AUDITORIUM NEXT MONTH.
FOR FURTHER DETAILS, D-I-A-L-G-O-D.

Fuss popped another stick of Juicy Fruit in his mouth and chewed nervously. He picked up the phone and dialed the letters. The line was busy.

8

He waited at the bottom of the church's cement steps. Everyone else had left and he knew she was still in there. What was left of the moon was a silver sliver, barely enough light slipping off it to see more than ten feet. Inside the church the lights had been off longer than a half-hour. He could see up to the top of the steps, over the closed door, where letters of an old sign long since torn down left their sun-faded outline, still spelling clearly *FIRST MEXICAN BAPTIST CHURCH*. She walked quickly down the steps, her arms full of little soft-covered blue books. She would not have noticed him standing in the shadows if he hadn't suddenly lifted his hat.

"Mr. Fuss?" The silver light cut across the blue of her eyes, which seemed to glint like a startled animal's. "Is that you?"

Fuss almost choked on his gum. He swooped his hat all the way off in greeting, his words coming out hoarse and hesitant. "Yes, ma'am, I mean Miss La Rue. I thought being so late and dark, you might allow me to accompany you home. The Barrio is not the sort of place a lady should be walking through alone at this time of night, especially since we are so close to the Zona Roja."

"Mr. Fuss." Kathleen watched him screw the hat back on his head and tip the broad brim low over his eyes. "I have walked home every Saturday night for the past six months through this neighborhood without one incident. Surely you don't believe all the slanderous stories printed in the *Examiner* about white women not being safe in the Barrio? I think I have much less to fear from Midwestern sailors than the good people around here."

"Well, ma'am, there is a war going on and, ah, during wartime people do things they might not otherwise do, and, ah, what with the odd-night Civil Defense blackouts just going into effect again, I thought—"

Kathleen walked straight to Fuss and looked up beneath the felt brim hiding his eyes. "Mr. Fuss, are you trying to pick me up? Do you take me for some kind of Tallulah?"

"No, ma'am, I was just trying—"

"Because if that is your intention, forget it. I haven't the energy or inclination for such frivolity. I am a dedicated lady, Mr. Fuss, dedicated with soul and body to my vocation."

"I'm dedicated too; that's why I thought in the interest of—"

"Is this the reason you have been coming to these meetings, thinking you could pick me up? Sitting in the back pew all these weeks with never a word, never a question. You think I don't notice you back there? You don't look at anybody else, you don't talk to anybody. You just buy the new weekly study books and go on your way."

Close up, with her standing beneath him, staring directly

into his eyes, Fuss was surprised at how much taller she was than he always thought. The top of her head reached above the loose broad knot of his necktie.

"If you've been waiting around to pick me up because you think I'm a terribly lonely, silly, frustrated, and stupid female, Mr. Fuss, then you're dead wrong."

"No, Miss La Rue." Fuss tapped his hat to leave. "I never once thought those terrible things. It was just extra dark and I thought—"

"You thought you could pick me up." Kathleen turned her head so the silver light caught the animal glint in her eyes again. "After all, as you say, it's wartime."

Fuss lowered his head, the brim of his hat covering his entire face, the shame in his voice cracking his words guiltily. "I honestly meant no offense, Miss La Rue." He turned to leave.

"Wait."

Fuss felt her fingers lightly touch his sleeve in the darkness. It seemed the touch of a small child. He raised his head and her hand was gone, clutching the load of books to her breasts.

"You can escort me home." In the silver light her red lips seemed purple. "After all." She smiled. "It really *is* wartime."

Fuss fell into step with her as she started to the corner. "How did you know my name?"

"Last month" . . . she spaced her words, her breathing becoming heavy as she walked, "don't you remember, in the legislative hearing room? We were both subpoenaed."

"Oh, yes, that . . . I almost forgot."

"And I suppose you also forgot we both sat through days of preliminary hearings for the Zoot-suit murderers' case?" Kathleen looked at him suspiciously. "This way, Mr. Fuss." She turned sharply around the corner onto Flores Street.

Fuss tried to think of a way to erase the sudden look of suspicion from Kathleen's face. He stopped and blurted out, "Would you care for a stick of Juicy Fruit?"

Kathleen looked at him even more suspiciously, then laughed. "Of course."

Fuss peeled the foil off a wrapper, slipping the gum through his fingers up to the purple of her lips. Kathleen smiled, her soft lips parting, her tongue quickly taking the gum into her mouth.

"What am I thinking of?" Fuss took the load of books from her, freeing her arms. "What kind of a stiff am I for not offering to carry your books?" He balanced the books against his chest and popped his gum loudly as they walked alone down the dark sidewalk, toward the crowded figures in the shadows of the distant corner. From the outline of shadows, oversized slouched hats, broad-shouldered sport coats, high-waisted baggy pants radically tapering in tight around the ankles, the occasional glint of looped chains dangling from hips, almost scraping the sidewalk as they swung back and forth, Fuss knew what was ahead: a gang of Zoot-suiters.

The high wail of an air-raid siren screamed from the distant direction of the blunt, cement needletop of the City Hall downtown. The Zoots were like a startled, roaming band of zebras hearing a lion's blood-curdling roar. They broke and ran, their oversized shoes slapping like hard hooves on the sidewalk as they disappeared into darkness.

"How much farther do we have to go?" Fuss's arms ached from the books weighting his arms.

"You're not worried about the air-raid siren, are you?"

"No, it's just another Civil Defense drill." Fuss shifted the load of books, trying to keep his awkward grip on them.

"Then slow down. I can't keep up with you."

Fuss waited for Kathleen to catch up. He had lost sight of her. The silver slice of moon had drifted behind the full height of a downtown skyscraper, casting the empty streets into absolute blackness. Kathleen's breath came to him in the darkness, a slight whistling wheeze, almost the exact insistent pitch of a steaming tea kettle.

"Ah, there you are." Kathleen's words broke the wheezing of her breath. The light touch of her hand traced the outline of Fuss's arm like he was a statue. She moved away. He heard the sound of keys jangling and the metal of a key scraping into a lock, then a doorknob twisting. Her hand came back to him and she pulled him through the open door, locking it behind them. She reached above her head, groping through the air until she found the pull chain for the light switch and tugged it, illuminating a long curved flight of stairs, ascending steeply into further darkness. "You'll have to let me hold on to you." She slipped her hand underneath Fuss's arm. "It's a long way to the top; it always exhausts me."

Fuss took the steps slowly, pausing at the top of each landing as Kathleen leaned against him, her body feeling like it was going to slip away as she gasped for breath.

At the top of the third landing, Kathleen unlocked the door to her apartment. "You wait here." She turned to Fuss, then disappeared inside.

He heard the striking of a match. Light flickered along the narrow hallway of a large apartment, then brightened. He saw her coming, holding a candle before her, its dancing red flame the same color as her lips and hair. He followed her down the hallway into a warm living room. She lit more candles, until the shapes of two overstuffed yellow chairs with intricate lace doilies dripping over their arms and backs became distinct. He sat down.

"Here, let me take those books." Kathleen smiled apologetically at Fuss. "I'm so sorry you had to carry them all that way." She took the books from his arms. They were tied in bundles of ten, each one identical, with bright blue bindings. Embossed in gold on the covers was the globe of the earth supported by two clasped hands. Circled around the globe was the vivid legend *MANKIND INCORPORATED*. She set the books neatly along the wall, piled ceiling high with stacks of the same bright blue books.

"How many of those are in print?"

Kathleen knelt on one knee before the books, looking proudly along the length of wall almost hidden by solid blue bindings. "The International Registration Bureau claims there are over two million. Someday it will replace the Bible. The Latin Service Bureau has sold a thousand in six months, but we are still far from the ultimate goal of universal salvation."

Fuss watched Kathleen carefully as she stood up, giving a little gasp as she took in more air, her hands nervously straightening the cotton dress. She was so thin the hipbones below her narrow waist stood out sharply against the loose material of the dress. "Why don't you turn on the lights, Miss La Rue?"

"Because I read in Walter Winchell that when the black-out drill is on it's better to use only candlelight. It's softer than electric bulbs and harder for enemy bomber pilots to see from a distance."

Fuss shifted uneasily in his chair, trying to think of something more to say before she asked him to leave. "I'll have to try that with the candles, a neat trick, anything to support the war effort." He fumbled in his coat pocket. "Care for another Juicy Fruit?"

"No, thank you, Oscar." She spoke his name intimately, as if she had known him for a very long time. "But I would like it if you would—"

"That's okay, I've stayed too long already." He jumped up from the chair and tipped his hat. "I'll leave now."

"No." She laughed. "Sit down. You were so kind tonight and I was so suspicious, uncharitable really. What I was going to say was I would like to invite you to stay for a nice cold bottle of Coke."

"I'd love one." Fuss fell back into the deep chair and slipped another stick of Juicy Fruit into his mouth, delighted with his good fortune. He listened contentedly to Kathleen humming in the kitchen, hearing her lift the top of the icebox open, the short hiss of carbonation escaping from the tops of two Coke bottles. He twisted his head around, trying to read as quickly as possible in the flickering candlelight titles of books behind the glassed-in doors of the library shelves:

INTERNATIONAL BANKERS CONSPIRACY,
REMARKS BY DEPT. A

NU'ERA TOOLS: LETTERS FROM
A WORLD SAVER TO HIS SON

I, UPTON SINCLAIR, GOVERNOR OF CALIFORNIA,

AND HOW I ENDED POVERTY

THE HIDDEN RULERS: DEALERS IN DEATH

WE ARE NOT CATTLE: REPORT TO
INTERNATIONAL VIGILANTES BY DEPT. A

THE TRUTH ABOUT ENGLAND

MAN THE UNKNOWN

Fuss hadn't heard of most of the titles, let alone read the books. But he had read in the newspapers about Dr. Alexis Carrel, the man who wrote *Man the Unknown.* Carrel won the Nobel Prize for devising a technique of suturing blood vessels during surgery. He achieved greater fame with his crusade to have all those guilty of insane or criminal acts, or born with serious mental or physical handicaps, disposed of in inexpensive euthanasic institutions supplied with proper gases. It was odd, Fuss thought, watching Kathleen return smiling from the kitchen, she was just the kind of physically unfit and defective person Carrel would like to see winnowed out of the human race.

"Here you are, Oscar." Bubbles of dark carbonation fizzed over the top of the glass of Coke Kathleen held before him.

Fuss sipped the cold drink, watching Kathleen over the

rim of the glass as she sat in the fat chair across from him, crossing her thin legs beneath the cotton dress. He noticed how delicate the bones of her hands were, standing out against the flesh of her fingers as she held the moist glass to her lips.

"You do much reading, Miss La Rue?"

"Yes, every spare moment I can get is devoted to my education."

"Have you read this extraordinary book by Dr. Carrel?"

"Of course. I've read everything on these shelves. Wisdom is armament." She pursed her red lips so they barely touched the cool rim of the glass.

"Have you . . ." Fuss's eyes scanned the wall of blue books behind her. "Have you been a member of Mankind Incorporated for many years?"

"No, not really, although it seems like a lifetime. I don't consider myself even being alive until I joined the ceaseless quest for universal peace. I've given up everything for it, and it has given me so much in return. We have a plan by which student ministers can willingly donate fifty percent of their income to the pursuit of perfect understanding by supporting the experiments the Sponsors instituted. But I gave everything I had. I don't want to be part of the dog-eat-dog profit system. My humble actions and small efforts will bring the day closer when there is a guaranteed same-size paycheck for everyone, from the President to a ditchdigger, all equal."

Kathleen's voice was so soft with strong confidence that Fuss found himself falling toward her in his mind. He watched her lips move, trying to remember when he had felt in such a strange way before; it was all so secure, familiar. As she craned her neck forward to take another sip of Coke, he remembered. It was the same far-off sweet brush of air he had felt when his mother bent over him in bed as a child, her close tender words sending him securely into the dark unpredictable voyage of another night.

"Do you mind me asking all these questions, Miss La Rue?"

Kathleen ran her thin fingers along the sheer white of her temple, the tapered fingertips darting out of sight beneath a fall of red curls. "I never tire of speaking my beliefs. It is a sin not to."

"Are you from Los Angeles?"

"Oh, no, I've only been here six months. I'm from up north. I lived in San Francisco all my life until I went to college in Berkeley. San Francisco still exerts a great, almost desperate pull on my life. It was there, after the 1906 earthquake, the Sponsors decided they must act before the Hidden Rulers split the earth asunder. Once the inevitable extermination of the Hidden Rulers occurs, San Francisco will become the center of the universe's stabilizing vibrations. The Sponsors brought the One True Voice to San Francisco while he was still a boy for thirty years of instruction in the select International Legion of Vigilantes. The Sponsors entrusted him to become Department A, delivering their Word across America. When I met him on the campus at Berkeley, he stunned my life. It was as if he unlocked the door to my heart, walked up the steps of my being, and kissed my very soul. I was fortunate, I was saved. But so many have not heard the Word, so many who don't know the end is near."

Kathleen stared deeply into her glass of Coke, wrinkles of concern etching across her smooth forehead. From the expression of dread on her face, it appeared she was witnessing within the glass an exploding cosmos that could only be saved by Department A, the One True Voice. Fuss was afraid to break her concentration by asking another question, his entire body giving an involuntary twitch as she unexpectedly turned her eyes upon him and broke the silence.

"This is not a mad dream."

Fuss gulped the last of his Coke and coughed noisily,

□ 45

trying to switch the subject. "Why did you leave San Francisco?"

The wrinkles in Kathleen's forehead faded, her skin peacefully regaining its smooth surface. "Do you know the poem by Carl Sandburg about fog coming in on little cat's feet?"

"No."

"Well, no matter. In San Francisco the fog doesn't come in on little cat's feet. It roars in like a lion; it spills over the hills and covers the houses something fearful, drowning people in a damp gray blanket. Sometimes you don't see the sun for days, even weeks. Everything is cold, isolated."

"So you left the north for sunny Southern California?"

"No, too much sun can also be dangerous. I left because of my calling. There are fields to be tilled everywhere we find disharmony and distrust. After being here only a few months, I realized if I'd stayed in San Francisco it would have killed me."

"The fog?"

"I'm asthmatic. I need dry, warm places. Dampness rots my lungs, robs my breath. I'm also hyperallergic to cats and dogs."

"You mean, not only can't you be around cats made out of fog, but you can't be around real dogs and cats as well?"

"Yes, and many other things are just as dangerous to my health, so many things I don't even know them all, probably wouldn't until it was too late and I had a fatal attack. It's kind of like living with a knife to your throat. You never know when you'll have the attack that will rob your life's breath and not have the proper medicine to fight it off."

"You're kidding! You mean this asthma condition of yours could kill you?"

"Yes." Kathleen's eyes played over Fuss's face like she was talking to a small, disbelieving boy. "But that is the least of my worries." Suddenly a look of concern wrinkled the smooth skin around her eyes. She stood up and held her hand out solemnly for him to shake, like a businessman concluding an arduous meeting. "You must leave now. You shouldn't be here, really."

Fuss stood to leave, taking the hand offered. Her grasp was slight and slipped quickly from him. "What *are* your worries, Miss La Rue?"

She opened the apartment door, her body blocking the flickering candlelight at her back as she ushered Fuss out to the top of the staircase descending into darkness. "To see justice in this country, Oscar. This war is the last chance for mankind."

In the empty streets leading away from Kathleen's apartment Fuss could see the sliver of moon cutting a pretty figure over the cement needle of City Hall. Around City Hall the outline of Barrio tenements stood out, shabby buildings stacked clumsily against the sky four and five stories high, their impermanence mocking the heroic proportions of the dominant needle.

9

Cruz no esta aqui!" The woman slammed the door in Fuss's face.

Fuss banged on the door again. He was tired of banging on doors all morning; he was tired of beating the pavement up and down the Barrio streets and having doors slammed in his face. He kept beating on the door in front of him, trying to knock it right off the hinges. He had to get to at least one of his boys. They had all stopped coming to practice. He thought they must be on to him, worse, fallen in with the older Zoots. He kept banging on the door. He heard babies crying inside the apartment.

A young girl held the door open a crack against Fuss's pushing, straight black bangs cut bluntly across her high sloping forehead, a baby balanced on one hip. She was barely sixteen years old, her broken English competing with the wails of the child.

"Mama, she say no Cruz. No aqui. Please not here."

Fuss wedged his foot inside the door, then flung it back and shoved into the room. Small, dark-faced children playing on the bare wood floor were unconcerned with Fuss's foreign presence, unconcerned by the storm of Spanish swearing shouted at Fuss from the clutch of women in the kitchen. With three families living in two rooms the children were not much concerned with anything but the possession of several pitiful toys they fought over. The mothers of the children were crowded together around the kitchen table. The woman who slammed the front door in Fuss's face waved a flyswatter menacingly before him like she was going to kill a big pest, screaming, "Fuera! Bastardo! Fueraaa!"

Fuss turned his back on the women at the table, fearful of their feminine wrath, the seething, unbridled hatred of their words lunging at him like beasts set free from some private hell. He stomped out of the stifling apartment, slamming the door behind him, running without thinking down the long five flights of stairs, almost bumping into the skinny teenage boy stepping from the brightness of the street into the dinginess of the apartment building.

"Cruz!"

The teenage boy lifted his head, brown eyes staring out in recognition from beneath the broad brim of an oversized fedora; he turned to run. Fuss grabbed hold of the long floppy tails of the boy's purple sport coat and pulled him back into the dark hallway, pinning the boy to the wall as he struggled against the grip Fuss had on his bony shoulders beneath the heavy padding of the coat.

"Hey, hombre, que pasa? Hey, what gives, man?" The boy snarled, his eyes narrowing, trying to look tough under the brim of a green hat, but he only looked like what he was, a frightened boy.

"You ask me what's happening!" Fuss shouted back into the tough expression confronting him beneath the hat. "Look at yourself! A real big hood, pachuco hat, Zoot suit with reet-pleats, dago chains hanging all over, a real hepcat! A smooth muchacho, a real street-cruisin' dude!"

"I got a right to dress the way I want. You don't stop me! It's a free country, ain't it?"

"No, I can't stop you, chico, but you know those coppers out there have razor blades on the bottoms of their billyclubs, and they'd just love for you to go cruisin' by to cut the clothes off your back, shave your reet-pleats wide open."

"I ain't afraid of no copper, I ain't afraid of no jefe."

"You're in a pinch, Cruz."

"Don't be no square peg, Fussy." Cruz shook his padded shoulders free of Fuss's grip and fluffed his long Zoot-suit coat like a cock strutting through a hen yard. "This is still America, ain't it? Young blade dress how he want."

"How come none of you blades have been to baseball practice—Hernandez, Tujillo, the whole pack?"

"I guess we got other business to take care of."

"You guess you got other *business.*" Fuss nearly spit his sarcastic words on the floor. "What is it you have better to do than stay out of jail?"

"It ain't no crime to wear a Zoot suit, it ain't no crime to cash it and flash it."

"Don't bitch up your life, Cruz. All you blades, you know the probation rules. Every day, three hours, you blades play ball with me. That's the way the probation judge laid it out, other-wise reform school."

"I ain't no criminal, no con-vic."

"Marijuana's a crime, carrying stilettos and fellettos to dag people with is a crime, and zip guns are a crime, so's street fighting a crime. What do you mean, you're no criminal? Lot of you blades been to Juvenile Court on all that kind of stuff. If it wasn't for the CYO going to Juvenile Hall and speaking up for you kids, you'd all be cooling your heels downtown in Juvie right now, and you know it. So don't bitch up your life, chico."

"I ain't. I'm hep."

"Then why haven't any of you blades been to ball practice? Not one of you show. How do you think we can beat Bakersfield again with no practice? You think the Yankees goof around before World Series time? Just dope it out for yourself, Cruz."

"I don't want to play ball. I want a job."

Fuss pulled off his hat, tracing a thumb around the inside band until it was free of sweat. "Baseball is a job. Look at your big brother, look at Angel, he's a model."

"Angel don't make nothin'."

"What do you mean? The Stars pay him twenty bucks a game."

"What's that? Big-league guys get hundreds."

Fuss slipped his hat back on and shrugged his shoulders. "You don't know, maybe Angel will play big league one day. Maybe he'll play with DiMaggio; he's good enough."

"Don't put the bite on me, Fussy, I ain't no pug. You know there ain't no Mexican guys playing big league. They don't let chicas patas play."

"That's just it." Fuss tried to force his lips into a smile of confidence. "You and Angel are no chicas patas, you're Americans, born and bred in Los Angeles. You're *eligible.*"

"Then how come we can't get work in U.S. factories? They truck coons by the melonload into California to work in shipyards and stuff, but you got a Spanish name around here, you don't work. They don't care which side of the border you born on anyway, they figure you a greaseball wetback."

Fuss shook his head. "No, that's not it at all."

"Why they won't let us work? We don't need a green card, we got American birth certificates. Why they keep us in the Barrio? We be better off down in Tijuana taking pictures of drunk sailors on donkeys."

"I don't know." Fuss looked straight at Cruz. "Honest to God, I don't have the answer."

"Then get off my back about playin' ball." Cruz pushed by Fuss and shoved the door open, the sudden shaft of outside light knifing into Fuss.

"Stop your motor a minute." Fuss tugged at the tails of Cruz's baggy coat. "Why have you blades stopped coming?"

Cruz moved his thin lips in a straight line of contempt, the slur of his four words coming out in one piece. "Because you're a *Commie—*"

Before the last word was broken off from the end of Cruz's sentence Fuss grabbed the floppy orange bowtie at Cruz's thin throat, whipped him around, and knocked him flat up against the wall. "So it's not the Zoots you've joined, it's the Sinarquistas! Say it, Cruz! Don't clam up on me! Admit it!"

"I ain't saying nothin'." The tears from Cruz's large, frightened eyes rolled down his cheeks and off Fuss's clenched fists at his throat. "You can't get me to cop to it! I'll kill myself first!"

Fuss ripped off Cruz's floppy tie and tore open his pink-and-black polkadot shirt, the buttons popping off like overripe cherries. He pulled the shirt open, exposing deep razor-blade cuts crisscrossing Cruz's thin, hairless chest, some cuts old and scabbed over, others open and festering. Cruz's face blurred before Fuss as his own eyes filled with tears. "You punk, Cruz! You dumb little punk! You've gone and bitched up on me! You've gone on the Horse! You're jacking it right into your bloodstream!"

10

The Horse is loose in the Barrio again."

"No job, comin' the Horse."

"The Horse is a killer."

"No job, she's a killer too."

"There'll be jobs, something's got to open up."

"If they can't be making enough job when they be making the wars, then will never be the job." Wino Boy spoke so thickly the words seemed to trickle as slowly as the red trace of wine from the corner of his mouth.

"It's that easy, huh?" Fuss angrily balled a fresh stick of Juicy Fruit and popped it between his lips.

"Amigo, life she's never what she's seeming." Wino Boy held the wine bottle up to the sun, peering into the empty green darkness of the glass. He tipped the bottle over. One blood-red drop fell to the hot sidewalk, evaporating into nothing on the cracked cement.

Fuss looked up to the end of the crowded street. On the roof of Butch Mendoza's poolhall workmen were covering over a *BUY US WAR BONDS* billboard with a bold black-and-white message: *DIALGOD*.

"Life, she's never what she's meaning." Wino Boy let the empty bottle slip from his limp fingers and roll off noisily into the gutter.

Fuss glanced down at the old man slumped against a boarded-over storefront window and shook his head sadly. "You're right. I thought I knew the meaning of everything, but the longer this war goes on, the less I understand people."

"We have a saying in Chihuahua." Wino Boy held out his open palm expectantly and waited for Fuss to put a stick of Juicy Fruit in it. "The man, who all the time thinking he has all the answers, no person's never asking him the questions." He chewed the gum Fuss handed him.

"Somebody's got to have the answers to why the Horse is loose in the Barrio. Nothing ever happens in the Barrio that isn't political."

"Si, en el Barrio, en la Zona Roja, la Virgin Mary."

"The Virgin Mary has always refused to even talk to me. Why now?"

"Because, compadre, the Horse is loose."

Fuss could see the near toothless smile of Wino Boy's face in the shadow. "What does the Virgin Mary care about the Horse being loose?"

Wino Boy's laugh came up out of the shadow. "Because the Horse steal this." His hand grabbed insistently between his legs over the half-open zipper of his pants.

"I don't have any friends left in the Zona Roja. Nobody there will talk to me since the night the FBI guys were shot. I'm afraid to even go in there. The whole place has changed since the war. The Barrio has changed so much, nobody trusts anyone anymore. People used to have faith things would get better."

"No jobs, no faith, amigo. Peoples no laugh when coming the sailors at night to taking their niñas. And you, amigo." Wino Boy squinted seriously at Fuss. "You no have the friends, people telling you are un Communista."

"That's crazy." Fuss doubled his fists and slammed them into his pockets. "I have a brother in the United States Navy. Why the hell would I be a Red?" He glared down at Wino Boy. "You know I'm lots of things, old man, but I'm no stinking Commie."

"Si, but Sinarquistas, they say different."

"Sinarquistas are Fascists; they say their own mothers are Communists. If Sinarquistas are on the square, why don't they come out into the public? Why do they always sneak around like cowards, never telling anybody who they really are, always having secret meetings, hiding behind closed doors, scattering leaflets in the night. Why don't they stand up and be counted?"

"Because they be arrested, amigo. Sinarquistas are no born stupid."

"Then let them come out into the open and take their lumps like men."

"And them." Wino Boy pointed to the new billboard blocking the sun in a giant square on the roof of the poolhall: *DIALGOD*. "Sinarquistas saying those too be Communistas."

"That makes about as much sense as *my* being Red." Fuss turned his back on the sign as if it didn't exist.

"Life is never what she's seeming."

"Come on, Wino Boy, stop giving me all this claptrap. You've got a grandson in this war, we're on the same team. Whatever you tell me helps the American cause." Fuss nervously peeled the wrapper from another stick of gum.

"If I no have to mooch all day and have moola to going to

the Santa Anita Racetrack and I be betting on the horses..."

"Who would you bet on?" Fuss interrupted Wino Boy impatiently.

"Sea Biscuit."

"Sea Biscuit?" Fuss repeated the words under his breath as if they were a question, quickly looking up and down to guard their secret meaning from anyone who might have overheard him. He knelt on one knee, whispering to Wino Boy intimately, "This Sea Biscuit is a real horse?"

"How much you be betting me?" Wino Boy's breath weighed heavily in Fuss's face.

"On what? I don't understand."

"This Sea Biscuit, is being a *real* horse."

"Okay." Fuss dug five dollars out of his pocket. "Here's a nickel note, that's all I'll bet till you tell me more."

"Ask la Virgin." Wino Boy's cracked lips clamped tight. "Now help me up." He grabbed hold of Fuss's shoulder for support.

"No." Fuss pushed the old man back against the wall. "I just gave you five bucks and all you can say is ask the Virgin. I already told you, I can't get to see the Virgin."

Wino Boy's shaky hand stretched out and tugged at the bottom of Fuss's coat. He pulled himself up on wobbly legs, wincing as blood cut from his feet while sitting against the building stung back to life. He didn't look at Fuss. He squinted at the black-and-white *DIALGOD* billboard blocking the sun up at the corner on the roof of the poolhall. He licked his cracked lips. His voice had no humor in it as he gazed at the sign. "Go to la Zona Roja, saying to those people you wanting la Virgin Mary so you can be making the bet on Sea Biscuit."

IJUANA TUXEDO JUNCTION TIJUANA
TUXEDO JUNCTION!
KU-KU RACHA DANCEHALL KU-KU RACHA
DANCEHALL!!!!!!

Waves of Shore Patrolmen and Military Police commanded the
Zona Roja. The bright streets were jammed with shoving people. Drunken sailors stood with their arms locked around lamp
posts as if clinging desperately to a ship's steel mast in a ty-
phoon. Dark-eyed Mexican women with glaring red lips and
wearing tight-waisted skirts blocked the noisy entrance to
Tijuana Tuxedo Junction, calling and whistling to young sailors surrounding them on both sides of the street. Cigarettes

dangling from the women's mouths bobbed and glowed like fireflies mating in a swamp, luring even the most hesitant and embarrassed of the sailors.

"Hey, buster, want to cut a rug?"

"Don't be a square, John, take a chance, buy a dollar dance!"

Fuss tried to push through the women. One in a red wig eyed him; for an incredible moment, in the pulsing cascade of neon light from overhead, he thought the woman was Kathleen La Rue. The red-wigged woman rammed her hip into Fuss's leg and jammed the six-inch spike of her high-heeled shoe down on his foot. Her breath smelled like a Baby Ruth candy bar. "How 'bout you, honey? Buck a dance, take a wild chance!" Fuss pulled his foot out from beneath the stab of the spiked heel. "Come on inside, civvie." The woman swung her purse recklessly by its long straps, arching her back so her large breasts almost pushed into Fuss's face, her bright brown eyes flashing the information that Fuss would never be so fortunate to see such a seductive pose again in his adult life. She looked like a farm girl swinging a rabbit by its ears. "Cuuuuuum onnnnnn kidoooooooh, give yourself a treat! Buck a dance, buck a drink, hard to beat!" Fuss pushed into the gang of women bartering and laughing with sailors weaving among them like punch-drunk fighters. The red-wigged woman caught up to Fuss, grabbing his coat and pressing her lips to his ear. "Wait a sec, civvie! If you come inside with me, I promise you, kiddo, if you can't get a boner, I'll let you cop a feel of my cookie. I'm hotter than a Spanish fly trapped in Betty Grable's pink panties! C'mon, civvie, my cookie's getting mushy! Treat yourself to a treat!" Fuss shook the clinging woman off and continued up the street, trying to stay clear of drunks stumbling out from clubs and squads of Shore Patrolmen walking four abreast, thick black billyclubs swinging at their hips. Hard white shells of Shore Patrolmen's helmets, with a black *SP* stamped on the fronts, reflected the frantic neon swirl of color around them. Fuss knew someone was following him; he almost felt the breath on the back of his neck beneath his hat. He spun quickly around. A short man nearly stumbled into him, then jerked back with a leer on his face, self-consciously patting the shiny wings of his heavily pomaded hair, the part down the middle of his scalp slashed straight as a white line down the center of a blacktop highway.

"What the hell do you want?" Fuss shouted in the man's grinning face.

The man looked over both shoulders and suspiciously behind him, then slipped a hand coyly inside his coat pocket, drawing out a pack of cards. "Beautiful Mexican cookie. You like to purchase Tijuana circus? Special to you today." Before Fuss could turn away, the man spread the deck in his hand like a rare fan and turned it over, exposing fleshy bits and pieces of a naked Mexican woman caught in different poses across the cards as she amorously ministered to her reluctant partner, a slack-eyed, big-eared donkey.

A sailor hung his pimply face over the man's shoulder. "Hot dog! Look at that big black enchilada on that animal, must be four feet from belly to floor! How much, senior—for the whole deck, I mean?"

The short man spread the deck wider for the sailor. Fuss turned and walked away, the sailor shouting after him, "Hey, civvie! I didn't mean to break up the deal between you and the senior here! C'mon back, you can buy them! There's more spic cookie where this came from!"

Fuss walked, faster, then started running to catch up with the shouting crowd at the corner. Beneath the white glare of his helmet a Shore Patrolman swung the length of his club menacingly, barking at the crowd to stay back on the curb. In the middle of the street spinning lights on top of a Shore Patrol jeep splashed its red color all over the old Packard three patrolmen had stopped, banging their clubs on the metal roof. Fuss made out two Zoots trapped inside the paint-peeled car, refusing to crank down the windows, slouched deep on the front seat, their faces obscured by wide brims of purple hats. One of the patrolmen smashed the driver's window open, to the applause of the crowd on the curb, and pulled a frightened Zoot from the car, slamming him up along the back fender, jamming a billy-club behind his Zoot's neck and knocking off the purple hat. The Zoot's hair was long and tied up in a black braid; the patrolman grabbed it in his fist, tugging like he was reeling in a reluctant fish, snapping the Zoot's neck back against the club.

"No nos vencerán!" The Zoot's terrified screams filled the street as he futilely tried kicking backward at the grinning patrolman who was choking him with the club.

Fuss knew what the Zoot was screaming. "You can't defeat us!"

A siren cut through the Zoot's screams, a black-and-white police car slamming to a stop behind the jeep, six police-men with shotguns piling out, one handcuffing the screaming Zoot while the others prodded the second Zoot from his sanctuary in the Packard. Even after the Zoots were handcuffed and locked in the backseat of the police car and it sped up the street, Fuss heard the shouts of the Zoots, their wild eyes glaring from behind the caged-in thick glass of the police car at the fist-shaking crowd. "No nos vencerán."

12

TONY TOMALE'S TATTOO PARLOR
TONY TOMALE'S TATTOO PARLOR
TONY TOMALE'S TATTOO PARLOR

The red-white-and-blue neon words blinked above the doorway of a small two-story shop. Fuss pushed the door open. A little bell tinkled over his head, breaking an atmosphere of intimacy in the hazy smoke-filled room. A young shirtless sailor sat crosslegged in a straight-backed chair, a dark fat man bent before him, delicately darting a needle into the pale skin of the sailor's chest. The fat man's arms came out of his white T-shirt like enormous blood sausages, the tight skin covered with a tattooed menagerie of lions, tigers, parrots, and dragons, fenced in at each wrist by a tattooed identity bracelet declaring

MAZATLAN 1922. Each of the man's fingers was ringed elaborately with a woman's name: *LINDA, DOLORES, TONIA*. Fuss could read the names clearly as the steady fingers pricked the needle into the sailor's pasty white chest, embroidering into soft flesh the picture of a muscular arm with a snake ferociously wrapped around it. The hand of the newly tattooed arm was choking the snake, which astonishingly had the human face of a Japanese, fierce razor-sharp fangs jutting from his mouth. In bold letters, like a newspaper headline, beneath the bizarre struggle being enacted on the sailor's shaved chest was the inscription *NIPS AND YANKS—A FIGHT TO THE FINISH*. The sailor's eyes were inky and luminescent, drifting around the room. A sloppily rolled brown cigarette dangled carelessly from his slack mouth, its ashes falling unnoticed into the black hair of the fat man bent to the task before him. Fuss smelled the wet, grassy odor of marijuana in the thick haze of the room.

"Are you Tony Tomale?"

"Does Jell-O roll off a tit?"

"Tony, I'd like to see the Virgin Mary."

The needle in Tony Tomale's fat fingers moved steadily as he answered Fuss without looking up. "You got a nickel, price of a phone call, you call up the Virgin."

"Isn't this where the Virgin lives?"

"Is a Chinaman's asshole slanted?"

"Look." Fuss reached into his pants pocket, taking out five bills. "I don't have a nickel but I do have five bucks. What do you say? Will it get me in to see the Virgin?"

Tony Tomale laid down his needle and fished another one up from a bowl of alcohol. "The Virgin is a class act, buddy, not some Flores Street dude cruiser."

"Well, then." Fuss reached deep into his pocket again. "How about ten smacks? Cash on the barrelhead."

"Say, dog balls, why don't you go over to the church with your ten spot and light a candle? Tell your troubles to *that* Virgin."

"I want to bet on a Horse."

Tony Tomale dropped the needle into the bowl of alcohol, his head swinging around on his bull neck. He stared straight at Fuss. "You really want to bet on a Horse?"

"Sure, a real Horse. I've got the dough."

"You really think this is that kind of place?"

"Sure, sure, I've got the dime, you've got the time, brother."

"You've got the *dime,* I've got the *time.*" Tony Tomale shook his head disgustedly, pushing himself up slowly from the creaking chair. "Okay, sports fan, I'll go talk to the Virgin."

Fuss watched Tony Tomale disappear through a doorway dripping with rattling strings of bright plastic beads. He heard him laboriously climbing stairs, each heavy step thudding down a long hallway. The sailor's head slumped forward, his chin resting on his brightly colored chest, inky eyes glowing with appreciation at the arm and snake locked in flamboyant indelible combat on his hairless pale white skin. Fuss heard thudding on the staircase again. Tony Tomale swept the beaded strings across the doorway back with his fat hand like he was chopping through a canefield.

"Okay, sports fan, go on up. The Virgin is waiting."

Fuss went through the beaded curtain; the long hallway was brightly lit. The fast sound of a clarinet on a record player turned down low grew louder in his ears as he trudged to the top of the landing. A sailor in full-dress white uniform was tilted back in a chair, propped against the wall outside an open doorway where the music was coming from. The cloth of the sailor's white cap was pulled down tight over his forehead almost to his eyes. The sailor jerked a thumb over his shoulder toward the music, and Fuss went in.

The dim room flickered from hundreds of candles flaming in soot-ringed bell jars. The smell of incense was thick and syrupy in the stuffy air, mixing with the sweet scent of burning beeswax, wafting over the form of a barely breathing body propped up on stacks of lacy peach-colored pillows strewn over the satin sheets of a large bed. Shiny black patent leather high-heeled shoes were strapped to the softly breathing body's thin ankles. Sheer black nylon stockings made a whispering sound as slender legs rubbed together beneath a pink Chinese robe, fastened high around the neck of an olive-skinned face half obscured by a silver sleeping mask in the shape of two startled cat's eyes. Fuss watched the pout of the face's pink lips as they seemed to tremble in time to the clarinet music on the record player. A thin manicured finger raised, its bright black polished nail wagging back and forth in time to the music.

"Listen to Benny Goodman blow." The voice was low and sultry. "Listen to Benny boy blow that black snake." It was unmistakably the voice of a man.

Fuss moved his feet uneasily, but not in time to the music. "I was told I could make a bet on a Horse here."

"Oh?" The Virgin Mary pulled off the sleeping mask. The sharp lines of his oiled golden face were clearly visible, thick blue mascara exaggerating the almond shape of his eyes. "We sell lots of things at lots of prices, but we don't sell Horse."

Fuss fidgeted more uneasily as the sailor from the hall came in quietly behind him. The heat from the candles made Fuss feel like he was in the boiler room of a ship. "I was told I could make a bet on a Horse called Sea Biscuit."

"Sea Biscuit? Oh, my, Johnny." The Virgin Mary looked wide-eyed at the sailor and laughed. "Did you hear that, Sea Biscuit? Oh, my!" The Virgin Mary's laughter was nervous, almost girlish, but not coquettish.

"What's the joke?" Fuss turned around and asked the sailor, who seemed to be inching uncomfortably closer to him all the time.

"The joke's on you, dear." The Virgin Mary stopped laughing, slipping a small pearl-handled derringer from beneath a lacy pillow and aiming it between Fuss's amazed eyes.

Fuss was afraid to take his eyes off the pistol so he didn't see the sailor move, but he felt the sailor suddenly grab him from behind with a viselike grip, locking his arms down. Fuss tried to shake the sailor off.

The Virgin Mary's thumb clicked back the derringer hammer. "Don't get hasty, dear."

Fuss stopped trying to break the sailor's iron lock.

"That's so much better, dear." The Virgin Mary slipped off the bed, slinking up to Fuss. In his high-heeled shoes he was more than six feet, taller than Fuss. "Now, dear." He nuzzled the barrel of the pistol under Fuss's chin. "Why don't you be a good scout and tell us who sent you here? Was it the Sinarquistas?"

"No."

The Virgin Mary dug the tip of the barrel into Fuss's jawbone. "Listen, you dirty little dope addict, somebody had to put you on to me. There isn't one boy in the street who doesn't know the Virgin Mary hates heroin, hates Horse. It's not a love potion like cocaine; it kills you between the legs. I don't like my sailor boys dead between the legs when I get them, understand?" The Virgin Mary pressed the barrel harder. "I like my seafood served nice and crisp when I reel it in. Know what I mean, dope addict?"

Fuss tried to answer, but the pistol barrel was jammed so far under his chin it pressed against the base of his tongue, slurring his words painfully. "I didn't come here for Horse . . . I came here for Sea Biscuit."

"Isn't that cute?" The Virgin Mary released the pressure of the metal barrel. "You don't want to connect, all you want is to bet on Sea Biscuit." He rammed the barrel harder into Fuss's chin. "Now who sent you to me to make this bet?"

"I'm not after to connect!" Fuss heard Tony Tomale thudding up the steps. "Wino Boy told me to come and ask to make a bet on Sea Biscuit."

"Tony, darling." The Virgin Mary slipped back from Fuss, fluffing the blond curls of his wig as he waved the small pistol, motioning Tony Tomale into the room. "Tony, would you be a darling and show our little sports fan here what we do with liars?"

Tony Tomale moved his bulk directly in front of Fuss, the shiny metal sliver of a tattoo needle held delicately in the sausages of his stubby fingers. He moved the sharp silver needle to Fuss's face.

"Now, dear." Virgin Mary puckered his lips at Fuss and blew him a kiss. "Tell us the truth or Tony darling is going to give you a new face. How would you like to look like Rin Tin Tin?"

"I'm telling you the truth." Fuss tried with the full power of his back muscles to break the hold the sailor had on him. The needle in Tony Tomale's steady hand came closer to Fuss's face. "I was sent here by Wino Boy. He said you knew everything there was to know in the Barrio. I want to know who set the Horse loose again. It's all over the streets out there. I'm not a pusher. I'm a Catholic social worker. I'm trying to stop the Horse from killing those kids. They're your people being killed."

The Virgin Mary's lips lost their pucker. He took the tattoo needle from Tony Tomale and held the point straight to Fuss's left eye, watching the pupil pulse and dilate in fear beneath the sharp metal point. "Now listen, dear." His voice hissed in Fuss's face. "I'm going to give you the benefit of a Catholic doubt, but if you are lying to me and want Sea Biscuit for the wrong reasons, darling Tony here will hunt you down and darn this needle right through your eye and out your brain."

Fuss didn't move. He felt the sailor release his iron hold. The Virgin Mary turned and swished back to the bed, lounging across the sheet in a flurry of silk, satin, and nylon.

"What about my bet?" Fuss was still afraid to move, the Virgin Mary's pearl-handled pistol shining alongside a bottle of fingernail polish on the nightstand next to his bed.

"What do you mean, dear?" The Virgin Mary batted the thick lashes drooping from his heavy eyelids.

"Wino Boy told me to say I'd like to place a bet on Sea Biscuit."

"Oh, yes, *Sea Biscuit.* Dear, if you're really such a sports fan you must go to pier 128 in San Pedro, always before dawn. If you are a good little scout, learn your knots and say your prayers sooner or later you will see Sea Biscuit. I promise you, Sea Biscuit will win, place, or show."

Fuss moved cautiously toward the door, but Tony Tomale's hulk was blocking it.

"Dear?" The Virgin Mary's voice came up low and sultry. Fuss turned to see him slip his slender legs open with a whisper of nylon, a bulge beneath his pink panties. "Don't you think my cookie is better looking than a movie star's, like Rita Hayworth's or Barbara Marr's?"

"Yah." Fuss winked. "I think you're a real cute trick. But I think you ought to try a different toothpaste." He turned and shoved his way past Tony Tomale and out the door.

13

Morning light was beginning to streak the dirty streets of the Zona Roja with a tinge of steel gray. A single jeepload of helmeted Shore Patrolmen roamed up and down long empty blocks, on guard for the crumpled forms of any sailor they might have overlooked the night before, searching in side alleys cluttered with debris of empty beer bottles and the shifting flutter of loose papers scattering in a restless wind. There was not a taxicab in sight. Fuss kept walking toward the blunt concrete finger of City Hall emerging in early dawn's gray distance. On the roof of Jimmy Zapata's bail-bond shop a black-and-white billboard stood out clearly in half-light: *DIALGOD*. A Shore Patrol jeep came around the corner before Fuss, its engine echoing off empty storefronts like the metal purr of a speedboat across a mountain lake. One of the Shore

Patrolmen from the passing jeep tipped a club to his hard white helmet in a mock salute. "How you doing, Admiral?" The Shore Patrolman's voice caught Fuss by surprise. Fuss saluted the man back and laughed. It never ceased to amaze him, whether the sailors had hard white helmets on or not, they were all so damn young, like his brother, Marvin, peachfuzz-faced kids. They better be good killers, because it made Fuss uneasy to think they were the only ones out there keeping America safe. Up toward the concrete finger of City Hall the yellow shape of a cab floated through a deserted intersection, not stopping for the flashing red light. Fuss called out. It was no use. He knew the cabbie couldn't hear him. The Shore Patrol jeep passed out of sight behind him; the streetlights flickered. He walked faster, reading the posters in store windows as he began to trot:

> JUNK MAKES WEAPONS,
> TURN IN YOUR OLD TOASTERS, SHOVELS, TIRES
> AMERICA CALLING,
> TAKE YOUR PLACE IN THE CIVILIAN DEFENSE:
> BUY WAR BONDS, SAVE FREEDOM OF SPEECH,
> SAVE DEMOCRACY

Every window had a large poster of a sailor drowning in a fiery sea before a sinking ship, pointing an accusatory finger above the words, *SOMEONE TALKED!*

Competing with the posters was a four-word slogan slashed in red paint on the sides and fronts of all buildings:

> SINARQUISTAS POR LA RAZA!

The yellow shape of a cab appeared again in the distant intersection. Fuss ran faster, shouting for the cab to stop. It kept going. He turned down an alley, hoping to catch the cab on the next street. At the end of the alley he was nearly breathless; breaking out on the street, he saw the cab rounding the corner and shouted. The cabbie saw him, clicking off the *UNOCCUPIED* light on the taxi roof and roaring down the middle of the street. Fuss couldn't understand why the cabbie was suddenly in such a hurry. Then he saw them, directly across the black pavement, the purple-green-and-yellow flash of their baggy suits bright as neon lights, brims of their wide hats like beaks of large angry birds as they kicked and screamed at a form in white cowering on the sidewalk before them. Fuss ran across the street, the cab skidding to a stop behind him. One of the Zoots jerked around to the intrusive sound of the cab; he saw Fuss running toward him and reached beneath his floppy coat. The click of a stiletto in the Zoot's hand released a sudden silver flash of an eight-inch knife blade.

"Back off, dude! Back off! It ain't your fight!" The Zoot waved the blade before his face, swaggering like a bullfighter straight toward Fuss. "Back off or I'll dag you!"

Fuss heard the cab door swing open behind him, the cabbie shouting at the top of his lungs, "Get in, buddy! Get in!"

"C'mon home to mama!" The Zoot jabbed the knife at Fuss, making a loud sucking sound with his lips as his hand slashed the blade before him, trying to distract Fuss's attention from the sailor in white on the ground. Fuss saw blood running between the fingers of the sailor's hands, protectively clutched over his face to avoid kicks coming at him from all sides.

"Get in the cab, buddy!" The cabbie honked his horn at Fuss.

The Zoot with the knife snapped his head around and looked up the street. The squeal of a Shore Patrol jeep's tires racing around the corner pierced through the roar of its engine.

"Get in, buddy, *now!*"

Fuss turned, looking at the open door of the cab, then back to the Zoot. Fuss screamed, not at the Zoot with the knife but at one of the two other Zoots kicking the dazed sailor. "Cruz!" He jumped in the cab and slammed the door. The cabbie punched the accelerator, swerving the cab up on the sidewalk to miss the nearly out-of-control jeep skidding to a stop in the middle of the street.

Fuss realized what he had just done, his chest still heaving as he tried to fill his lungs with air. "What are we running away for? We have to go back!"

"Go back! Are you crazy, buddy?" The cabbie fixed Fuss's panting image in the rearview mirror. "Go back and you get involved. Go back and you end up having to give testimony. You want to give testimony? I'll stop the cab and you get out. Me, I got a job to do every night. I intend to spend my days sleeping, not giving testimony in some court. You want to get out?"

Fuss looked through the back window, the sky was almost clear with the light of morning. "No, I can't, I have to be somewhere."

"Where to, bud?"

"San Pedro, pier 128."

"Okie-dokie, San Pete it is."

The city rolled out flat, away from the sun threatening to break over jagged purple peaks of the San Gabriel Mountains, into mile after mile of dry weed fields dominated by black-silhouetted factories, bare interlocking steel fingers of high cyclone fences surrounding each one. Short hills started up in the distance, pocked with forests of oil rigs pumping on the horizon. A few lights still blinked in the town of San Pedro, sprawled disorderedly along low hills against the perfect blue of the Pacific Ocean. Small one-story houses began to row out along the deserted highway. Some houses had patches of green Victory gardens stamped like miniature oases in front yards; others had royal-blue flags proudly hung in windows, each gold star on the flag indicating a son, brother, or father in uniform overseas. Behind the houses giant crisscrossed steel skeletons of the shipbuilding yards rose abruptly, forging a commanding attraction across an endless bleak landscape.

"Yah, I was in Number *One*."

Fuss became aware of the cabbie's voice. It had been

droning on like the slap of rubber tires against pavement beneath the taxi ever since they left Los Angeles.

"Leatherneck I was, fought the Heinies. But I'll tell you,
buddy, if I wasn't over the hill as a good dogface, what I would
give to get a crack at these greasy little slanteyed Jap bastards."
He angled the rearview mirror to get a closer look at Fuss. "Hey,
how come you ain't in the service?"

"4F."

"4F, what a waste. Must be tough to sit the big one out,
huh? I bet you wish you were over there right now sticking
those Nips, huh?" The cabbie winked in the mirror.

"No. My younger brother's sticking it to them for me."

"Navy or Marines?"

"Navy."

"Buddy, you wouldn't catch me on no washtub out there
in the drink in times like these, takes real guts. Those swab
jockeys got to be made of steel to fight them Jap subs and Zeros.
Problem is, most times you can't never see the yellow Jap bastards till they hit you. You tell your brother I think he's doing
a fine job. Maybe he'd like to meet my daughter when he comes
back. Want to see a picture of my daughter?" Before Fuss could
answer the cabbie had his wallet flipped open and dangling
over the seat in Fuss's face. "Ain't she a move star, though?"

"A regular June Allyson." Fuss tried to smile apprecia-
tively at the picture of a woman in her early thirties, her hair
pulled up in two knots above her ears, fizzed like an out of
control spray of fireworks.

"Real attractive, ain't she?" The cabbie slapped his wallet shut with a grin. "I keep her out of trouble over at the USO
rec hall in Azusa. She meets a lot of nice servicemen there, and
I don't have to worry about some civvie getting her PWOP and
jilting her. A serviceman's got his regular wages from Uncle
Sam, and if he don't come back from overseas old Uncle is real
generous with his war widow's insurance. You know what that
means, PWOP?"

"No." Fuss shook his head. He didn't know and he didn't care.

"P-W-O-P! Pregnant without permission, buddy! That's what them Wackies and Wavies call it. I thought you said your brother was in the Navy. He should tell you about things like that."

"He is in the Navy, but they just yanked him out of boot camp and stuck him right on a carrier. I haven't seen him once since. Where he is now he couldn't get a fish pregnant if he wanted to."

"Don't you worry, day comes when they tie up the boat in downtown Tokyo he'll get all the Jap nookie he can eat. That's the way it ended when I was in Number One. That's the way it's going to end in Number Two."

"Tell me." Fuss leaned forward against the back of the cabbie's seat. "Do you see much of the kind of stuff we saw this morning in the Barrio?"

"I see stuff that would make you puke. A lot of gals marry servicemen; soon's the guys ship out of town, the gals go down to the Zona Roja and turn a few tricks. I ain't just talking about Mexican gals neither. I see all colors doing it. Some kind of disease or something, makes you want to puke."

"I didn't mean that. I mean what *we* saw."

"Since I become a cabbie I seen everything there is for a man to possibly see, and since this war begun I seen all the *rest.*"

"Have you seen Zoots beating up sailors?"

"I seen Zoots beating up sailors and sailors beating up Zoots, so what's new? And why not? If you was a sailor, say your brother as an instance, and come home to find a bunch of greasers that didn't want to work hanging around in gangs on the street corners of your town dressed in those jungle bunny suits they wear, what would you do if you was a white man? I heard on Walter Winchell just the other day, Uncle Sam's gonna outlaw them Zoot suits those spics and niggers wear anyways; they use up material that could go into making more uniforms for our boys overseas."

"You really heard that?"

"Hey, buddy, don't you know?" The cabbie screeched to a stop before the high wire mesh of pier 128 and turned around with a dead-serious expression on his face. "Walter Winchell never lies. Winchell gets all his inside stuff from President Roosevelt himself. It's the straight poop."

14

The wire-mesh gate of pier 128 was open; Fuss went through. Down the long distance of the broad pier blank salt-streaked walls of packing sheds blocked access to the sea. Stacked on pallets high as three men were large wooden crates, each stamped *HANDLE WITH CARE—AMERICAL TUNA, SAN PEDRO, CAL.*

"You can't go any farther, fella."

Fuss looked over to the man in a green guard's uniform staring out at him through an open window of a small guardhouse inside the wire-mesh gate. "Just looking, no harm."

The guard sipped from his thermos of coffee, wispy tufts of steam inching up his nose. "Restricted property, 'less you got an appointment."

"Sure, I have an appointment."

"Why didn't you say so?" The guard unhooked a clipboard hanging from a nail above his head and flipped through the pages of names. "Who with?"

"Who with, what?"

"Who do you have the appointment with?"

A lift truck roared from the other end of the pier, its steel-forked fingers weighted with a pallet of loaded crates, the heavy timbers beneath the truck's wheels thundering like the thick skin of a giant drum.

"What was that you said?" The guard shouted into the roar of the lift truck.

Fuss waited until the lift truck stacked its load and backed off, roaring out of sight into the packinghouse. "I said I have an appointment with the owner."

The guard racked his clipboard back on the nail. "Then you've got a long wait. He's out of town on business, won't be back till tomorrow."

Fuss backed out the gate. "Guess I got the date confused. Tell him I came by, will you?"

"Sure thing. What was the name?"

"Archibald." Fuss tipped his hat and smiled. "Archibald Fitzgerald, State Fish and Game Department."

"All right, Mr. Fitzgerald." The guard saluted Fuss with a patronizing wink. "Will do."

The sun was bright. Whatever it was Fuss was to witness at dawn he had missed; it was already midmorning. He noticed the tower of a grain silo sticking above the warehouse roofs at the end of the pier next to the Americal packing plant. He heard steam blasts of big cargo ships and honking and braying of tugs working the crowded harbor. Above all was the clamor of warship yards, the steel din filling the narrow streets Fuss walked through into the center of San Pedro. He checked into the Tide's Inn Motel, down the street from the bus terminal. He had the desk clerk call *DIALGOD*. The line was busy. He thought of his brother, Marvin, lost somewhere out in the Pacific, the last one in the family he still had communication with. He pulled the shade over the window of his motel room and fell wearily across the bed without taking his clothes off. The vision of Cruz's chest crisscrossed with razor cuts refused to leave his mind. But Cruz's face wasn't his own; it was the grinning face of Marvin. Fuss wondered if the Shitter had gotten to Marvin yet. He thought of the Shitter, another one alone out there in the wide blue Pacific, some scared kid maybe, or even an officer, letting everyone know just what he thought of the Navy, of the Japs, of the war.

A knock came lightly, like the tentative peck from a small bird on a windowpane, but it was enough to jar Fuss awake. He jumped up from bed, grabbing the doorknob and pressing his back up against the door. The knock came again, right on the other side of his ear, a little tapping like a bird far away in a forest.

"Who is it?"

"Can I come in?"

Fuss didn't recognize the woman's voice. "Are you the maid?"

"No, brother. I'm Tokyo Rose. I thought you'd like some home-front morale boosting."

Fuss thought he heard laughter. He cracked the door open and peeked out. A woman in blue coveralls with a red-and-white bandana knotted around her dark braided hair smiled straight into his eyes. He opened the door a crack more to see if anyone else was standing in the hall. The woman slipped right in. He closed the door quickly behind her.

"I'm Rosie the Riveter." The woman pressed close to Fuss. She turned her lips up to him and winked. "Don't you know who Rosie the Riveter is?" She slipped her arms around Fuss's neck. "Why don't you lie back on the bed like a big ol' Victory ship, then I'll do a job on you for the good of ol' Uncle Sammy."

Fuss pried the grip of the woman's fingers from behind

his neck. "Lady, I think you have the wrong room!"

"Every room is the right room."

Fuss grabbed the woman around the waist; she didn't have anything on under the coveralls. He lifted her up and set her down at arm's length from him. The top of the coveralls were unzipped from her neck, down to the deep V of her very large breasts. "I know you got the wrong room, lady."

"Come on, Mac." Her fingers fiddled with the zipper between her breasts. "Don't be a palooka; give a working gal a break."

The sudden rasp of the zipper was loud in Fuss's ears as it traveled down to the woman's waist, exposing her bare stomach, one finger lodging lightly in her belly button.

"How about it, Mac?"

"How much?"

"Ten."

"Five."

"Oh, brother!" The woman started to pull the zipper back up. "Who do you think you are, Andy Hardy?"

"Okay." Fuss held his hand up in surrender. "It's a—"

Before Fuss could get the last word out the woman was on him, her mouth coming straight over his lips, sucking the air from him. He tried to feel her loose breasts but she belligerently pushed his hand away, pressing her body against him, her own hand going beneath the coveralls. He felt an urgent movement on his chest as her fingers stroked freely over her breasts, pinching the thick nipples. His own breath came wildly back from her mouth. She panted loudly, her free hand going between his legs, clinging desperately like a starfish to a smooth rock. She slipped the hand fondling her breasts deep inside her coveralls. She gasped, moving her fingers between her legs, raising up on the quick rubbing of her hand as she squirmed against Fuss. He locked his arms around her arched back, bucking against her as she moaned in rhythm to the frantic stroking of her hands probing between both their legs.

Her lips sucked off of him, slipping free from the bite of his teeth, her eyes wide open and on him as she brought her hand back up from between her legs, over the hard thrust of her breasts, and covered his mouth. The damp smoky scent of her slippery fingers quickly filled his nostrils. She rubbed the taste of her slickness roughly over his lips. The starfish suction of her hand between his legs spread across his belly, far into his groin like a hot wave. She forced open his lips, driving her tongue through damp fingers deep into his mouth. All across his belly the hot wave was very wet, very urgent. She pulled back from him, cocking her head to one side like she was about to scold a very bad child.

"Oh, shoot, you got your pistol off already!"

Fuss stood alone in the middle of the room, shaking, barely aware of the sweat coming down along his cheeks. In the spotlight of small scattered bits of sunshine knifing into the room from behind the window shade the heaving of the woman's large breasts seemed very far from him, as if she was an untouchable passionate actress on a distant stage. He couldn't stop his hands from trembling. He wanted to step into the spotlight and cover her breasts with his hands, make her tremble beneath him, break the power she held over him. She had manipulated him like a puppet, jerked the right strings to vent his lust. She had sold him the sizzle without the steak, made a joke of his vulnerable manhood. He wanted to penetrate her flesh until she cried his name. But she didn't know his name, and like all the others he had taken quickly in a great fumbling of false emotions, she didn't want to know it.

"Well, I guess that's it." She zipped her coveralls carefully over the full swell of her breasts. "Andy Hardy meets Rosie the Riveter."

"I don't know what came over me." Fuss heard his voice come out awkwardly into the stillness of the room. "I usually don't—"

"Forget it, Andy. We all have our odd days."

"But I've never—"

She put a finger to her lips and blew out a big "Shush! No harm done, the country will survive. You've been a good scout. Now, if you'll pay up, little Rosie will be on her merry way."

Fuss reached into his pocket. "How about five bucks? We only did it halfway."

"Now don't be a naughty boy, Andy." The woman placed her hands on her hips, tapping her foot in rapid bursts of irritation. "Be a good sport. You know what the generals say. Napoleon never got all the way to Moscow, but he was man enough not to ask for half his army back."

15

Kathleen La Rue was above him. Way above him. The sun was behind her red hair. The kind of brilliant sun he had never seen as a boy on the farm in Oregon. A desert sun, fierce as a hot breath from a snarling Gila monster. He was so far away, the rope of his voice couldn't reach her. He kept calling, calling, and calling, but he couldn't catch the meaning of his own words. He was in the bottom of a deep pit, an enormous split in the earth, a grand canyon. It was dark where he was. It hurt his eyes to look at her against the sun. Her face was so pale, her wild curls a thousand red snakes surrounding the white face of an angel. She was so far away, so much above him. Her anguished lips opened slowly, a compulsive sad cry screaming down into the canyon to him, reverberating off the steep cliffs, groping for him thickly in the darkness. He felt like his heart was broken in two. The hurt boiled up out of his chest and stung his throat like someone trying to strangle him. Her cries were so terrible, taking forever to reach him, so distant he was helpless to suppress them, each one coming stronger than the last.

The cries in Fuss's head broke from his dream. He sat up suddenly in the darkness of the room. Outside, the steady, mournful cry of a foghorn came muffled and distant through the drifting blanket of fog. He glanced at the luminescent green numbers of a ticking clock glaring at him from the nightstand: 4:30. He climbed out of bed and quickly slipped on his pants. He had almost slept through the dawn. He didn't know what he was supposed to see with the dawn, but he was determined not to miss it a second time.

The streets of San Pedro were empty. Fuss made his way quickly to the docks. It was difficult to see through dense fog from one block to the next, but the sound of a distant foghorn in the harbor guided him. Block after block through dark neighborhood streets brought him closer to the docks. The sky began to shimmer, the rising sun tearing cold gray blankets of fog right off roofs of warehouses. He was afraid he had missed the dawn again. But it wasn't sun beginning to sear through the fog. He heard the clamor, a steel pounding and incessant wail of drills. Suddenly through the dark gray curtain of fog brilliant lights strung like Christmas ornaments in a forest of giant steel girders illuminated the predawn sky. Blazing lights stopped Fuss in his tracks. For more than a mile, hulking four-story steel hulls of half-completed Victory cargo ships were lined like steel-ribbed primordial creatures in the steep cement guts of the mammoth Cal Shipyards dry docks. Jeeps of heavily armed Shore Patrolmen cruised along the scene of frantic activity, each dock protected by twelve-foot-high wire-mesh fence stretching into the distance where the blaze of lights gave way once again to fog. Hundreds of people worked the graveyard shift, swarming around steel hulls like ants at a July

Fourth picnic, showers of welding sparks shooting off everywhere in a mad display of fireworks. All the women were dressed in blue coveralls, red-and-white bandanas knotted around their braided hair.

Fuss cut up alleys, went down back streets, passed deserted factories and sleeping neighborhoods to avoid the searing light of the shipyards. Fog gently enveloped him, its soft gray moisture a lazy falling miniature rain, making him almost invisible as he slowed his walk. He emerged before the stillness of the Americal packinghouses barricaded behind a steel wall of wire-mesh fence. The faintest glimmer of light fingered from the guardhouse through mist, giving Fuss just enough illumination to see where to put his hands in the steel crisscrossing of the fence. He pulled himself up, climbing hand over hand, slowly, until reaching three strands of barbed wire running dangerously along the top. Fuss's pants snagged on the barbs as he tried to slip through the taut strands of wire. He hung, caught on barbs cutting into his flesh, small pricks of blood running hot on his legs, his pained breath exhaling white in the gray fog. He waited to see if the guard in the house heard him. The sharp ring of a telephone startled the quiet of the guardhouse. Fuss wrestled his pants leg free of the steel barbs. He barely heard the guard laughing to someone on the phone as he dropped to the pier.

Fog was so thick Fuss saw only ghostly outlines of seagulls swirling and dipping over choppy water, crying out in anticipation of their morning meal. Fuss hid in a mound of coiled mooring rope stacked high against the wall of the packing plant. After an hour of waiting the smell of oil in the rope was making him sick. He didn't know how much longer he could hide out in the rope without throwing up. He watched anxiously for the first sign of dawn. He knew when the sun seared away the fog he wouldn't be able to get back over the fence without the guard discovering him. It was difficult to determine if the fog over the gray water of the harbor was ten feet before him or hundreds of feet away. It was impossible to know if the fog was rolling back or if the heave of the waves was tricking him into thinking he saw farther into the harbor than he actually did. Then he heard it. The throaty sound of an engine exhaust muffling through water. Then he heard another, until an entire chugging chorus of engines surrounded him and he could see them all. Like hellish creatures appearing from clouds of a prairie fire, the tuna boats bobbed free of fog, bent iron fingers of net wenches cutting through cold air like twisted flagpoles on the decks of a wrecked fleet. The cry of seagulls split the air; they swirled in reckless feathered clouds, dipping down into the foaming wakes of the boats to devour guts of the catch being dumped overboard.

The boats passed out of sight, on to the far side of the pier, their sound almost totally blocked from Fuss by high walls of the packing plant. He dug deep in his pocket for a stick of Juicy Fruit. Was this it? He peered into the fog bank that was now definitely drifting back over oil-slicked water as the heat of a new day began to assert itself. Was this all there was? Was this what the Virgin Mary wanted him to see? Tuna boats? He couldn't put any of it together. What did any of it have to do with anything? He pushed himself up from the coil of rope. The sun was winning its war with the fog. Dawn was breaking. Suddenly the sound of another boat cut through the distant fog bank. He slipped back into his hiding place. Probably one struggling tuna boat catching up with the fleet after a long night's fishing. But it wasn't a fishing boat.

The sleek surprise gliding out of the fog dazzled Fuss with its whiteness. From where he was watching, it appeared to be over a hundred feet long; its new paint seemed wetter than the water it cut through. The yacht was a total apparition, as if she were queen of the sea and had been waiting all this time in the bank of fog to see if her family of tuna boats would come home safely to put in with their precious cargo. But the queen of the sea did not follow her children. The yacht put by the tip of the pier, the smooth cut of the prow ignoring the packing warehouse where fishing boats had tied up, heading straight before Fuss to the far end of the next pier, coming alongside an enormous cargo ship taking on grain through long steel chutes running down from a towering holding silo. The yacht bobbed the length of the cargo ship, uncertain as a kitten at the feet of an elephant, then cut away to berth; men with ropes on the pier signaled her to come about.

A man emerged from the yacht's cabin. He seemed to be the only one on board. Spluttering exhaust from the dying engine stopped. He grabbed hold of ropes thrown to him from the pier and secured them to the yacht, then swung off onto the pier ladder, climbing twenty steep feet to join men above. He looked down at the yacht, his white hair slicked back in wings beneath a blue sea captain's cap, his face deeply tanned and distinguished looking. He said something to the men on the pier; hurriedly they untied the yacht's securing ropes and threw them off into the sea. The yacht bobbed uncertainly, several currents taking advantage of its sudden freedom. It edged away from the pier like an abandoned child. High overhead, from the top of the cargo ship, the unexpected long iron arm of a boom crane appeared. Swinging from the tip of the crane's boom, rubber-encased steel netting hovered above the yacht. Heavy netting plummeted into the water, barely missing the yacht. Deftly as a mother plucking her precious child from the bath, the netting scooped up the abandoned sleek white prize, hauling the yacht dripping and swinging over the top of the cargo ship to nest in the soft grain continuing to cascade into the cavity of the hold.

Crouching alongside the packing plant, heading for the barbed-wire fence, Fuss kept mumbling two things over and over so he would never forget them: the maritime number of the yacht he glimpsed as it sailed dripping into the air, and the name of the cargo ship the yacht miraculously vanished into, *Vera Cruz Ally*.

16

The Hollywood Stars were cooking. Angel was red hot and throwing comets. Out on the mound the breath from Angel's nostrils steamed into cold evening air as he stamped angrily at the earth. The Bees were frightened, afraid to swing at the ball because they kept eating empty air, afraid not to swing because the furious pitches came curving dangerously at them, like the arc of a great blade that could slice a man's head off. The Bees swung in self-defense.

"I tell you, Fuss, this Fresno bunch is cowed. Angel's been punching the ticket on each one of them."

"He's been hot like this for two weeks, Senator."

"That boy you're looking at out there is the star Star. He's going to pitch this bunch of bums all the way to the Coast championship."

"If he's not drafted first."

"He won't be." Kinney turned to Fuss, his lips curved in a sly smile beneath dark glasses. "I'm taking care of it."

"If Roosevelt can't keep a big-league pro like DiMaggio out of the draft, how you going to pull it off with an unknown West Coast player? Half the teams he plays against don't even know his last name."

"All things are possible in love, war, and politics, Fuss." The smile on Kinney's lips grew larger as he slumped down in his seat, trying to make himself more inconspicuous to the surrounding crowd. "Love, war, and politics, Fuss, eternal sisters with no rules. You'll find that out someday. When you do, I hope it's not too late."

"Did you get the information I wanted?"

"We're working on it."

"Working on it! How much time do you need, Senator? The Jap army could be camped out on the Golden Gate Bridge by the time you come up with the information."

"Now don't get hasty, Fuss. We're working on it."

"I risk my life climbing over guarded fences in the dark, and you can't find out who a couple of boats are registered to."

"I didn't say we couldn't find out, I just said these things take time. There *is* a war going on, Fuss. Other matters are equally pressing. But I do think we'll have the goods on who owns the yacht within a couple of days. The cargo ship, on the other hand, is not so easy. Going through the Mexican bureaucracy is like pouring money down a rat hole. You have to bribe the left hand to find out what the right hand is doing. We do know one thing, though. *Vera Cruz Ally* belongs to somebody high up in the Mexican government. Look at that Angel out there, would you! Nobody can spit and polish a baseball the way that boy can. Once these hot-blooded Latins get cooking, there's nobody they can't beat."

"*How* high up in the government?"

"Fuss, I told you to hold your horses. We don't have that

information yet; besides, it isn't a crime to stuff a fancy yacht into the hold of a grain ship."

"Will you tell me, Senator, if you had a two-hundred-thousand-dollar yacht and wanted to take a cruise to Mexico, would you do it under fifteen hundred tons of grain?"

"Fuss, I'm not implying there isn't something fishy going on. I just don't see the connection between that yacht and the Sinarquistas. The Sinarquistas are Fascists, not Sunday sailors. We know they come from Madrid to Mexico City, then wetback it across the border into California. They don't sail up the coast in two-hundred-thousand-dollar yachts. They are Fascists, they try to set up a fifth column wherever they can. The way they traditionally do it is by organizing street gangs first, to gain control of thugs and bullies to do their dirty work later. They can't operate without control of the street gangs. Without support of the gangs there is no way for them to put an iron fist in their velvet glove."

"Angel struck out the side. Maybe he shouldn't look so good, the Army might want to draft him for one of its teams."

"What did you dig up on the La Rue girl?"

"She's a sad case really, she . . ."

"Wait a minute, Fuss, the hotdog kid is selling foot-longs up there. Get me a dog, would you? Mustard, hold the relish. You want one?"

"No, I don't want one." Fuss climbed from the box seats into the grandstand bleachers and brought back a drooping slab of pink meat wrapped tightly in a soggy bun.

"Great dogs." Kinney bit off six inches of meat, his words puffing around the load in his mouth. "Now, what's the poop on the girl?"

"I think La Rue's harmless. A lonely type, typical kind who gets involved in wacko cults. She has terrible asthma, a wonder she's alive really."

"Have you met the Voice?"

"No, but she promises me I will. Be patient, she says.

Everybody seems to have all the time in the world except me."

"You've got to get to the Voice. He's the ticket."

"He's certain to be at the Shrine next month. They're having some kind of big rally there, first in L.A. The girl's all excited about it."

"Is La Rue thick with the Zoots?"

"She spends her days pounding the pavement, proselytizing for her outfit. She'll put the bite on anyone trying to put over her beliefs."

"She getting any converts?"

"Not among the Zoots. I think they tolerate her because she acts crazier than they dress. She's unique."

"She having better luck with anybody else?"

"Older people mostly. Yah, I guess you could say she is getting through to some of them. She's filling up her meetings anyway. I think people come to hear what weird thing she's going to be telling them next. Last week she promised to give us a secret electronic gizmo the Sponsors invented. We attach the gizmo to our radios and hear Mankind Incorporated broadcasts, giving instructions about the final worldwide program of organization. The week before, she was excited about another mysterious invention the Sponsors cooked up at the lab in the center of the earth with the help of their metallic-headed little friends. This one was a beaut, a blue beam having power to melt steel from thirty miles away. She told us it had recently been tested in Seattle and stopped all motor traffic for twenty minutes; even police cars going to investigate the massive traffic tie-up were stranded and helpless. I checked the Seattle papers back over the past year, couldn't find one reference to a weird thing like that happening. God knows where she gets this stuff."

"What about the Doomsday Vibration Machine? Some kind of apparatus capable of suspending animation that can be used to immobilize entire armies and make their eyes pop out. Does she ever talk about that?"

"I tell you, Senator, her outfit has more crazy ideas. I mean, they believe the earth is a glass crust and there are these tiny metallic-headed supermen living in the middle of it controlling balances of nature, like gravity, ocean tides, earthquakes, that kind of stuff—but I don't recall her ever speaking about some powerful secret Vibration Machine."

"La Rue's never talked about vibrations?"

"She's talked about what she calls a theory of vibrations, how love has a high vibration rate, and hate has a low one. She says all these vibrations are of the same universal substance, coming from the sun. According to her, we can get to a point where we'll actually see these vibrations; they'll become visible. Eventually we'll be able to see if someone is thinking good or bad things about us."

"But no Vibrating Machine that can destroy all weapons on earth, stop armies in their tracks, suspend airplanes in air, freeze movement of ships on the seas?"

"Not a word."

"What about a film called *Dealers in Death?* Supposed to document how Hidden Rulers of the world, including Roosevelt and Hitler, are plotting the final holocaust. What about that?"

"I never heard her talk about it. She says the Hidden Rulers have a very low vibration rate, and the One True Voice an extremely high aura of vibrations. She's more concerned about the day when she can control her aura of vibrations so she'll be able to leave her body and travel to another person's healthy body, or another planet even. I think that's the real reason she believes in all this malarkey. Figures one day it'll free her from her own sick body."

Kinney rolled the empty mustard-stained hotdog wrapper between his palms and tossed it to his feet, shaking his head in disgust. "Jesus, Fuss, the garbage some people will wade through if they believe it will cure what ails them."

"It's a free country, Senator."

"That's right. Sometimes, though . . ." Kinney stood to

leave in the blare of seventh-inning-stretch organ music. His shoulders seemed to slump as the screeching tune of "Yankee Doodle Dandy" echoed across the dusty diamond and empty outfield bleachers. "Sometimes I just wonder if it's worth all the spit and blood to keep it free for *every* Tom, Dick, and Harry."

i Guy,

*Thanks for the pinup of Betty Grable. What a pair of
bazookas that dame's packing. I'm telling you, any little
titbit like that makes a swab jockey's job just that much
easier. When you know how sexy the home fronts are on
a gal like Grable, it's a lot easier to fight for them. Hey,
did I tell you? I got a signed autographed pic of Henry
Fonda when he was here. Great guy really, all the guys
thought he was real regular. Nothing much exciting on
the old tin bucket. Oh, yah, the other night I was having
that dream again, you know, the one about fire on the
water. Well right in the middle, when a bunch of guys
was hollering and screaming and dying around me, I
smell something funny, real terrible like burning cat*

hair, you know? But it wasn't that, it was something else closer by. I woke up and sniffed around. Sure enough, the guy in the berth across from me was sound asleep with a big mound of shit on his bunk and a little greeting tacked to it. Guy wakes up kicking and screaming, getting shit all over everything, terrible mess, everybody laughing. The note says, "Marvin Fuss is next. Good luck and sweet dreams!" And it was signed, "Your Pal, The Shitter." So every night after chowing down I been coming right back to my bunk and camping out on it. This is one swab jockey the Shitter is not going to take off guard!

> *See you guy,*
> *Marvin*

P.S. Started your Victory garden yet? Remember vitamins are for victory.

Fuss put the letter down and dialed the telephone. "Operator, I've been trying to reach a number but it's always busy. Could you check on the listing for me, please, to make certain it's active?"

"What's the name of the party, sir?"

"*DIALGOD.*"

"One moment. Yes. I show it active; the number hasn't been changed. Would you like me to dial it for you, sir?"

"Would you, please?"

Outside the window Fuss's eyes traced the once bright ropes of Christmas decorations. He remembered the December day more than a year and a half ago, before Pearl Harbor, when he watched a crew of men work their way down the street all morning, laboriously looping silver ropes with dangling, almost life-size plastic Santa Clauses from the slick legs of the palm trunk tops. After the bombing of Pearl Harbor no one came back to take down the decorations. They faded in the hot summer sun, the strong winds battered the plastic bodies of Santa Clauses, covering them with dust.

"Sir?"

"Yes?"

"Still trying."

"I'll wait."

Fuss was depressed. He was tired of the lousy war; he wanted it over. He wanted his brother to come home. He could get him a job. He wanted the city to take down its lousy Christmas decorations. Outside the window it looked to Fuss like the city of Los Angeles had decided to hang every Santa Claus in the world by the neck in mass execution on his street.

"Sir?"

"Yes, operator?"

"I'm sorry, but all the circuits to *DIALGOD* are busy."

18

They're such nice kids, all of them."

"That's the thing, Kathleen. I just can't believe they're killers. But somebody pulled the trigger that gunned down those two FBI agents."

Kathleen dipped her finger into the muscle of crosscurrent created in the wake of Fuss's steady rowing. Briefly her finger left a crooked little trail in the water behind the gliding boat. "Oscar, all through that long, awful trial I kept thinking to myself, over and over, as I watched those Zoot-suiters sitting silently in their blue jail clothes, handcuffed together like they were no more important than common cattle, I kept thinking it was all such a nightmare. Those boys are just children. They're certain to die in the gas chamber at Alcatraz."

"In the electric chair. They will die in the electric chair;

that's how they do it in a federal prison. It's the state of California that sends people to the gas chamber."

"Some of them could barely speak English, it was pitiful really. They couldn't even follow what the district attorney was saying about them. It was so awful. A disgrace. Even if one of those boys did shoot the two FBI men, how can they condemn them all to die? Only one could have pulled the trigger, not all twelve at the same time. I was right there, and I didn't see *one* of them fire a gun. But I guess the Sinarquistas teach them how to do things like that."

In the sunlight Kathleen's red hair went purple against the blue water. Even in the shade of a wide straw hat her face was flour white, almost colorless. She seemed someone never intended for the outdoors, only magically to be transported from house to house. She breathed so deeply, so strenuously, even while relaxing in the boat. Fuss noticed the small pointed puffs of her breasts, rising and falling against the thin cotton of her long dress buttoned high to her throat, keeping every possible ray of sun from touching her pale flesh. Her heart was always racing, beating wildly beneath her breasts, like a small bird fluttering its wings against bars of a cage. Fuss couldn't keep his eyes off her as he rowed smoothly to the middle of the lake. There was something compelling about the frailty of her health, a strong magnet pulling him implacably to her in the strangest way. He could not look at her without uncontrollably feeling the heat of hardening flesh move between his legs. The weaker she seemed to become, the more excited he became.

He had always had an acute attraction for broad-boned women. Women with their feet solidly planted on the ground beneath them. Women he could hang on to for a wild ride. Women he could kiss in the dampness of their armpits and they would laugh in his face, throwing their heavy arms around him, bucking even harder beneath him. He had never been attracted to a small-breasted woman, no matter how pretty she was. He felt if he leaned over in the hot sun and unbuttoned

Kathleen's dress from around her throat, spreading the thin cotton down over the bone white of her shoulders and kissed her under the arms, she would cry or even simply faint. He felt there was something unhealthy about his attraction to her, something fatal in her absolute frailty of body. Her illness had become an aphrodisiac to him. It surrounded her like the sweet musty scent of a rotting tree in the forest. He could not bear to take his eyes off the involuntary trembling of her bright red lips. The sweat of his palms, in a tight-fisted grip around the hard wood of the oars, made him aware he was holding on to something significant, substantial, but very slippery. When she turned her eyes to him, in the shade of her hat, her azure gaze fell upon him easily, the red lips momentarily stopped trembling, her relaxed body peaceful as a beautiful sleeping angel.

"Tell me." She spoke in her usual way, breathless, as if words were not powered by the strength of her lungs but were given energy from some deep well of alien source. "Tell me, dear Oscar, about yourself." Her eyes glowed in the shade of her hat. "You are such a mystery to me."

Fuss twisted the oars into the water, making the boat spin in a slow arc toward the lake's center. He rested the oars and wiped his slippery palms across the knees of his pants. "Me, a mystery?" He heard his laughter trickle self-consciously across the still surface of the lake. "No, I'm not the one who's much of a mystery. My life is very simple. I'm a simple man."

"No one is simple, Oscar, in the grand scheme of the universe."

Fuss leaned uncomfortably back on the hard rim of the boat. "I'm afraid that when the universe got around to me, things weren't so grand anymore."

"You should take more pride in yourself. You are always sitting back and watching others, asking questions. You should try to control events around you."

"I can't control myself, let alone others." Fuss felt his

hands shaking. "You see?" He laughed, holding his hands up. "I told you, I can't even control myself!" He clasped his hands together like a small boy in prayer.

Kathleen dipped her hand beneath the surface of the water; it looked like a pale blue fish. "Somehow, you don't seem to fit in the Barrio. You seem out of place there. You don't even seem to fit in Los Angeles."

"That's because I'm like everyone else, I'm not from Los Angeles."

"Oh." Kathleen brought her hand up, letting the clear beads of water drip off her fingers back into the lake. "How did you arrive here?"

"My father."

"You came with your family?"

"No, I followed my father."

"Your father came here first, then your family followed?"

"No, my father abandoned my family."

"Oh, Oscar, no wonder you always seem so nervous. They say children from broken homes are always nervous, that they have a hard time learning to trust people and feel they can't control events."

Fuss pushed himself up from the hard rim of the boat. "My father was a farmer up in Oregon. He was a simple man. He had two sons, four daughters, and six hundred acres of land in the Beaver Dam country, some of the richest truck-farming land in the world. But a small farmer's life is no better than a gambler's. House odds are always against the gambler; nature's odds are always against a farmer."

"What happened?"

"In 1925 onions were eleven dollars a hundred. My father borrowed against his already mortgaged land and put all six hundred acres in red-eye onions, but smut and cutworm ruined the crop. Next year, because of a bumper crop down here in California, the price of red-eye onions went down to ninety cents a hundred. My father just walked off the farm, walked away to the promised land where house odds are a little better, California."

"You mean he didn't take the family?"

"No, he just walked away. Leaving my mother with the mortgages and us kids."

"How awful."

"Awful, but not unusual. Farmers see things live and die, then reborn every year. I guess they figure they can do it too."

"Did you work the farm?"

"I did what I could. I was fifteen, my brother Marvin was only six, the girls were all in between."

"How terrible for your mother."

"Yes, and it was even more terrible a year later. I just got up and walked away, just like my dad had."

"You didn't!"

"I did. Actually, I wasn't walking away from responsibilities of the farm. I was determined to find my dad."

"Did you ever find him?"

"We knew where he was. We had an address on one postcard he sent back. He wasn't trying to hide or anything like that. I found him here in Los Angeles, way out on Fairfax Avenue, you know, where the Jews live. I found him living in a cheap apartment with a woman. He was friendly enough to me, real glad to see me as a matter of fact, and he asked about everybody up in Oregon. It was funny how much he really seemed to care, but after dinner he took me aside and said, 'Oscar, all a man really wants in life is enough to eat and enough sex. All the rest of it is bullshit. Someday you'll understand.'"

Kathleen's eyes questioned Fuss from the shadow of her hat. "Do you think you'll ever understand?"

"I understood right away. That night I was sleeping in the living room. There was only one other room in the apartment, and that was the bedroom. I woke up hearing fighting back there, lots of loud cursing and thumping. The woman started screaming at my dad, 'Either that little son of a bitch goes before morning or I do!' "

Kathleen said nothing. She looked across the lake to a small boy toddling down from the shade of park trees, leaving a trail of broken pieces of bread along the shoreline, ducks and geese creating a loud commotion, quacking and honking furiously as they paddled from all directions to glut on the sudden feast.

"Before morning I left. I never saw my father again; I understood his words."

When Kathleen turned her face back to him, Fuss saw the stain of tears in the shadow of her face.

"I didn't go back to the farm. I got lots of crazy jobs. I took anything. First one I had was for Jack Warner."

"What could a sixteen-year-old boy do for a big movie producer?"

Fuss laughed. "Babysit his son, Jack Junior. Junior was exactly my age, always trying to sneak off with some starlet or another from his father's studio. There was always the threat of a paternity suit. My job was to stay with Junior at all times. I was a hired shadow; wherever he went, I went. Every Saturday afternoon we drove the limousine down from the Beverly Hills mansion to see one of the old man's movies. Since the old man made the movies, he knew exactly how long they lasted and always called the ticket girl to ask if we arrived at the theater, so there could be no hanky-panky. But Junior was one up on the game. He'd give me twenty bucks to keep my mouth shut, slip out the side door of the theater, and take the limo to meet some hot date. He always got back just as the movie ended."

"I bet I know what happened next."

"What?"

"One day the limousine got a flat and Junior was caught in the backseat with a starlet."

"How did you know?"

Kathleen tipped her straw brim up slightly. An oblique shaft of sun subtly lit the lower half of her smiling face.

Fuss slumped back against the boat's hard rim, nervously plucking at the worn wool of his pants stretched thinly over his knees. "After that I got a job with the actor Pepe Maria y Maria."

"You don't mean the vulgar Cuban comedian who used to stuff basketballs into his mouth?"

"That's him, and he really could do it. It wasn't a trick, only it was a soccer ball painted like a basketball he used. His way of making a living was no more vulgar than most others. He was an average guy, a baseball fanatic. He hired me to play catch with him."

"That's all, play catch?"

"That was it. I was big enough, strong enough, played baseball in Oregon. Pepe took me everywhere, to the studio, his three ex-wives' homes, everywhere. I would wait for him until after he got out of his agent's office. He'd come out mad as a hornet every time and throw the ball to me hard as he could for hours, working his anger off. He wasn't such a crazy Cuban after all. But one thing he gave me to use later in life was Spanish. I learned all the swear words first, as he hurled the hard balls at me. Slowly I learned the rest of it. Ever since, I've been able to get jobs where Spanish had to be spoken as well as English."

"And that's how you got the job working with young boys in the Barrio?"

"That's how. Not very complicated, is it?"

"You are not such a simple man after all, Oscar Fuss." Kathleen let loose of her wide straw brim, her white face disappearing once again into complete shadow. "And these stories you just told don't lessen the mystery about you." She fell silent. The water lapping alongside the boat murmured around her. The lightness of her hand came up to Fuss's face. Gently her fingers traced the scars down his cheeks. "Are these the scars you got from Barbara Carr the night of the murders?"

Fuss placed his hand carefully over hers, as if trapping a butterfly. "Yes. She scarred me for life. But it's of no consequence if a man shows his scars. With a woman, it's different; she should never show she's been wounded."

"Your ideas about women are very odd, Oscar. You think we should all be perfect. That is what mystifies me most, your belief women are without sin. The way you came to the rescue of Barbara Carr, it was so gallant, so—noble." Kathleen's voice lowered, barely discernible above the murmuring water. "That is what I have come to cherish in you most, your sense of greater nobility."

19

So you're Oscar Fuss, huh?"

"That's right."

"Prove it."

Fuss took out his wallet and passed it up to the Sergeant behind the high desk.

The Sergeant flipped the wallet open, mumbling as he copied information off the driver's license onto an official release form. "Oscar Fuss. Address, 5676 South Spring Street. City and county, LA, LA. Here you go, bud." The Sergeant pushed Fuss's leather wallet to the desk edge with the point of his pencil like it was a dead brown rat. "You're the right guy all right."

"Where is he?"

"Your little pal is coming. We rounded up about eighty of

'em last night. Usual thing, street fighting. They carry those big clubs sewn into the pants legs of their Zoot suits next to their flies. Sometimes I think the clubs really are supposed to make their girlfriends think they have eighteen-inch hardwood peckers. I guess it takes a lot to impress those little Black Widows how tough you are. The Zoot we got for you had no identification on him when we brought him in. We didn't send him over to Juvie because he looked over eighteen, so we booked him in here for the night. Lucky you was there on his one phone call or the little Beaner would still be in the stew. I tell you, I think it's a big mistake letting these young pachuco punks out in the custody of you social workers. They're nothing but baggy-pants little dandies, Zoot-suit punks. It won't be long now before Mayor Bowron unties Chief Horell's hands; then we'll tackle this disease with real action, not just slaps on the wrist." The Sergeant jabbed the sharp point of his pencil in the air. "Sit down over there and rest your load, it's going to be a while."

Fuss followed the direction the Sergeant pointed; he walked through swinging green doors and took a seat in a small waiting room. A solid metal door with a round barred window at the top opened behind him. Cruz was prodded into the center of the room by a guard pressing a billyclub to his back.

"How do you like your little taco-breath baby now, daddy?" The guard winked at Fuss.

Cruz's eyes were on the floor, his head bent as if the thin links of cheap silver-coated chain hanging from his oversized green coat were a burden too heavy for his narrow shoulders to support. He would not raise his eyes to Fuss. He still wore his baggy purple Zoot-suit pants, pegged in like toreador pants at the ankles, the wide-brimmed fedora clutched in his shaking hands. The only thing different was that his black hair, usually swept in neat oiled waves to a perfect V at the back of his head, was now cut away; bristling nubs were spotted over the denuded curve of white scalp, nicked with angry red scissor cuts.

The guard touched his club to the top of Cruz's shaved head in a grand gesture worthy of a queen beknighting a heroic warrior. "You'll notice we gave him a white man's haircut, cut the duck's ass right off him. We figure it's his contribution to the war effort. The amount of oil this baby greased his hair up with every morning could lubricate a whole tank battalion for a month. Now he doesn't have to steal four bits for his yearly haircut." The guard clicked his heels and spun around. "Bring him by for a fashion lesson anytime, daddy. We aim to please." He chuckled and pushed out the metal door, letting it clank loudly behind him.

Fuss took Cruz's hat from his trembling hands and set it gently on the boy's head. Cruz still would not look at him. "Could have been worse, you know." Fuss sighed. "Could have been what you were dishing out to that sailor couple of weeks back."

Cruz turned his brown eyes up to Fuss. There was a watery film across them threatening to break at any moment. "What makes you think they didn't dish it out?" Cruz spit at the metal door the guard had disappeared through, the wet wad splattering against the small glass window. Cruz's top lip curled angrily above the soft pink of his gums. "What makes you think you know so much? You Commie coward!"

Fuss grabbed the boy around his neck and slammed him against the door with spit dripping down it. "Listen, I'm damn sick and tired of this Commie business. You know better! What the hell, who is it keeps coming down here at all hours of the night to bail you blades out? Huh? Who is it does those things when he knows what you blades are all into? Who gives you money and covers for you with the probation officer?" He pushed Cruz's chin up with his fist. "I know you blades don't get a fair shake. You think I'm blind? You think I'm deaf, dumb, and don't have a pot to shit in? Well, let me tell you something. If it wasn't for me you would be dead in three days. They would have found out you're on Horse and put you cold turkey." Fuss felt sick pushing a little kid around, he felt disgusted with himself. He couldn't look in Cruz's face; the boy was trapped, terrified, crying. Fuss shoved Cruz down in one of the chairs. What he was going to do next made him want to throw up. He hated himself for it. But there was a war on. "Okay, Cruz, I know I've been a little tough with you, but it's not a pretty picture out there. You know in the end I'm on your side. Now tell me, how much to get you hopped up?"

Cruz looked mockingly into Fuss's eyes. "What? Are you going into the business? You!"

"Nobody can hear us in here. Tell me, how much to connect?"

"What should I tell *you* for?"

"Because I want to make a deal."

The expression in Cruz's eyes changed completely. "No shit, you want to talk turkey?"

"I don't want you to bitch up your life is all. I want to see you get out of the Barrio, get a good job someday. Get married in the Church. Move out to San Fernando Valley and raise a family."

"Yah, well they'll give Emperor Hirohito an honorary degree at UCLA before that happens."

"I'll give you dough to connect."

"What's the catch?"

"That you promise me this is your last time. You're young, you're not hooked. You don't have to bitch up your life; be proud of yourself."

"I am proud."

"Baloney. You listen to the Sinarquistas. They tell you to spit on America. They teach you are different people from Anglos, even though you were born here. They tell you they can win here same way they did in Spain. They talk about pride, the cause, La Raza, but they don't care about that. They only care about defeating the American way. If they really cared for your people so much they wouldn't have let Horse loose in the

Barrio, hooking young kids. Who does that kind of thing? Gangsters. A mobster does that kind of thing, no matter what his politics are. A Hitler does that kind of thing."

"So you're *different*? You're offering me a fix if I'll play it your way on the square. You're just like what you say the Sinarquistas are."

"I'll give you something more than their empty talk about the glory of the Spanish race."

"What?"

"In two weeks you'll be eighteen. Don't bitch up your life. I'll get you a job."

Cruz shook his head. "You must really think I'm some dumb Beaner to go for that. I want a job in the shipyards. That's where the good money is. You know there are no jobs like that for us."

"I didn't say I'd get you a job in the yards. I said I'd get you a *job.*"

Cruz leaned his head back against the wall; his laughter came painfully from his dry throat. "Sure, shoveling horseshit on some rich man's roses."

"It's an honest day's work. I've done it."

"No dice. I want a factory job."

"Okay." Fuss nodded his head. "I'll get you a factory job."

"You promise?"

"Cruz, have I ever lied to you? I'm a Catholic."

"Thirty bucks for the Horse then."

"Thirty bucks for the ride, the *last* ride." Fuss reached into his pocket. "All right, here, thirty bucks." He handed over the money.

Cruz took the money and began counting as he chuckled. "You sure know how to come up with the bucks, Fussy, mon. You got more jack than FDR. How come a guy like you can always make change for a fifty?"

"I've got money because some are born smart, chico. Shut up and stash it before the guard comes back." Fuss stammered.

He wanted to change the subject fast. "And one other thing—"

"Oh no, Fuss, I ain't going to start dressin' like no square John. I'm happy being a Zootie."

"That's not what I had in mind." The skin around Fuss's eyes tightened; his gaze pinned Cruz to the wall. "I want to know your connection."

"Are you crazy?"

"Are you stupid? You think I'm giving you money for a kick of Horse, then you're going to go cold turkey for the promise of a job? How am I to know you quit using? If you tell me your connection, that's the kiss-off. I'll know you're on the square."

"I can't do that. Besides, it's never the same person, and it's always in a different place."

"Then protect yourself. Don't tell me who it is, chico, just tell me *where* it is."

"I can't do that. I've got to live in the Barrio."

"Look, Cruz, I'm no cop, you know that. I just want to see who it is, that's all. Just see."

"But if it's just him and me, he'll know I squealed. I'm one dead muchacho."

"Cruz, I give you my word. I'll just watch. Nothing will happen."

"You promise the job, no bull?"

"I promise the job."

"You better not be lying, Fussy, mon. You know how many people are in my family. You know my brother Angel doesn't make enough off his baseball to feed himself, and nobody give him a job."

"I know."

"They draft my big brother, Roberto, so he can get killed by Japs on the ocean, but none of us can get jobs in shipyards or nothin'. You need something from me, now I get a job. That your big idea of a fat democracy?"

"Nobody said America's perfect, Cruz, but it's a free

country, that's what counts. I didn't promise you I could change the system for everybody. I'm not Roosevelt, but I can promise you a job."

Cruz tightened the wad of bills in his fist, jammed them into his pocket, and stood up to leave, his eyes mocking Fuss. "Like they say on the radio, don't call us, we'll call you."

20

1 have a dream that when the war is over I can buy a car and drive all the way to the Grand Canyon without stopping."

Fuss sipped at his Coke. The sun pouring through the ghostlike flutter of the curtains behind Kathleen sprayed its golden glow along her slight, relaxed silhouette in the over-stuffed chair. He circled his fingers over the cold edge of his glass. "Why don't you buy a car now? What's to stop you?"

"What's to stop me?" Kathleen patted her red curls tenderly as if they were alive and needed attention. "Only the fact, dear Oscar, if I did have a car I could never get enough gas-ration cards to travel all the way out there into that vast desert."

"I know where I can get my hands on some extra A-ration cards. How many would you need?"

"Oh Oscar, an A-ration card is worth only three gallons a week. I would need at least fifty gallons to make that trip."

"Impossible."

"I know." Kathleen shrugged her shoulders philosophically. "It's hopeless."

"What do you want to go all the way out there in the middle of the desert for anyway?"

"Because of the air." Kathleen straightened up excitedly in the big chair. "Because the air is so good and pure and sweet, and I can breathe it without wheezing. It's like honey poured all over my lungs and I can just breathe and breathe and breathe it. And there's something else too." She looked at Fuss suspiciously, the slightest trace of a frown forming on her lips.

"What?"

"You're such a dear sweet man, you're so kind to me, so heavenly polite to me. I'm afraid if I tell you this terrible thing about me you will leave and I will never see you again."

Fuss reached out his hand and lightly touched Kathleen's knee, timidly, patronizingly, like it was the head of a newborn baby he couldn't believe he was touching. "What would there possibly be about you that could come between our friendship, Kathleen? I'll accept anything about you at all, anything in the world." Fuss lifted the glass of Coke to his lips and smiled reassuringly at her across the glass rim.

"I smoke marijuana." She spoke the words softly, her expression of concern not changing.

Fuss nearly choked on his Coke. He cleared his throat, trying to speak easily, trying to hide his shock. "Well, Kathleen, that's a, ah, surprise. Yes." He clicked the ice in his glass. "Yes, indeed, that's very original."

Kathleen clasped her hands together in her lap, her slender fingers worming nervously together. "I'm not a hophead like some people in the Barrio, or anything dreadful like that, and it doesn't turn me into a monster."

"Kathleen, I can't believe you, of all people, would . . ."

"It's medicine. My doctor gives it to me for my asthma. Do you know, there's been considerable research done on the subject in Switzerland at one of the big sanatoriums. The doctors there found it relaxes the lungs, or expands their breathing capacity, or something like that."

"Does it do that for you?"

"Yes, but . . ."

"But what? You can trust me."

"But I'm afraid of it. I'm afraid maybe one time I'll smoke it and get hopped up and do something crazy like jump out of a window or something."

"So why continue to use it, if you're afraid?"

"Because my doctor prescribes it, and it makes me feel," she turned her eyes away from Fuss, *"better."*

"Well." Fuss cleared his throat again. "No reason to feel ashamed for anything a doctor prescribes to make you feel better." Fuss was irritated with the sound of his voice; it seemed cavalier and phony.

"Oscar, you're so heavenly kind to me. Can I ask you a very deep favor?"

"I won't deny you anything, Kathleen, anything."

"Would you let me smoke it in front of you? I'm afraid to smoke it without someone very close nearby in case something goes wrong."

"Sure, sure, Kathleen." Fuss sipped nervously at his Coke. "You go ahead and have some if it's what the doctor ordered. I'm around this kind of thing all the time in the Barrio, part of my job. Even Black Widows smoke it. They don't do all those crazy things to become Black Widows the papers say, like burning houses and beating up white men, but they do smoke reefers, no denying that. So go ahead, feel free, feel natural about it. I can't be shocked."

"Oh, Oscar." Kathleen stretched her slender fingers out until her bright red nails stroked the sleeve of his coat, softly as water in a stream running over a moss-covered rock. "Thank you for being so understanding." She got up and went into the kitchen, opening and closing doors, her voice calling nervously back to him, "Would you like another Coke?"

"No, no thanks. I'm swell." Fuss tried to keep his voice calm and steady. He clamped his eyes shut. He just couldn't envision someone like Kathleen with a reefer between her bright red lips. It seemed so alien, like a five-year-old child sitting at a bar.

She came out of the kitchen and sat in the overstuffed chair, folding her legs beneath her long dress. The sun was intense behind her, its golden arm coming through the window, running a thousand bright shiny hands intimately over the curves of her body. She puffed tentatively at the tight yellow rolled cigarette held securely in her lips. Fuss couldn't hear her breathing. She was inhaling smoke deep in her lungs. He saw traces of smoke swirl from her nostrils, curling recklessly into the sunlight. Fuss breathed easier himself and relaxed back into the chair.

"Bright Angel Rim."

"What, Kathleen? What was that?"

She turned her head slowly to him and smiled. "You are so *heavenly* kind to me."

"What about the bright angel? Kathleen, you're not hallucinating, are you?"

She shook her head, her laughter bubbling around the cigarette. "Dear Oscar, how I wish I could. Bright Angel Rim is along the north side of the Grand Canyon. You can't imagine on this earth so many colors in one place. Colors more grand and meaningful than all the colors in the rainbow. Intense hues, lighting up the length of the jagged canyon rim like fluttering bright angels swarming suddenly from a crystal clear sky, escaping from an enormous glass jar in the heavens, a bell jar like children catch butterflies in during summer heat. But enormous and clear. All those angels with their gay colors, dazzling life into that vast dark canyon. Five hundred feet down they go, unafraid, along the steep cliffs of the canyon. A thousand feet down they plummet and swirl. So far away they go, but never lose their color, a million diamonds scattered like dust in a dead universe."

Fuss was alarmed at his own breathing; it almost stopped as Kathleen spoke. He quietly watched her. The intense sun behind her hurt his eyes, but it cast her face in deep shadow. She seemed distant, so far away, way above him. He was on the river bed of her enormous dark canyon, and she was far above him, watching down from the rim, the sun behind setting fire to the red curls flaring wildly around her head like a nest of snakes. He yearned to call her, call to something inside of her, touching her obscure face with his voice. But she was so distant, on the edge of a dangerous precipice, tiny and barely significant, the faint diamond glitter of a fading bright angel.

"Oscar?"

"Yes?" Fuss straightened up in the fat chair, his breathing coming normally again.

"Did you hear what I said?" The cigarette was gone from Kathleen's hand, stamped dead in the ashtray.

"Yes, certainly, all of it."

"It looked like you were somewhere else."

Fuss laughed and straightened his tie. "Only with the bright angels."

"I think you've been working too hard." Her lips were very soft in their concern. "I think it would be wonderful if we could both go to the desert, forget this war, live like normal people."

"Yes, wonderful, swell." He turned his palms up and laughed. "But like you said, we don't have the A-cards."

"No." Her voice was very sad in the sunlight. "But we could dream about it. We could focus all our vibrations on the war ending and us going to the desert, just the two of us alone in that vastness. There's mysterious medicine in the desert."

"What do you mean, Kathleen?"

"My doctor told me the Zuni Indians out there have a kind of sage plant they smoke in secret rituals. He says it is good for the lungs, better than marijuana even. He says the Zunis who smoke it never have any lung problems. But they won't tell anybody where they get it. We'd have to hunt for it. Do you think"—her eyes became very excited again as she shifted in the sunlight—"if we found it and smoked it, it would be a crime?"

"No, of course not." Fuss rubbed his lips and laughed. "If it was a crime they would have all the Zunis in jail."

"I suppose that's true, but," Kathleen's voice turned sad again, "we could never find it." She absentmindedly brushed her dress out smooth in her lap.

"Think I might know where we could find something just as good."

"Oscar, do you really? If we found something, anything, I would never have to smoke marijuana again and be frightened I might do some crazy thing."

"I know where there is a blue sage, not a sage really, a big lavender bush. The Mexican brujas in the Barrio use it to cure people who get pneumonia, make a hot tea out of it. I found it growing last summer by accident."

"Where is it?"

"On Santa Catalina. I took some of my CYO boys over there last summer and I saw it growing in a steep canyon behind Avalon."

"But we can't get to Santa Catalina. We don't own a boat."

"There's a ferry."

"Really? I've never heard of it."

"That's because you don't go dancing. There's a ferry goes out to the island every weekend to dance concerts at the Avalon Ballroom; sometimes Harry James's big band even plays."

"I don't have anything against dancing."

"Well, then, what's to stop us? Let's go next weekend."

"I'm not very good at fast dancing. I don't have the lungs for it."

Fuss jumped up and beat his chest excitedly like an ape in the middle of the jungle. "Don't worry, you can lean on me. I'm strong enough for the two of us. I'm sure Harry James won't mind."

Kathleen took Fuss's hands and let him pull her up. "You're not kidding, you promise we'll go?"

"I always keep my promises."

"How far is the island?"

"Twenty-six miles across the sea, just like the song says. *Twenty-six miles across the sea, San-ta Cat-a-lin-a is awaitin' for me, San-ta Cat-a-lin-a, the island of row-mance row-mance, row-mance....*" Fuss took Kathleen in his arms and danced her around the room to the tune he was singing.

"Oscar, you sit right here." Kathleen pushed him down into the chair excitedly. "I'll go get us two more Cokes and we'll plan the trip all out."

Fuss heard the icebox door open in the kitchen and Kathleen's happy whistling of the Santa Catalina song before he heard the crash of Coke bottles on the floor. He sprang from the chair, but Kathleen was already staggering back out the kitchen door, her face ghostly white, her hands clutching her chest.

"Kathleen, what is it?"

She pointed back into the kitchen, her words coming up in a dry, empty wheeze; she couldn't talk.

Fuss ran into the kitchen. An enormous bright orange Angora cat was curled on the table, its silky fur fluffed comfortably as it purred up impassively at Fuss. Fuss grabbed the cat by its tail and flung it out the open window onto the iron bars of the fire escape, then slammed the window shut and ran back into the living room. Kathleen was sprawled in the fat chair, her legs spread carelessly out before her, her eyes wild with fright. Fuss barely understood the words gasping from her parched lips.

"In—the—icebox. Get—it."

Fuss opened the door to the icebox. He saw a small plastic bottle with a red spray cap; behind it were several rows of glass vials containing a yellowish fluid, next to them was a hypodermic needle. He grabbed the plastic bottle and read the label: *BREATHALATOR*. He took the bottle to Kathleen, the dry breath coming from her in frantic waves of wheezing as she put the red spray cap in her mouth, pressing the bottom of the bottle, drawing short hissing bursts of medicine deep down into her lungs. Fuss knelt before her. He felt helpless as she sucked at the bottle, helpless and far away. He was afraid to touch her, to comfort her, afraid it would mysteriously make her condition worse. He waited patiently. Her hand slumped with the empty bottle to her side as she breathed rapidly, the wheezing subsiding until her breath came normally, leaving her paler than ever, almost lifeless in the fat chair. She seemed so pitifully thin. When Fuss heard her voice again it was like a miracle.

"You're so kind." She extended her weak hand, bent at the wrist.

Fuss took her hand. In her wrist he felt her blue veins throbbing. "I didn't know what in the world to take out of the icebox. I was just hoping it was the right thing, because you couldn't talk."

"You did the right thing. The hypodermic syringe is for adrenalin; it relaxes the lungs. If I have a severe asthma attack, worse even than this, I must inject six cc's in my arm. Otherwise I could die in four minutes. If I'm at death's door"—Kathleen's eyes widened at the thought—"I must inject the adrenalin straight to my heart. Sometimes an adrenalin shot to the heart can kill you. Thank God, I haven't had to use the adrenalin yet, but there's plenty there just in case."

"And all because of a cat?"

"Other things too. It's a terrible way to live. If you are not forever vigilant and get careless, leaving a window open just a crack, or something simple like that, then it can be the end. It's like living with a loaded gun aimed at your head all the time. You never know when something as dangerous as the neighbor's cat will slip in."

Fuss stroked her weightless hand. The only sign of life in it was an erratic fluttering of the pulse. "Are you all right now?"

"Yes, dear Oscar." Her hand came up to his chin, the lightness of her touch guiding his face closer to hers "Promise me . . ." The movement of her pale lips almost touched his.

"Anything in the world, Kathleen."

"That you will always be heavenly kind to me."

"I promise." His lips touched hers and they opened beneath him, widening and trembling as his tongue felt into her mouth. He had never desired anyone so much. She tasted like medicine, a tonic. Her weakness became his strength. A madness came over him. He wanted to suck her very soul into him. His hands went roughly behind her back, circling her arching frail body. He clung to her like a desperate man, the veins bulging in his neck as his fingers dug into her resilient flesh. She pushed him away. Blood banging at his temples nearly blotted out her words.

"Be kind . . ."

21

All right, Fuss, here's the information you wanted on the yacht. Still no confirmation on exactly who owns the cargo ship."

"The yacht's more important now; that's something in our own front yard."

"The yacht is registered to," Kinney's voice dropped to an almost inaudible whisper in the dark confessional, "Americal Yachtworks. Now, that little fish is inside Americal Tuna Processing Company. If you follow the string all the way out, you find both these little fish inside Sea Biscuit Enterprises. Here's the queer catch: the president of Sea Biscuit is a retired admiral who lives up in Beverly Hills. He's the obvious owner of the yacht; he's probably the big fish with a hook in his mouth."

"Goddamn."

"Watch your language, Fuss, you're in a Catholic church."

"Sorry, Senator, but it's incredible, my tip was right."

"You mean what Wino Boy told you about betting on Sea Biscuit if you were looking for the Horse connection in the Barrio?"

"That, and more."

"Well the tip could have been hot, but so far you haven't come up with anything concrete, and I still don't see the bigger connection with the Sinarquistas."

"We knew in the beginning, Senator, the way the Sinarquistas got influence in Zoot gangs was by getting control over the Horse flow."

"But we know for a fact, all our investigations prove out, the Zoots weren't using Horse before Pearl Harbor."

"That was before the war, Senator. Before the pain of having brothers and fathers die while being barred from good jobs. Before the Sinarquistas showed up promising to save American Latins from Yankee imperialism. Before the cynicism."

"Sure, but the gangster who got involved with the Sinarquistas, the guy from Buenos Aires, what was his code name, the one called Big Banana?"

"Chiquito Banana."

"Him, we know from FBI reports he's out of the country. FBI figures he got booted out of the California front by higher-ups in Madrid because his heroin tactics backfired. He hooked young kids and the Zoots turned on him."

"But the FBI has no way of knowing if Chiquito Banana is back in the Barrio doing business at the same old stand. Maybe the Germans are backing him now. What do the Germans care how many kids in the Barrio they hook if it advances their political goals?"

"Maybe. But the problem is the FBI never had a photograph of that guy Chiquito Banana. They don't even know what the guy actually looks like; he could be anyone. All they have are five pictures of different men. One they think is Chiquito Banana; which one is anybody's guess. The only fact on the guy is he left the Barrio last September."

"Can you get me those FBI pictures of the five guys?"

"You think Chiquito Banana is connected to Sea Biscuit?"

"Maybe."

"I doubt it. When you get outside and look at the paper I gave you with the address of Sea Biscuit Enterprises, you'll know why. The address is in Beverly Hills. Not many Fascists up in Beverly Hills. Tons of Commies, but few Fascists."

"I don't exactly know where this Chiquito Banana is, Senator, but I have a feeling he's back."

"Well, when the FBI confirms that, fine. For now, your job is to stay on top of this Mankind Incorporated thing."

"I need those FBI pictures."

"Okay, you'll get them. Now tell me, are you any closer to the Voice?"

"Next week he's at the Shrine. I'm certain I'll see him before or after the rally, crusade, or whatever they call it."

"Good. It's this Doomsday Vibration machine has us worried. I know it sounds wacko like you say, but so did Hitler when he started talking about flying V-1 rocket bombers with no pilots. What about the girl? Does she suspect anything about you?"

"No, but the Zoots started avoiding me after the preliminary hearing on the FBI killings. Since I testified at your closed hearing and started seeing La Rue, the Zoots have become more suspicious. I don't know how much longer I can keep the shell game up; none of my probation boys come to baseball practice anymore. How am I supposed to have any credibility as a Catholic social worker if I never work?"

"That's no problem. Social workers never seem like they are working. All they do is go around sticking their noses into other people's business. Long as you continue to make a pest of yourself people will think you are the real ticket."

"I don't know if that's so certain. People aren't so dumb as you think they are. Sometimes they surprise you. One of my probation boys who's gone over to the Zoots, Cruz Parra . . ."

"You mean Angel Parra's little brother?"

"Yah."

"Jesus, him too?"

"Him too, and he's started to call me a Commie."

"That's not so unusual. If he's a Zoot, the Sinarquistas have probably gotten to him by now. He probably calls his Mama a Commie too."

"But why me? What am I doing different now than I've ever done?"

"I told you, Fuss, he's probably a little Sinarquista robot."

"Anyway, the whole business is beginning to make me sick."

"There are far worse things than being called a Commie, Fuss. After all, what if you were one?"

"No, that's not what makes me sick. It's this Cruz kid. I've known the kid's family for three years; now they won't even talk to me. They're like most people in the Barrio—they're decent people, damn poor, but decent human beings."

"They're a lot better off here than in Mexico. Here there's always seasonal work."

"That's not the point. If you're starving and can't get a job, it makes no difference where you are."

"Come on, Fuss, save your sermonizing for Kathleen La Rue, that's her line of business. Me, I have to go, have to be up in Sacramento by tonight to prepare for arguments on that Italian bill we want to get through. Right now I'm more worried about the wops in our own backyard than the spics." Kinney slid the screen closed.

"It's not sermonizing when you feel sick in your stomach for killing a kid."

"What do you mean, *killing* a kid?"

"The only way I could get information out of Cruz was to give him the money to buy a kick of Horse."

"You did that?"

"I did it, but I made him promise me it would be his last kick."

"You know it won't be. If he's hooked now and he gets a free kick, it'll just make his mouth water for more."

"I know. It's a risk I had to take. It makes me sick to think he'll die all junked up." Fuss heard Kinney's chair scraping beneath him as he stood to leave.

"You must remember this." Kinney's voice whispered down at Fuss. "I don't like involving innocents any more than you. The business of war is not pretty. To win we must expend ourselves more than the next guy. It's like a train ticket; the guy willing to buy the most expensive one is going to get the longest ride."

22

owering palm trees were waving in the wind all over Beverly Hills like hula girls hired for the rich. The cab driver squinted through his windshield at the skinny trees, their skimpy palm frond skirts tearing and fluttering in the wind. "Damn wonder these freak trees don't snap in two in weather like this. Every time you think the wind has the better of one of them and is going to rip it right out of the ground, it pops back up like some kind of queer jack-in-the-box. These trees are real queer. Ain't like your basic Eastern tree what loses its leaves every winter. Hell, they don't lose nothin'. They say palms here don't even have no coconuts growing on them like over in Hawaii. But brother you wouldn't catch me walking under one, be just my luck to get bonked on the noggin with a queer coconut. Kill you dead as a doornail, like a Jap sniper dropping a grenade on you is how good a job it would do. How much farther? You got ten bucks on the meter now."

"Turn right, up here on Tremonto, and slow down." Fuss was busy trying to read house numbers, but it wasn't easy. Many were set in Spanish tiles on ivy-covered pillars leading up driveways that snaked out of sight behind curves of mammoth flowering bushes and sharp rows of blue-fingered cacti.

"Right here? This the one you want?" The cab driver slowed at a steep intersection with five narrow roads spurring off it, each road disappearing into a jungle of growth.

"Yes. One of these is Tremonto, isn't it?"

"How the hell do I know? You think I live up here? Think I'm Ralph R. Rockefeller or something?"

"Try that road off there to the left, the one with the jacaranda tree."

"The what kind of jack tree?"

"The tree with the big purple blossoms on it."

"Listen, mister, you give me white man's directions. I don't know a jack-a-miranda tree from a jack-o'-lantern." The driver swung the wheel sharply, leaving a thick track of rubber behind him as the cab's tires gripped the steep black pavement speared between the perfect cut of English hedges. "Who the hell lives up here anyway, big movie star or something?"

"Did you see that?"

"What?"

"Stop the cab and back up."

The cab driver backed slowly down the hill, stopping before the intricate iron scrollwork of twenty-foot-high gates blocking a narrow driveway.

"Get out and see if the gates are open."

"That's a queer thing to do. Ain't the people who you're going to see expectin' you, so the gates wouldn't be locked?"

"Just try them."

"Damn queer thing." The cab driver pulled in before the gates and yanked the emergency brake, but before he could get out the gates began swinging slowly back with a faint little buzzing sound. "Hey, what do you know, one of those electric-eye jobs!"

Fuss handed the fare over the seat to the driver. "This is far enough. I'll walk the rest of the way from here."

"Sure you don't want me to drive you? No extra charge. I'd like to see the house, must be some mansion with a gate like this protecting it, must be somebody famous like Lana Turner or Barbara Carr."

"No." Fuss got out and slammed the door. "I'll walk."

The cab driver backed out of the driveway entrance, calling through the open window as he turned and headed down the street, "Damn queer thing is all I got to say!"

Fuss started up the winding driveway beneath thick broad-trunked trees locking branches over his head in a lush maze of green blocking out all sunlight. He heard a noise behind him and jerked around. A faint electric buzz drifted up the driveway toward him as the heavy iron gates swung closed. Sweeping red wings of tiled roof soared through the air long before he could see the house itself. Trees began to spread open and pull back from the driveway, finally surrendering to the stone expanse of a piazza spouting blue sprays of water ten feet high from a sculpted marble fountain in its center. Fuss pressed a small black button next to the towering carved doors of the house before him. He heard ringing chimes inside, echoing loudly like church bells over the roofs of a Mediterranean mountain town.

"Good afternoon, sir."

Fuss pulled his hat off and nodded to the woman standing before him in the open doorway, her hair pulled tightly in a knot atop her head like a gray fist. "Oh, yes, I'm here to see the president of Sea Biscuit Enterprises."

"I'm afraid Admiral Nemark is resting."

Fuss twisted his hat in his hands absentmindedly like it was a wet towel. "I'm, ah, really sorry but . . ."

"You don't have an appointment. All the Admiral's appointments are before luncheon."

"Well, no, matter of fact I couldn't get through to him and the matter is rather urgent. State business, really."

"State business?"

"Yes, ah, you see it concerns his tuna-processing plant, Americal."

"Go on." The woman's expression was sharp as the starched creases in her black-and-white uniform.

"State of California, ma'am. I'm with the Department of Health. It appears there's been a case of botulism reported up north in a Monterey restaurant, and one of the items served was Americal tuna."

"You wait here." The woman turned quickly away, the heavy doors thudding closed in Fuss's face; behind him short bursts of wind picked up the watery spray from the fountain and splattered the back of his pants. The doors opened again. The woman ushered Fuss through. He followed her for what seemed a mile, through sitting room after sitting room. The thick cushion of Persian carpets beneath his feet made him feel like he was floating. All around him were life-size bronze castings of naked Greek boys, about to hurl ebony javelins through ceiling-high windows across a garden dropping off in giant green strides of lawn. One garden terrace after another followed down the mountainside, appearing to stretch across the entire city skyline below, twenty miles to the blue haze of Pacific Ocean horizon. Once, in *Collier's* magazine, Fuss saw photographs of newspaper tycoon William Randolph Hearst's castle. The Hearst castle crowned a mountaintop above the ocean, but it seemed smaller than where he was now. The man who could afford all this must consider the price of the yacht Fuss saw dumped into the grain hold of the cargo ship nothing more monumental than a nickel phone call.

"Would you please step this way." The woman stopped at the end of a long room; behind her appeared a gigantic picture of Washington, D.C., showing that city in flames, British warship barges anchored calmly in the Potomac River.

Fuss passed the length of the painting, stepping into the dark recesses of a paneled library with rows of leather-spined books, their gold embossed titles aimed at the man sitting behind a desk so large it could have had a sail hoisted on it and cruised the seas to China.

"I am Admiral Nemark. You are the state official with the alarming news?" The man behind the big desk rose quickly. Fuss noticed the silver wings of hair swept back under the blue bill of his yacht captain's cap. He was the same man who abandoned the new yacht to the grain ship.

"That's correct, sir, and I'm afraid the situation is more than serious." Fuss took out a pencil and notebook and started writing rapidly so the Admiral couldn't interrupt him with questions. "Now, there are certain facts and dates we will have to immediately be apprised of. If you'll—"

"Why wasn't my plant manager called?"

"Well, Admiral, he was informed a short while ago."

"Why the devil didn't he call me then?"

"Because we wanted to inspect the operation immediately to ascertain if any of the tuna on the premises contained poisonous bacteria."

"Inspect the premises! My good man, you're standing there telling me you went into my plant without a warrant of inspection or proper authorization and started breaking open crates and cans without informing me!"

"That's exactly what we did do."

"What the devil!" The Admiral sank down in the padded leather of his chair, the distinguished lines of his lean face shadowed and darkened into crevices of concern.

"We had to act hastily. One person was dead and three more hospitalized up in Monterey."

"And what the devil did you find?"

Fuss tapped his pencil against the notebook and looked

directly at the Admiral. Although the man was in his late fifties, he was fit as a panther, ready to leap across the desk and sink his teeth into Fuss's neck.

"Nothing. We found only good wholesome tuna in the cans."

"What the devil were you looking for?"

"A certain strain of botulism, but that particular bacteria could not have incubated in your canned tuna under the packing conditions employed."

"So?" The Admiral's breath came more calmly. "Are you informing me I'm off the hook?"

"So to speak."

"So to speak what? Am I, or am I not clean?"

"We did find one or two minor health violations which we will—"

"Blast it, man, one or *two*? I defy you to find that few in any other tuna-packing operation from Monterey to San Diego. This is wartime. Sometimes little health regulations get overlooked in our zealous pursuit to move tuna from the ocean to the table quickly as possible. You won't find a more hygienically run ship than our Americal plant. It's shipshape, has been since my father's day. Clean as a shark's tooth. We use only the most modern methods of canning. It's not Russian herring we're packing, you know. Excuse me."

The Admiral picked up the ringing telephone. As he spoke softly into it Fuss turned his back on him, trying to give the impression he wasn't eavesdropping. Fuss glanced over the photographs covering one entire wall; aircraft carrier ships, convoys of destroyers, submarines, the Admiral graduating from Annapolis, and one photograph that seemed out of place amid the glossy sea of photographs populated only by naval men and their seagoing regalia. The glossy picture clearly depicted a delighted Charles Lindbergh being decorated with the Service Cross of the German Eagle by a most improbable Santa Claus, Nazi Field Marshal Hermann Göring, chief of the German Luftwaffe. Fuss stepped closer to the curious photograph to determine if it was a fake. He slipped a piece of Juicy Fruit into his mouth and chewed thoughtfully, pressing his nose next to the glass protecting the photograph. He couldn't determine if anything had been retouched, or if Lindbergh's head had been transposed onto the body of a German war hero. Yes, the photo was real. Fuss turned around, chewing steadily on the gum as he tried to ignore the pistol the Admiral had leveled at him.

"That's a very intriguing picture, Admiral. Did Lindy give it to you himself?"

"Who the devil are you?"

"I told you, Admiral, I'm with the Department of Health."

"I know from my telephone conversation with my plant manager that isn't true. Now you speak plainly or this gun is very likely to go off, and the police will come to pick up one very dead liar."

"My name is Fuss, Oscar."

"Go on."

"I investigate un-American activities."

"Who the devil *for?*"

"State Senator Kinney. He heads up the secret joint fact-finding committee funded by the state legislature."

"I've never heard of such a cockeyed committee."

"If you don't believe me, Admiral, you can call Senator Kinney up in the state capitol at Sacramento right now."

The Admiral rested the handle of the gun on the desktop. "If this is true, why would you sneak in here to spy on a retired rear admiral of the United States Navy? Why wouldn't you be out spying on Communists? These Beverly Hills are full of them. These mansions around here are nothing more than glamorous Liberal fronts. If you want to spend your time spying on un-American activities, why don't you try breaking into a few of them?"

"Well, sir." Fuss spit his gum out, wadding it into a sticky ball between his fingers. "Excuse me, can I drop this in that ashtray there on your desk?"

"Yes, drop the damn stuff."

Fuss plopped the gum into the silver ashtray and sat down on the edge of the desk. "The reason I came in like this is I didn't see any real reason to alarm you at this point in our investigation."

"Investigation, man! You don't have to investigate me! You don't have to subpoena me! I'm a patriot. I'll gladly share with any fact-finding committee any and all information I have on subversive activities in this country." The Admiral shoved the gun carelessly away from him like a half-eaten plate of food. "And I can tell you, Mr. Fuss Oscar, there's one hell of a lot more Reds in our own backyard than just what's running loose right here in Beverly Hills. If something isn't done about it pronto, mister, there's going to be the devil to pay. Here, you look at this, today's headlines in the *Examiner.*" The Admiral pushed the front page of the newspaper at Fuss.

Fuss glanced down at the headlines:

ZOOT-SUIT GANG RAPE AND ROB NAVY WIFE
CONTINUED VIOLENCE IN EAST LOS ANGELES
PACHUCOS RUN DOWN MOTORCYCLE COP

Fuss looked back up at the Admiral. "You know how many rapes there are every day in a city this size during wartime, Admiral?"

"As many rapes as there are Pachucos allowed to roam the streets."

Fuss pushed the paper back across the desk. "Headlines like these are meant to sell newspapers. Every time the LA cops come up empty handed without a suspect for a rape they immediately pin it on the Zoots. The fact is, it's usually the sailors cruising the Barrio's Zona Roja who do the raping of teenage girls unlucky enough to live around there. That's one of the biggest reasons for the war going on between sailors and the Zoots."

"You're nothing but a naive boy scout if you believe that's the case, mister." The Admiral tried to control the angry shaking of his hands by picking up the gun, rubbing the cold barrel quickly up and down between the circle of his fingers. "Every day now, these kinds of headlines." He banged the gun down loudly on the newspaper. "Zoot-suit Pachucos are being used as a Communist front; they're getting bolder every day. It won't be long before the Commies get the Zoots to start a war right here in America. You take me to your committee. I'll tell them a thing or two. I've been telling the public since before Pearl Harbor, myself and men like Colonel Lindbergh, we are fighting on the wrong side in this war. The enemy is not the Fascists who have tried to contain Communism in Europe. Only the Fascists have ever had courage to fight the Communists where they threaten most, on the home front."

"You know who the Sinarquistas are?"

"Yes, I most certainly do. They are Mexican Fascists."

"Do you know they are operating in America?"

"Just what I've been saying, only the Fascists are man enough to stand up to a Communist threat like the Zoot-suiters. More power to them. The Zoot-suiters have already killed two FBI men."

"You know what some newspapers say about the Sinarquistas? That they are the ones behind the Zoot gangs. They're using these boys as part of a Fascist plot to develop race hatred on the West Coast."

"They've got it all wrong; it's Communists behind the Zoot-suiters. The Reds are the ones trying to get white to fight brown. If I were Attorney General Biddle, I'd ask for permission from Roosevelt himself to let loose all our servicemen stationed around here on these gangs, turn them out in the Barrio to clean up the problem once and forever."

"Thank you, Admiral." Fuss stood up and walked to the door. "I apologize for the ruse earlier."

"You tell that committee of yours." The Admiral came around the desk and rested his hand in a fatherly fashion on Fuss's shoulder as he showed him through the door. "You tell them anytime they want the true facts on what this war is really all about, I'll be happy to donate my time to them."

"Oh, one other thing before I go, Admiral. Does the name Chiquito Banana ring any bells?"

The Admiral stopped before the painting of Washington, D.C., rubbing his chin as a blank look came across his face; behind him the capital of America was still in flames. "Chiquito Banana? No, I'm certain it doesn't. I forget faces sometimes, having been a career officer commanding so many men, but a name like that I'd never forget. Why?"

"Just curious, Admiral. The FBI thinks he might be involved in covert Sinarquistas operations here on the West Coast."

"No, Mr. Oscar, I wouldn't have knowledge of a thing like that, but I will tell you one thing you can take back to your committee."

"What?"

"If I ever meet this Chiquito Banana after the war's over, I'll pin a medal on him."

23

Mankind must unite if it is to have a hope, a chance, a possibility for *survival!*" Kathleen looked so far away. The harsh spotlight shooting down out of the high rafters of the Shrine Auditorium pinpointed her on the barren stage like a butterfly needled inside a large glass display case. The enraptured crowd before her in darkness hung on her every gasping syllable booming from enormous loudspeakers in every corner of the great domed auditorium. The crowd was dead silent as Kathleen sipped at a glass of water, light dazzling the curls of her red hair like a radiating halo. "And if we heed the Sponsors' word . . . join the Valiants at the gates to Brotherhood City of the Future . . . desire with all our spirit to become pioneers in the new age of peace . . . then we must prepare for moral, physical, and spiritual combat such as mankind has never witnessed. Forces of Good and Evil have never fought as they fight now." Kathleen pulled back from the lectern. Even from his seat high in the crowded balcony all Fuss glimpsed of her was the haloed brilliance of red hair; strong light penetrating from the darkness erased the paleness of her skin. Her face appeared invisible. Only her words came forth, disembodied, slowly, deliberately, articulating an urgency that charged the air of the hall like a clouding summer sky preparing to storm and aim fabulous bolts of lightning into damp earth. Breathlessly she announced, "He is here among us today. The One who can translevitate to any spot on this troubled globe within three hours, from Moscow to Cairo, New York to Rio, Peking to Paris. The omnipresent One who carries the torch of knowledge made manifest to the original Sponsors. The One . . . True . . . Voice. The Voice of the Right Idea."

Kathleen walked off stage. The spotlight did not follow her. The great golden fall of the heavy brocaded curtains pulled back behind her, exposing a man alone, standing in the far recess of the stage like he was at the mouth of a vast cave, like he was the first man on earth, except he was wearing a neat blue business suit, his back to the expectant crowd, who after three hours of waiting patiently through speeches were still fresh and anxious, perched on the edge of their seats, a thousand hungry birds in a mammoth nest, waiting to be fed, waiting for the One True Voice to speak, to acknowledge their existence.

At the back of the stage three separate movie screens unrolled like glittering silver flags. The silhouette of the One True Voice reflected its slender black image on all screens, the shadows of his hands spreading as if to embrace the entire auditorium. Across the audience bright eyes of light shot from three film projectors onto each movie screen, filling the stage with the faces of Hitler, Churchill, and Roosevelt. The

words of a title marched across the faces until it towered on
the stage:

DEALERS IN DEATH.

The title faded before large crowds applauding the three
leaders in each one of their screened sections, people cheering frantically and silently. There was no sound, except for
words from the Voice. As the real crowd in the auditorium
watched cheering crowds on movie screens, they gasped at
the first words of the Voice.

"You need Us . . . We need You . . . Now!" The words of
the Voice did not boom from loudspeakers or scream from the
stage. They came like the breath of a baby, the wings of a dove
striking air in peaceful flight, fingers of a lover moving intimately on naked flesh. "This is a challenge to mad ambition."
The Voice tingled every spine in the house. "Accompanied by
an invitation to sane men and women." Each word was spoken
as if from the lips of several different people: father, mother,
lover, friend, brother, wife, husband, sister, ally, confidant.
"Give instructions to a wise man and he will yet be wiser.
Teach a just man and he will increase in learning." The three
screens loomed with the images of Christ, Gandhi, Buddha. "Be
a Way Shower, a Spiritual Doer. Act in accordance with revela-
tions for survival made by our International Vigilantes. Defy
warlords and money changers who do the work of Hidden Rulers, who released sparks of this war by a worldwide holocaust
of bombs, gases, poisons, death rays, germs, and shattered
dreams."

Hitler reappeared on one of the screens, locusts of airplanes darkening the sky above him. Churchill joined Hitler on
the next screen, christening a fleet of destroyers. Roosevelt
flashed on the next, passing review of West Point graduates. All
three faces dissolved in flames. New faces emerged, saluting,
smiling, reviewing: Mussolini, Franco, Hirohito.

"Men are not inarticulate beasts of the field, incapable of voicing protest against injustice. Intelligent creatures must drag from cover forces of greed, insane ambition, and cruelty. On that immortal December day in 1885, when our Sponsors established the International Institute of Universal Salvation and Administration, the end was marked for centuries of domination by worldwide rich families."

The imposing faces of John D. Rockefeller, J. P. Morgan, William Randolph Hearst flashed on the three screens.

"War on warlords has been declared. Our Sponsors have proof every national government, political party, major utility, and natural resource is controlled by Hidden Rulers who plan revolution and war."

The silver screens flashed vast horizons of factories: Krupp munitions factories in Germany, Kaiser shipyards on the California coast, steel plants of Hiroshima, Japan.

"No other way than by murdering educated and religious classes could Hidden Rulers hope to gain world control. They had to take control before their wars exhausted all precious earth resources. Greed and cruelty are bred by a system of private profits and unscrupulous competition. Fabulous families of wealth fear that their unquestioning patriotic minions, their pathetic worker ants, their armies of self-made moral idiots will also dream of owning the last of earth's resources. Our Sponsors know this beautiful home planet is equally everyone's. They aim accusative arrows not at individual hearts but at the true monster's heart: class antagonism. Let arrows fly into the fetid heart of the private-profit monetary system, then there will be no nations, only one world home: Brotherhood."

The movie screens went dark. The Voice's words came from pitch blackness, soothing like the voice of an adult calling out to a terrified child afraid of the dark.

"How do we wrest control from Hidden Rulers? By dedication to the Thirty-Day Program our Pacific Coast bureau chief, Kathleen La Rue, described earlier. The inevitability of an eight-month work year, free health care, global home for the aged, is our universal society promise. More crucial to you gathered here is how to battle against this latest attempt to annihilate us. Tonight I will speak of things shocking and hideous, miraculous and true."

Fuss barely made out the shadow of the Voice outlined on all three empty movie screens. He strained to hear the sounds of the Voice floating softly above rows of people afraid to move for fear of destroying the path of words.

"The world is ready for the free Thirty-Day Program. If we fail, it will take thousands of years before civilization is restored to spiritual justice. If one piece of equipment developed by our Research Department falls into wrong hands, if our Sponsors' principles are decoded by wrong-thinkers, then civilization will remain a starving illiterate mass."

The sound of bombs falling drowned the words of the Voice. Bright spears of projected light struck the silver screens. Planes flew, bombs whistled and exploded, warship guns pounded and thundered across the screens before the Voice in a roar of destruction. Then the Voice's words rose steadily, surmounting the fearful sound of falling bombs, until dominating the man-made din of disaster; on the screens images of holocaust appeared without letup.

"They tried to pry from me secrets of the future. They subpoenaed and interrogated, trying every devious trick to intimidate me. They brought me before their clandestine committees because they knew I had the power to know when war in men's hearts would break into a war of the worlds. These sinister Senators who led mankind into mindless world slaughter asked if after Japan bombed Pearl Harbor the bureaus of Mankind Incorporated were ordered to lay in supplies of food and clothing, secure blankets and water, make maps of airplane factories, shipyards, police and radio stations, hospitals, roads, railroads, and bridges. The interrogators questioned if this planning was for a takeover of America."

Roosevelt came onto three screens before the Voice, talking and smiling to Churchill, talking to a smiling Ambassador Kichisaburo Nomura of Japan, talking to a smiling Charles Lindbergh—Lindbergh talking and smiling with Willy Messerschmitt on tour of German aircraft factories.

"I confronted the sinister Senators. Why would Mankind Incorporated sow confusion in America? History would record, and dead sailors witness, that President Roosevelt knew the Japanese secret codes and plans and provoked them into bombing Pearl Harbor, leaving his naval fleet unprotected, inviting catastrophe. Roosevelt dispersed our young manhood on two sides of the world to fight, ordered bombing of Tokyo because he desires the Japanese to retaliate by bombing unprotected American cities. Roosevelt plans to bring America into line with other dictatorial states. Why would Mankind Incorporated engage in seditious activity when the saboteur of peace is Roosevelt himself? We prepare for the day in this country when there will be an uprising of fifth columnists synchronized with an invasion from outside. We rely on no man's army. We have no need to sabotage, since we already hold in our hands power to bring about a new world. We have equipment capable of suspending animation in a human being, disarming whole armies. If it was not for this equipment, Hitler would already be in America. Hitler fears us more than all armies combined. Imagine all technology of modern warfare rendered useless. Hitler can. Imagine humanity's reaction to a plan rendering useless all machines of death. Mass cooperation will be the reaction. The Sponsors developed a weapon the size of a card deck that can be screwed into an ordinary lightbulb socket. A weapon so awesome its radiating power can destroy everything within a hundred-mile radius. The Army generals were shown this weapon; Henry Ford was given a demonstration. They knew it would put warmongers out of business. This weapon was intended not as a death ray but as a life ray. Its radiating energy can be harnessed to power civilization. In the past inventions like this have been stolen and stored away by Hidden Rulers who fear to lighten the workingman's load, lest he have time to think of his enslavement. People realize Roosevelt has placed himself above God Almighty. People realize they have no protection from a government that is not trying to stop war. People have been left with no protection. America's fighter planes are gone, armies and warships are gone. We could be bombed into atoms. The Hidden Rulers are laughing. They have you buying war bonds to support the war effort. War bonds don't end war; war bonds prolong war. Hidden Rulers have made our nation into a whorehouse, forcing our daughters into USO work to entertain sailors, forcing our daughters into the WACS, the WAVES. Where in history do women go into battle with men, unless it is to be camp followers and spoils of war? Where are your children? Your sons are dying on indifferent battlefields and impervious oceans; your daughters are dying of sin. Where are the children of the rich? Wars rage all around, but Rockefellers still ice-skate in Rockefeller Plaza. You must take your place in a new civilization. The dog-eat-dog profit system that has the world running blindly on a timetable of chaos is doomed."

Bombs falling like eternal rain before the Voice stopped. The screens emptied to a sizzling silver, gradually turning to a brilliant field of blue, blue of deepest ocean, blue of clearest sky, of infinite universe with one tiny speck of gold, growing, spinning toward the audience, becoming massive, the golden globe of earth, supported by two giant clasped hands, surrounded by mammoth letters, letters forming words that seemed to take wing and fly into the darkness of the tense hall as the Voice gave them life:

THIS IS NOT A MAD DREAM!
HEAVEN HERE AND NOW!
MANKIND INCORPORATED!

Light flicked on, stunning the crowd in sudden brightness. The Voice had disappeared from the stage. Everywhere people jumped to their feet, chanting, *"Heaven here and now!"* The words rang out with fervor, like invisible roses thrown onto the empty stage in passionate homage to the Voice, to curry his favor, prove his sermon had found its target. Fuss tried to make his way down the aisles, but they were clogged with people clapping in unison. The clapping was steady and rhythmic, coming from every direction, bursting like insistent gunfire. The crowd wanted the Voice. They wanted him back on stage; they demanded heaven here and *now*. Fuss sensed the shifting mood around him. People were on their feet, their chants directed at the empty stage becoming screams. They wanted the Voice back because he belonged to them; they demanded his return.

Fuss shoved his way through aisles. People were becoming desperate, sensing the Voice would not return. Some jumped on the stage, raising fists to lead thunderous waves of chanting and clapping. The crush of the crowd moved in Fuss's direction. It seemed everyone had the idea to move toward the stage. But it wasn't the Voice Fuss wanted; it was Kathleen. He was afraid she would be trampled in the rush. He knocked people aside to make it down steps into a broad corridor leading backstage. People split into chanting mobs, running in senseless wedges against one another as they tried to reach the stage. In the winding corridor the way was lost; no one knew which direction to go. Fluorescent lights along curved ceilings reflected their growing fear. Fuss was caught in a tide of panicked people heading away from the stage, down beneath the auditorium into narrowing passageways. There was no turning back. Ahead, shouting voices echoed their excitement to Fuss. A way out had been found. Fuss followed the tide, it carried him through a door marked *FIRE EXIT* into the night air. Everyone was running toward an Airstream trailer standing to one side of the parking lot in a rutted field of weeds. The trailer was humped like a whale, its thin metallic skin reflecting moonlight as a swarm of people banged on its sides, rocking it back and forth, chanting, *"Heaven here and now!"*

Fuss couldn't get near the trailer. People were running from every direction to pack around it. The door opened. Fuss barely discerned the figure of the Voice in the doorway, talking. A hush came over the crowd. Then the door closed and the chant went up again with a roar, people smashing their fists against the trailer like it was a great tin drum. The door opened again. Fuss strained to make out the figure in the doorway; it wasn't the Voice. A murmur went through the crowd and there was total stillness. Fuss heard the sound of words from the figure in the doorway, but he could not understand the meaning. A fear went through him, sweat breaking out beneath his suit. The thin, distant figure in the doorway with the faint red glow around her head was Kathleen. There was no way to reach her. Fuss was terrified the crowd would tear her to pieces to get to the Voice. It was impossible to save her.

The sound of Kathleen's words ended. People did not move. The door closed. She was gone. People turned away from the trailer, pushing Fuss aside as they walked off in silence. He couldn't help grinning, smiling uncontrollably as he looked back to the shining trailer. Kathleen had turned the crowd. He didn't know what she told them, but it was powerful.

24

he Beavers were eating the Stars alive. Sweat was dripping like rain down the sides of Angel's face. He swung his arm wildly around, kicked his knee up before his face, and fired the ball at the Beaver third baseman with a bat cocked over his shoulder at home plate. The crowd was on its feet, screaming and booing long after the crack of the bat sent the ball straight up and over the *AMERICANS SMOKE LUCKY STRIKE GREENS* sign painted on the centerfield fence.

"They're going to yank Angel now, Fuss. Here comes the manager to the mound."

"I don't understand why the FBI just doesn't smash him."

"Angel doesn't want to leave. Portland's gotten four hits off him from the bottom of their lineup, and still he doesn't want to leave."

"There's no need for me doing this tango any longer, Senator. It's pointless to play footsies in such a dangerous situation. This man is a threat to the nation."

"No, they're not taking Angel out. The manager is giving him one more shot."

"This man is clearly seditious."

"Have some popcorn, Fuss." Senator Kinney held the stuffed bag in front of Fuss's face. Behind the Senator's dark glasses his eyes focused on Angel rearing up again like a terrifying marionette, his fastball slicing through the strike zone easy as an ax through butter.

Fuss pushed the bag away from his face. "I didn't come out here to eat popcorn. I came out here to pass information. To warn you of a seditious character."

"Take the popcorn, Fuss."

Fuss grabbed the bag angrily. "Senator, I—" The bag in his hand was heavy; a thick metal lump bulged in its lower half. Fuss thought he knew the feel of the metal shape. "What's this for?"

"We know your man is dangerous. We know you're getting close to him. Close and warm."

Fuss wedged the bag carefully between his legs on the wooden seat, the cold metal of the gun pressing against his thighs. "Why doesn't the FBI just bring him in?"

"Fuss." The Senator shook his head wearily. "How long have you been working for us on the home front?"

"A year, a year and a half, and I say bring the weirdo in."

Kinney settled back in his seat as Angel struck out another Beaver and retired the side. "A year and a half maybe? Then by now you should know what your job is."

"I know that, I just think—"

"I don't care what you *think,* Fuss. I care what you *report.*"

"So I've reported there is no question in my mind Mankind Incorporated is an un-American activity. I have reported the Voice is a subversive force on the home front."

Kinney turned the hard glare of his sunglasses on Fuss. "Now listen to me. What I'm going to say makes a good deal of horse sense. If a man one day jumped up before President Roosevelt when he was throwing out the first ball at a World Series and shot him dead, do you think the FBI would kill that man on the spot?"

"Yes."

"No. No because then they would never know why the man shot the President of the United States. The FBI would want this man alive, because any man who shoots a king or a queen, a sheik or a shah, a prime minister or a president, is politically motivated. Kill the assassin and you kill the possibility of discovering his motivation. Of course the Voice is a crazy weirdo, but he is not silly, he is not stupid, he is not a lunatic. He is a danger to our country, an immediate threat to our way of life. The Voice has been investigated in the past, but only now has he focused what before *seemed* harmless hogwash. Only now has the Voice shown himself to be clearly un-American."

"So you want me to keep investigating?"

"That's why the FBI hasn't brought him in. The Voice is fronting for someone, and we're all trying to find out who." The Senator reached between Fuss's legs and grabbed a small handful of popcorn, flicking the puffed kernels into his mouth. "You know, Fuss." Kinney licked his salty lips. "We are just as anxious to smash the Voice as you are, smash right through his front and find out just what the hell is behind it all. There's big money behind it, we know that. They don't peddle enough of those little blue Mankind Incorporated bibles of theirs to pay rent on the places they preach out of in just this state alone. Now tell me, what about the progress of your relationship with the girl?"

Fuss watched Angel sucker a Beaver for an outside pitch

and hit a soft line drive right into the mitt of the second base-man. "Good. She doesn't suspect anything."

"Do you see her regularly?"

"Almost every day. The only day last week I didn't talk to her was Sunday, the day the Voice was at the Shrine. She promised to meet me after his talk to introduce me to him. But there were a couple of thousand people trying to get to the Voice. Things got real crazy. It was impossible."

"What about her own meetings? Do more people come?"

"All the time. Especially since the Voice was at the Shrine. She promises the Voice will make an appearance in the Barrio soon. I think she's gaining real converts. I didn't think so before, but now I do. There are lots of poor people willing to listen to anyone who preaches that their sons and husbands are just so much cannon fodder shot from the guns of big bankers. People will believe anything in wartime. They get confused, issues get confused."

Kinney scooped some more popcorn from between Fuss's legs. "You're not getting attached to her, are you, Fuss? La Rue is pretty in her own odd sort of way."

The muscles in Fuss's thighs squeezed involuntarily, pressing against the thick gun. "I do my job."

"Good." Kinney smacked his salty lips loudly. "That's all that counts. Everybody pulls his fair share of freight and this war will be over before you know it. You can't beat a united home front."

"Only one thing."

"What?"

"I don't know how long I can keep my front up."

"With the girl?"

"With everyone."

Kinney stood to the music of the seventh-inning stretch and patted Fuss on the shoulder. "It won't be long now. We've got the Japs and the Jerries on the run. Oh, I almost forgot." He slipped a hand inside his coat pocket and brought out a heavily taped envelope. "These are the photographs you wanted. One of these five guys is Chiquito Banana. Study them carefully. If you're on to the top banana with this Cruz kid you've set up, you're going to have to know your apples from oranges. This Chiquito Banana is no street-fighting Pachuco punk like you've been used to dealing with. You're going to need all the protection you can get."

"What about the Admiral? Anything further turn up on him? He's chin deep in this somehow."

"Don't worry, FBI guys got such a tight tail on him they can tell you how many times a day he goes to the bathroom."

Fuss slipped the thick envelope carefully into his coat pocket as Kinney started to walk away.

"Oh, yah." Kinney came back, looking around at the fans in the bleachers above him suspiciously, then leaned over to whisper through his cupped hand into Fuss's ear. "Enjoy your popcorn."

25

Hundreds of midget Santa Clauses hung between palms swayed in the dry wind. Outside Fuss's dusty window the lights down on the street were just beginning to come on, illuminating dark faces of boys playing stickball on the buckled pavement. The real contest for the excited boys was dodging cars that interrupted their stickball game, treating every new vehicle that threatened to run them over with contempt and shouts in loud Spanish, flashing their brown eyes triumphantly as the drivers honked and cursed them. The boys played each car like it was a dangerous bull that had to be contended with every evening if the larger games of life were to continue the next day. Watching the boys took Fuss's mind far away from worrying about his brother—whether Marvin had drowned in a sea of fire or died peacefully in his sleep, unaware Jap torpedoes were ripping through the giant steel hull of the aircraft carrier. Fuss was worried. He hadn't heard from Marvin in three weeks. But sometimes the Navy censor held up all letters, especially if there was a battle going on, or one about to begin. Everything in the war seemed an afterlife to those fed only news from newspapers or letters, which always gave the facts after the fact. The ringing phone jarred Fuss off his chair. He ripped the receiver off the hook and pressed it to his ear. "Yes?"

"Hello, Fussy mon?"

"Yes, this is Fuss."

"Cruz, mon, Cruz." The voice was excited, loud, like it was shouting through the apartment door.

"Yes, Cruz. Where are you?"

"Doesn't matter, mon. Where am I going to *be?*"

"Where?"

"Listen carefully."

"I'm listening with both ears."

"Hollywoodland."

"Hollywoodland?"

"Seven o'clock. Tonight."

"Where the hell is Hollywoodland?"

"Be there."

"Cruz? Don't hang up! Where is—" The phone went dead. Fuss jumped up. He glanced at the clock above his hotplate on the sink counter: 6:01. Fifty-nine minutes to go clear across town to Hollywood, and he didn't even know where it was in Hollywood he was going. He slammed the window shut, as if it somehow was saving time. In his excitement he couldn't remember where he had hidden the gun Kinney slipped to him in the popcorn bag. Each day he moved the gun to a different location in the room, sometimes hiding it from himself. He looked under the mattress, behind milk bottles in the icebox, in his old spiked baseball shoes in the closet. He looked in the medicine chest, then dumped out the garbage bag beneath the sink. The gun clanked out on the rug with empty cans of tuna and Campbell's tomato soup. He tucked the gun beneath the pants belt under his coat. He felt like an idiot. He didn't even have a holster for the damn thing. He ran stiffly downstairs into the middle of the street, the boys shouting at him for breaking up the eighth inning of their game. The driver of a cab, passing through the intersection at the end of the street in front of the red-and-white swirl of an electric barbershop pole, slammed on his brakes. Fuss ran to the cab and jumped in.

"Where to, champ?"

"Hollywoodland."

"Hollywoodland?" The driver flicked down the lever on the meter box, the numbers loudly ticking off as he started into the traffic. "Beats me where that is, champ."

"I thought you guys were supposed to know everything."

"Only my wife knows everything, champ, and she only tells me the half of it." The driver ran his hand fondly over the short bristles of his graying hair like he was petting a tooth-brush.

Fuss was sick and tired of cab drivers. He wanted to buy a car. But what good was a car when you couldn't get enough gas to use it? "Look, friend." Fuss handed a ten-dollar bill across to the driver. "I'm in a hurry. Couldn't you just call in and ask if they know where Hollywoodland is?"

"Sure thing." The driver snatched the bill and clicked the meter off, honking his horn as he tore around three automobiles in front of him, racing through the yellow light of another intersection. "This is 968, over! 968!" he barked into the mouth-piece of his two-way radio, flipping the callback switch.

"Yes, 968!" The callback voice answered immediately through loud static from the radio.

"I'm on New High Street heading west! I have a pickup to Hollywoodland. Can you direct?" The driver flipped down the switch and filled the cab with humming signals of dead airwaves. . . .

"Ah Hollywoodland? Doesn't show on our map! You sure it's not Hollywood Hills?"

The driver looked back over the seat at Fuss. "You sure, champ?"

Fuss nodded his head. "Certain."

"That is correct info!" The driver barked delightedly into the mouthpiece.

"Then drive around until you find it!" The static voice shouted back.

The driver slowed the cab and swerved sharply around a corner. "Let's go up Sunset Boulevard to Hollywood, fastest way."

"Fast is not fast enough."

The driver jammed the accelerator to the floor. "Hey, you see that old church?" He jerked a thumb out the window at the high brown adobe walls of a church, its slanting red-tiled roof reflecting the sunset.

Fuss barely glanced out the window at old Mexican women with black lace mantillas covering their heads walking up the steps, through arched doorways into the church. It was the same church where Fuss met Kinney every other week in the confessional at three o'clock. "Sure, I know the church. Just step on it, would you? I'm not a tourist from Buffalo on a sight-seeing trip."

"My wife says it's the oldest church in Los Angeles, built by them Spanish conquestors even." The driver honked his horn and swerved out to pass a milk truck in front of him.

Fuss thought the faster he talked to the cab driver, the faster the cab seemed to go. "Old? Boy you better believe that church is old. Oldest place in the city. It's called Nuestra Señora la Reina de los Angeles. Watch out for that old Chinese lady over there coming out of the market!"

"You speak Spanish, huh? What does that mean, Noostra Rayna whatever?" The driver sped through a red light just as the Chinese lady stepped down from the curb to cross in front of him.

"Our Lady the Queen of the Angels."

"No shit?" The driver looked at Fuss in the rearview mirror. "That's pretty, Queen of Angels. Ain't no angels left around here." He clucked his tongue and looked out the side window. All around the cab Chinese people hurried home from work before stores with bright lettered signs:

HUNG LEE IMPORTERS
KWON LUNG SUPERMARKET
HOT DUCKS DRUGS

"No angels left here, chief, only Chinks."

Fuss twisted uneasily in his seat. "Just keep your eyes on the road, would you?"

"This whole Chinatown area nearly burned down five years ago, in thirty-eight. Too bad it didn't all go. I'm not partial to Asiatics. My wife is right. Japs, Chinks, all those yellows are in this war together. It may not look it right now, but you'll notice your colored peoples will always stick together against whites in the end. You ever notice that?"

"Yes, I've noticed that about Hitler."

"What do you mean?" The driver looked into the rearview mirror.

"Forget it. Can't you make this old tub go any faster?"

"I'm doing forty now in downtown traffic! This isn't exactly a new Packard I'm driving!"

In the distance Fuss noticed broad skirts of palm trees silhouetted in the haze of sunset behind low buildings along the broad boulevard. Above the tall palms sparkling white bungalows with red-tiled roofs climbed jaggedly up hillsides like a primitive Mexican village hurriedly sketched against the backdrop of a cosmopolitan city. The full height of the palms came into view as the cab sped by Echo Park. Behind a small white boathouse the smooth expanse of lake was ringed by more palms. Flocks of pigeons, the underwhite of their wings flashing in last light, circled calm water toward the far shore where Fuss once rowed Kathleen. He thought of Kathleen's face, obscured beneath the broad brim of the straw hat, sunlight etching her body outlined sharply against the long thin dress, the brilliance of her red lips, and the breathlessness of her breathing. The thought of Kathleen's bright lips was dazzled from Fuss's mind by the abrupt reality of a golden dome, rising atop an enormous oblong building that unfolded against the sky like a concrete tulip. The gold of the dome flared blood red in the sunset.

"My wife says that temple was built in 1922 by Aimee Semple McPherson, the preacher woman. My wife says Aimee built it as a monument to herself so she would never be forgotten in this town, even after she walked into the tide and drowned herself out in Santa Monica."

The cab driver's sudden pronouncement jerked Fuss to attention, but not to admire the incongruity of the temple they passed by. He was struck by the stark immediacy of a forty-foot-high black-and-white billboard perched opposite the temple on the roof of a mattress factory: *DIALGOD*. The billboard faced off against the gold dome of Aimee Semple McPherson's Angelus Temple in what appeared to be a holy duel of monolithic design against monolithic statement. Fuss settled back into his seat nervously, the gun rubbing irritatingly against the skin of his stomach; the cab driver kept a suspicious gaze on him through the mirror.

"Watch out for that truck!"

The cab driver wheeled sharply back into his own lane just as Fuss screamed at him, then gunned the engine and shot down the narrowing boulevard, walled in on both sides by one squared-off block of apartment buildings after another, marching endlessly, their five-story height only occasionally broken by a single-story grocery store offering a sudden relief of darkening sky behind it, like a perfect row of teeth with one tooth knocked cleanly out.

"Pull over here, driver!"

The driver pulled over in the middle of a block of stores, scraping along the high curb to a stop before a busy drugstore; above its swinging glass doors an elaborate neon scroll announced: *SCHWAB'S PHARMACY.*

"What do you want to stop here for? You got a headache or something? Need an aspirin?"

Fuss swung open the door. "Everybody who comes to Hollywood to be discovered as a movie star always ends up at Schwab's; they know everything about the town. Who better to ask?" Fuss jumped out and pushed his way through the swinging doors into the crowded store. Cash registers clacked and rang like a bank of overworked typewriters. A long row of people had their backs to Fuss, thumbing through racks of glossy magazines flashing the perfect faces of movie stars on their covers. A soda jerk raced up and down behind the counter, scooping ice cream and racking tin containers of milk shakes into buzzing mixers. Teenage girls in preposterously padded brassieres shouted orders at the soda jerk as they spun recklessly on high stools. Fuss demanded the attention of the salesclerk at the first bank of cash registers. He pushed in front of a sailor with an armload of magazines. "Can you tell me where Hollywoodland is?" he shouted at the woman clerk in pink-and-white uniform dress.

The clerk's hands stopped playing over the register keys, the glare of her eyes appraising Fuss coldly like he was far less important than the scoops of ice cream the girls at the counter were gleefully digging spoons into. "You'll have to wait your turn."

"Look, lady." Fuss pressed closer to her. "I haven't all day. I have a cab waiting outside!" He pointed urgently through the glass doors at the black-and-white checkered cab idling alongside the curb.

The clerk grabbed the magazines out of the sailor's hands and slammed them on the counter before her, almost on top of Fuss's fingers. "I don't care if Clark Gable is your cab driver." She started punching the register keys. "You'll just have to wait!" She winked at the pimply faced young sailor in recognition like he had just popped up newborn between her legs. "*No* one cuts in front of a United States serviceman."

Fuss looked up at the clock above the shelves of toothpaste. It was ten minutes to seven. He turned and shouted straight into the backs of men before the magazine racks. "Does anyone know where Hollywoodland is?" None of the men turned around, as if used to people coming in and rudely shouting while they singlemindedly thumbed through page after page of pulp, hoping to catch a glimpse of Betty Grable's shapely legs swelling out of a wet bathing suit, or the broad blond smile of Lana Turner, her bigger-than-life breasts stretching beneath a sweater exactly like the giggling girls at the counter wore. "This is an emergency! Hollywoodland!"

"Hollywoodland? Brother, did you say Hollywoodland?" Down at the end of the magazine racks a man spoke without turning. From the back he appeared to be wearing a white linen suit. As he faced Fuss he displayed in full the linen of his outfit, but it wasn't a suit; it was a closely fitted white robe worn casually as a bird wears feathers. The flow of the man's gray beard and long hair was tailored neatly around the glow of his healthy face, creased in an open smile wrinkled from decades of exposure to bright sunshine. "Hollywoodland. Yes, I know it exceedingly well, brother."

Fuss took the man by the arm, surprised to feel the muscles beneath the crisp linen still lean and taut in one so old. "Come outside and tell my driver how to get there." Fuss pulled him through the swinging doors. "He says he knows!"

"Indeed I know, all right." The man raked slender fingers thoughtfully through his beard. "But it's been eons since any inhabitants around here have spoken of it. I thought one and all had forgotten. But you can't kill grand schemes and dreams. No, brother, you just can't devalue them; they'll always come back to haunt you like an albatross."

"I'm sorry to interrupt." Fuss pressed the man's arm harder. "But we're in somewhat of a hurry to get to this Hollywoodland. I'd like to sit around here for eons and listen to you reminisce about it, but just tell the driver where it is."

"Brother, I don't have to tell him, I can *show* you." The man smiled. "You can see it right up there, from the corner."

"Let's go." Fuss grabbed the man's arm again and pulled him along the crowded sidewalk.

"You used to have to go by the old Krotona Palace to get to Hollywoodland, in the old days." The man spoke quickly in a strong voice, determined that his history of the past could help Fuss to reach his destination more easily. "Of course, brother, they've torn down the palace now, ripped out the gardens and fountains. Made the entire place into another one of those cancerous apartment complexes. The Krotona was like a classical apparition from India magically transmigrated to the once lovely hills of Hollywood. I heard the master, Krishnamurti, there for the first time, in the early twenties I think. What a boy! So beautiful. So godlike. So honest and direct. The true Star of the East. He was brought to America by that Theosophical woman. What was her name? Yes! Besant, Annie Besant. Very rich she was. Rich and dogmatic, a spiritual didact."

"Here we are at the corner." Fuss nearly pulled the man into the intersection of honking cars. "Now, where is it?"

"There." The old man swung his arm up like Moses pointing to the burning bush. "Mack Sennett, you know, the Jewish comedic genius who invented the Keystone Cops, it's his old real estate development. It was supposed to be the new Beverly Hills. But old Mack was hoodwinked by the duplicity of Hollywood city fathers. The august city fathers wouldn't allow Mack to suck off their main water line."

Fuss followed the direction of the old man's arm, the tips

of his fingers waving toward the Hollywood Hills in the absolute last light of day. "Where? What are you talking about? There's five square miles of houses and apartments up there."

The old man raised his arm higher. "Way up, almost to the top, below the flashing red light of the RKO radio tower. Don't you see it, brother? Way up on top of Mount Lee."

Fuss saw it. A huge sign rolling through clumps of sage and spikes of yucca near the mountaintop. Nine wooden letters, each high as four men atop one another's shoulders, each letter painted white, sprawled improbably across the natural shoulder of the mountain. The letters seemed a tenuous but monstrous joke that could blow down in any retributary wind. But there they stood, naked as the last advertisement for a feeble civilization, dwarfing the simple beauty of the natural terrain, idiotic and splendid, washed in the ethereal glow of the dying sun sinking blood red into the ocean to the west:

HOLLYWOOD

Fuss was familiar with the letters. From the top of Mount Lee they dominated the city of Hollywood below. "You sure that's it?"

"Most certainly, brother." The old man dropped his arm and sighed. "At one time in history it spelled out in full *HOLLYWOODLAND*. Now it is just decomposing and falling apart, like everything else temporal and carnal glamorized around here. The last four letters have fallen down, but you can still see them if you get up close. The whole business is ready to topple over any day, surrendering to time and the elements, nature claiming her own. That's all that's left standing of an expensive dream, *HOLLYWOODLAND*." Cars were honking furiously around the old man. He shook his long gray hair sadly as Fuss ran down the dark sidewalk and jumped into the waiting cab without looking back.

"Turn right at the next block and head up into the hills!"

Fuss shouted over the whining of the cab engine as it lurched into the bright lights of evening traffic, squealing around the corner and racing toward Hollywood Boulevard, then slamming to a dead stop before a blockade of police cars. "This is crazy." Fuss pushed his gun deep beneath his belt as police ran from all directions, surrounding the cab.

The cab driver furiously cranked up his window to shut out the unexpected and seal himself protected into the castle of his cab. He looked into the rearview mirror and snarled at Fuss, his face sweating anxiously. "What are you? An escaped convict? My wife told me not to work that Mexican area downtown. She warned me something like this would happen if I cruised fares in the Barrio. I should of stayed out at Wilshire Center like she said."

"I don't know what's going on! I swear it!" Fuss slid down in his seat as one of the policemen banged the butt of a billyclub on the glass of the driver's window.

"Roll the window down in there!"

The driver obeyed the command cautiously. He lowered the window slowly. "Yes, sir, officer. Whatever you say. Would you like to see my driver's license?" The driver held his hand nervously on the window crank; if the blue-uniformed man tried to jump into the cab, the driver was ready to roll the window back up and catch him in it.

"No, no need for that." The officer smiled, tipping the thick vinyl visor of his cap. "No need for your license. You'll just have to back up and go around. Detour."

"What's the trouble, officer?" Fuss leaned on the back of the front seat, his body almost doubled over so the gun was impossible to see.

The officer pointed his club up Hollywood Boulevard, toward brilliant mile-long beams shooting into the air from cannon-sized klieg lights. "Barbara Marr. They're premiering one of her movies here tonight. It's her first picture since she was involved in those Zoot-suit murders last summer. We've got the boulevard blocked for ten blocks. George Raft is going to be here and everything; the fans are going wild. Sorry, you'll have to turn around and go back the way you came."

"Sure thing." The driver saluted the officer like he'd just received instructions to drive a tank over a mine field. He jammed the cab into reverse and backed his way slowly around the line of cars stalled behind him.

Fuss leaned farther over the front seat as the cab backed up, catching a glimpse up the boulevard of two neon signs hanging from the soaring sweep of a green-tiled pagoda roof over a surging crowd on the sidewalk: *GRAUMAN'S CHINESE*. The neon signs impressed their colorful glare on empty pavement in the middle of the boulevard reserved for a long line of limousines inching slowly between cheers and flashing camera bulbs. One of the women, her blond hair cascading as she stepped from a limousine and waved a sequin-gloved hand to jubilant fans, looked like Barbara Marr. He dropped two bills on the seat next to the driver. "Here's another ten bucks. I'll tell you exactly how to go, just get out of here fast as you can."

"That's fine with me, champ." The driver jerked the cab back into the flow of traffic on Sunset. "The faster the better. I've had some real pills want me to take them to Hollywood, but you and your little ferryland place you want me to take you to, you're the biggest pill yet."

At the end of steep short streets running blindly into one another, then looping back through darkness and spiraling along the unrailed edge of sheer cliffs, dropping like a series of unending soundless waterfalls down to the swift running currents of electric lights sparkling up from distant Hollywood, Fuss had the driver let him out. He followed the road until it deadended, the pavement giving way to hard gravel. His crunching steps echoed around him off the barren hillsides. He slipped the gun from under his belt, holding it before him like a flashlight with a dead battery. In the darkness the gravel road narrowed, a path of soft dirt starting beneath his shoes. He never took his eyes from the guiding light high on the distant ridge, incessant red blinking at the needle point of the steel-strutted RKO radio tower. He followed the red light faithfully, even when the trail narrowed, running off through thick dry clumps of ragweed in a hundred paths no wider than a rabbit. The soft dirt gave way entirely underneath him and he slipped. It felt like he was on the edge of a cliff, hanging only by the luck of the grass tufts clutched in his hands as he tried to keep his grasping fingers away from the gun's trigger. The lights of Hollywood twinkling below seemed to beckon him; the powerful beams of klieg lights fingered furtively from the faraway city, as if searching him out. Sprawled on the mountainside in darkness, dangling like a man from a thirty-story-high window, he felt like a fool. He pulled himself steadily up, regaining his footing on the steep incline. The howl of a coyote came, startling, like the cry of an abandoned or beaten child. The cry of the coyote carried away from the cliff, far beyond the bright lights of Hollywood and the glimmering ocean of Los Angeles lights, all the way west to Santa Monica and the infinity of a real ocean beyond. Fuss held his breath, turning an ear up to the mountaintop, trying to hear the coyote walking. He heard nothing until the cry came again, louder, anguished, a snaking lament carried way out over the city lights and crushed by the far-off metallic rumbling of traffic. "Cruz." The name came out in an involuntary hoarse whisper, as if in answer to the coyote. "Cruz?" There was no answer. Fuss felt his way farther, slowly, deliberately, inching toward the sign looming large and barely distinguishable, propped up from the sheer mountainside on soaring poles crisscrossed and strutted behind each letter, spelling out in the darkness

HOLLYWOOD

"Cruz?" Fuss waited for an answer. Cruz could be hiding behind any one of the twenty-foot-high letters, the shape of his body not penetrating from dark shadows of the supporting poles. Fuss sat wearily on the earth gone cold in the night air. Above his head the radio tower light rhythmically sprinkled the slightest glimmer of red across the enormous letters soaring out before him. He was afraid to go any farther. Anyone could be lurking in the shadows of the letters. He controlled the single access to the sign. He would wait for the light of morning, wait until the letters were exposed and he was certain no one was hiding there, or until someone came up the trail. He heard the anguished cry of the coyote and aimed the gun in its direction, holding off the unseen, the unknown. Even in his dreams, after he went to sleep at the foot of the giant sign and the coyote had long since ceased its solemn lament, and the rising sun stunned the vastness of the distant Pacific Ocean holding back the sprawl of highways clawing concretely out from the heart of Los Angeles, even then he did not know what he expected to find up there.

26

The island of Catalina came up out of the sea rearing and blowing like a humpback whale on the blue horizon. A strong Santa Ana wind whipped the sea into a frenzy of spray around the sudden heights of the island's barren cliffs. Beneath the bright flutter and rip of a hundred maritime flags strung from the S.S. *Catalina*'s three steel masts people crowded along the edges of the sleek white ship's four passenger decks. They cheered the sight of the island like castaways abandoned to a cruel sea who hadn't sighted land for days, rather than only several hours since leaving San Pedro. Fuss didn't care about the island. He was intrigued by the red of Kathleen's hair whipping and snarling in the wind as she leaned precariously out from the perch of the upper deck's railings. Kathleen was so thin and vulnerable, he feared she might blow away in the strong warm gusts swirling about the ship as it eased into the open sweep of Avalon harbor, or she might suddenly be swooped into the air by circling clouds of seagulls dipping and diving over the big white steamer like it was a giant iron-fin marlin to be feasted upon by the most tenacious and fortunate. Fuss stood behind Kathleen, closing his arms around her on both sides and locking his hands over hers on the railing. If a sudden wind was to spirit her away, it would have to take them both.

"Look! Look out there! Do you see them?" Kathleen's arm came up and she leaned back against Fuss, pointing in the direction of the island's curving harbor, all the way out to its end, a spit of land dominated by the five-story-high white dome of the Avalon Ballroom, perched improbably between land and sea like a sheik's stretched tent on the desert.

Fuss followed the line of Kathleen's arm across the water. Palms and flags fluttered around the dome of the ballroom. The small town of Avalon rose behind the ballroom, climbing steeply up the fall of cliffs protruding abruptly from the sea, then surrendering to steep terrain, a straggle of brave houses perched on poles eight hundred feet up the mountainside, as if prepared for the ocean to one day lap at their front doors. "What am I looking for?"

"You're looking too far, Oscar. Not all the way to the town. Out there, on the water." Kathleen placed her hand gently against Fuss's cheek, guiding his gaze to the sight the people on the observation deck above were screaming and shouting about. "Flying fish!"

Fuss saw them. Skimming over the white frothing tongues of the ocean's chopping waves, the fish were actually flying, sailing through the spray in a display of dazzling acrobatics, creatures not of land or sky, but wedded in breathtaking moments to a realm all their own, unique, without parallel. Fuss felt the slightness of Kathleen's body pressed against him, trembling with excitement at the fish flying by, freeing themselves from the depths of the sea, bounding from the ocean's floor, sailing toward the sun in a fabulous pursuit of freedom. He slipped his arms around Kathleen's waist. She did not object. All the way into the harbor he held her tightly, feeling himself tremble, trembling from fear of the unknown within her, the questions he knew must be asked, the answers he didn't want to hear. He held on to her as if it was for life, afraid she might escape the few moments they had together, like the flying fish long left behind in the wake of the steaming ship, living between two worlds, never questioning the impossibility of their existence, never testing the improbability of their realm, sailing forever through water and air.

In the Avalon Ballroom beneath banners of a thousand balloons Fuss thought Kathleen died in his arms. For hours he held her, breathless, dance after dance, the big trumpeting sound of Harry James's band breaking over them like stormy brassy waves. Everywhere sailors and soldiers laughed and shouted, hoisting their girls into the air like proud prizes just won at a carnival, offerings to be displayed on the altar of good times. The war was a million miles away in the ballroom. The packed swirling dancers made the vast domed building spin like a private planet, a reserved place in space where romance reigned, red lips of young women pressed against the faces of eternal partners. Drums, trombones, and trumpets of the band fired thundering rockets of sound, coursing through the blood of every tribal foot stomping on the dance floor. Against Fuss's cheek the slightest breath escaped from Kathleen's lips, a high whistling sound, almost a wheeze, her red hair covering her eyes, the dampness of her skin welding the two of them together, offering a physical promise far beyond a simple fusing of their flesh. For hours the balloons spun above their heads. The weaker Kathleen grew in his arms, the stronger Fuss became, until finally he carried her from the ballroom, spent and exhausted, the red curls framing the radiant smile of happiness on her face. He walked her slowly along the tiled promenade of the harbor. The sea had become gentle inside the island's protective arms, its soft rocking barely disturbing the rows of small anchored boats. Kathleen's body swayed beneath Fuss's tight hold around her waist as they passed lovers crowded together on concrete benches, holding hands, anxious to make plans for a future never to be. At the end of the promenade Fuss took Kathleen up a narrow dirt road winding above the last houses of the town and dropping suddenly into a purple canyon, hidden from the sea and blaring music of the ballroom below.

"What are those?" Kathleen pointed to a clump of rough spiked plants tall as a man, long tongues of pearlescent flowers blooming from the cluster of their sharp green fingers.

"It's a type of yucca, a yucca whipplei. The Spanish explorers named it the Lord's candle. Here on the island it blooms those thousands of little blossoms in the spring." Fuss took Kathleen's hand and led her along a steep trail descending into the canyon. "But that is not what will help your asthma. What we're searching for is cyanothus americanus."

"What?"

"The plant I told you about, remember? The plant we came here to find, the one the Mexican brujas make a tea from and believe will clear the lungs, help you to breathe easier. Better than your marijuana cure."

"What's a bruja? You never told me."

"A witch."

Kathleen stopped, stretching out her hand to stroke the blossomed tongue of a spiked yucca next to the trail. "This plant of yours, do you really think it could help me? I'd try anything, even a witch's brew, if I thought it would help me to breathe easier. I'm so dispirited taking medicines all the time."

"It's worth a try, Kathleen. Anything's worth a try. The Indians who lived here boiled poison oak leaves and drank the broth, believing it made them immune to poison oak rashes." Fuss waded off down the trail into thigh-high brush. "There are two varieties of the plant we're looking for. One has a blue flower, the other white. I just hope we can find the right one, since it's not in bloom now and won't have any flowers."

Kathleen plucked teardrop-size yucca blossoms and studied them in her palm, calling to Fuss as he went deeper into the canyon. "How come you know so much about this island?"

"Because"—Fuss pushed his way through a thorn bush grabbing at his flapping sport coat—"when I brought my CYO boys over here last summer I decided to study up on the place. This is the only nature lots of those kids will ever see. I like to be able to answer their questions, leave them with a feel for the specialness of a place. Most people don't know it but this island is more than twenty centuries older than the mainland of California, just twenty-six miles away, a freak of nature. There are plants here that exist nowhere else in the world. Ask me about the firewood trees on the way back and I'll—" Fuss stopped. Before him a broad hardwood bush that appeared to be dying from lack of water came up out of the ground in a swirl of stiff branches blocking his passage. He snapped off the brittle tip of a branch, a strong scent of resin racing up his nostrils, a scent so powerful it seemed like he had just uncapped a can of ether. Fuss plucked off the tips of more branches until his coat pockets bulged with them, then made his way back up the steep trail to Kathleen.

"Did you find it, Oscar?"

"Smell." Fuss reached into his pocket and held out a handful of twigs beneath Kathleen's nose. She pulled back suddenly and shook her head as if getting a whiff of smelling salts.

Fuss laughed, slipping the twigs gently back into his pocket, like they were eggs about to be hatched. "I'm not promising we have the right variety. Like I said, cyanothus is dormant this time of year, so it's impossible to tell whether we have the blue or white one. Come on, we better go back." He took Kathleen's outstretched hand and led her up the trail. "But it really doesn't make any difference which variety we have, because to be honest I don't know which one will do the trick for you."

"You actually expect me to drink that? It smells like gasoline."

"Or ether. You said you would try anything."

Kathleen stopped at the top of the canyon, the dome of the ballroom in sight against the calm sea below. "I will try it on one condition."

"What's that?"

The shuddering boarding blast from the steam whistle of the S.S. *Catalina* hauling anchor in the harbor drowned out the first part of Kathleen's words. "And besides that, you must promise to drink some with me."

"It's a deal." Fuss shook her hand solemnly. "We'll drink it together, then if it's hemlock we'll die side by side."

"Oh, Oscar, that's funny, the two of us dying in each other's arms like in some sad Greek tragedy. Come on, we have to hurry or the ship is going back to San Pedro without us." Kathleen put her arm around Fuss's waist for support as they ran down the steep road toward the harbor, all the while her strange breathless laughter ringing in his ears.

27

The five photographs tacked to the wall stared glossily down at Fuss. He studied them carefully, closely, with full attention, committing every distinguishing feature to memory. The dark mustaches of the two men on the end, the scar straight down the middle of the forehead on the man in the center, the slightly receding hairline creeping up the broad head of the one who seemed to be the oldest of the group. But it was the face of the second man from the end that Fuss kept coming back to again and again, the one who finally dominated his attention. That was him, Fuss was certain of it. He was Chiquito Banana. There was an unmistakable air of authority in the man's lean Latin face. The lips straight and strong with no trace of obvious malice, but the eyes potent, a gaze so full of life it followed Fuss around his small room from the glossy surface of the photograph. The man was handsome, in his early thirties, his thick eyebrows almost growing together, merging in a definite V above the fine slanting nose. This man had character, authority in the tight fist of his cleft chin, nobility in the arched bones of his cheeks. This man was a natural leader. Maybe the FBI didn't know which of the five men in the photographs tacked to Fuss's wall was one of the most dangerous Latin Fascists in California, but there was no question in Fuss's mind. None. And he knew sooner or later he would meet him, or at least see him. This man who was not above hooking young kids on dope to buy their political allegiance. This man who played on every physical fear and mental anguish of the people in the Barrio. This man Fuss wanted to ferret out of his rat hole. This man was the ultimate danger. Fuss didn't like why this man was the ultimate danger: the danger lay in the larger truth of his politics. Fuss was a good American. Fuss knew the Barrio was a deadend trap for the thousands who came across the border to find an honest day's wage. Why shouldn't they come with that hope? Everyone else came to America for the same reason. Was it a crime to want to work, speak another language, demand an equal wage? Fuss knew the Barrio was a giant, elaborate net, stretched across the east side of Los Angeles for one purpose: to trap cheap labor, migratory labor, labor that would stoop and pick in the hot summer fields, labor desperate and dying for a chance to work in factories, prove itself, that it could take it, take the low wages, the inhuman living conditions, the heat, the dust, seasonal work, overcrowding, the abuse. Take it and come back for more, because abuse had become in America the conditional price tag for hope. That's why this Fascist was dangerous, because many conditions of abuse he spoke about were true. There was no denying it. Fuss himself hadn't yet figured out why people of the Barrio were denied work in many war industries. It didn't make sense. It wasn't the American way; during a war everybody is supposed to work. If these people were asked to go and fight for America, die for America, why couldn't they work alongside anyone else in America? Everything seemed confusing, but in the end Fuss knew there was one constant in his own life: he was a good American. He knew the system wasn't perfect, but there wasn't a better one to replace it with. The Fascists and the Communists all had the same corrupt bottom line—kill individualism. Fuss would rather die protecting an imperfect system than live without freedom. Fuss knew what was dangerous about this man, this Chiquito Banana. He had seen the Fascists' pamphlets scattered every morning throughout the Barrio. The Fascists used small truths to mask the big lie. The whole world knew what the Fascists were. The whole world knew if America didn't defeat Hitler it would become one big Nazi slave camp. Some things Fuss was confused about, but about that he wasn't, about that he was certain.

The phone hadn't rung for days; no word from Cruz. Fuss was afraid to leave the house in case he missed the call. He left the house only to see Kathleen. He put out the word to Wino Boy to tell the Zoot gangs he wanted Cruz to call him, to let Cruz know he went to Hollywoodland, he was late, but he kept his part of the bargain, he got there. Cruz hadn't been seen on the streets for the last week. Fuss couldn't sleep at night. If it wasn't one thing it was another. He woke up from dreams about his brother screaming in a sea of fire. He woke up from seeing himself rip open Cruz's shirt, his narrow hairless chest crisscrossed with fine razor-blade slashes, festering and swollen from the heroin he powdered directly into his bloodstream. These Barrio kids were too smart to jab themselves full of needle holes in the legs and arms, the first places every probation officer looked to see if a kid had a monkey on his back. Fuss woke up seeing bombs fall like rain as the odd, sensitive words of the Voice rang in his ear, words enticing and cool, breathed in like pure oxygen through a gas mask. Fuss couldn't sleep worth a damn. Four o'clock in the morning and he was looking at the photographs of the faces pinned to his wall.

He tried to get his mind to relax, but who can relax when the whole world is at war? He tried to concentrate on the perfect pitches Angel could throw for the Stars. The game of baseball followed certain rules. Lines of performance had to be upheld, but there were always the two wonderful surprises: either smash the ball straight out of the park and make all rules meaningless or throw pitches so sincere and absolutely down the middle that the game became an excuse for poetry. Games were the reality of dreams. How the game of war should be played, Fuss thought as he studied the photographed faces of the men on his wall, is Hitler, Roosevelt, Stalin, Hirohito, Churchill, the whole pack of them, should get up some national baseball teams to manage, then square off against one another in the World Series of War, but with baseballs. It was four o'clock in the morning and Fuss didn't like his thoughts. They were stupid when he thought about them. But he couldn't get any satisfaction. The only whole, solid piece of sweet dreaming he was capable of was about Kathleen. Sweet, simple dreams about her small breasts or about the white of her slender calves as she walked before him up the stairs of her apartment, and the sound of her breathing, always breathless, unnerving, like her words just arrived after a night of exhausting lovemaking, her entire body still damp, her excited fingers trembling, seeming to trace the outline of another body in the empty air as she talked. But he didn't like to think of her feeble condition, dream of her spent body. When he did he went hard as a baseball bat between the legs, and he felt dumb and empty.

Fuss sat at the small card table. For the hundredth time he picked up the V-mail letter from Marvin. A false dawn staggered down the empty street out the window over the palms, a strange and faint light coming from behind the bouldered peaks of the San Gabriel Mountains. He pulled the light cord above his head and watched the strange light through the window. He didn't know what caused it; he had seen it before. Steadily, as the true dawn began to flood the sky, the strange light grew more distant, at the same time giving off a distinct color, like spilled red wine on a rug or blood on a sheet moments before the stain fades. He strained his eyes in the new light that poured through the window, reading over and over the words of the letter he already knew by heart. He didn't know why he kept rereading the letter. It depressed him, but it was the only form of contact with Marvin he had had for the past eight weeks. It depressed him that any time of the day or night Marvin's aircraft carrier might take a direct hit and go down. Why should Marvin have to worry about Jap subs, fight a stinking war, and still be obsessed with having to defend himself against someone like the Shitter? The Shitter wasn't such a joke anymore. The Shitter wasn't so cavalier and swashbuckling with his stinking protest against the Navy and the war. The Shitter was some crazy guy out in the middle of the Pacific Ocean who was terrorizing Marvin. The Shitter had become so real Fuss would wake up in the middle of the night, out of one bad dream or another, half expecting to see a reeking hot mound on his bed with a letter tacked to it: *Sweet Dreams, Oscar. Your Pal, The Shitter.*

What was more terrifying than the Shitter stalking the streets of Los Angeles was the fact that Fuss thought he might be the Shitter himself. That was the silly thing about it. If the Shitter singled you out of a whole shipload of other sailors, or if he picked you out of three million lost souls in Los Angeles, weren't you just as guilty as he? Wasn't the target himself the reason for the revenge? Didn't the target feel deep down inside, with not too much prodding, that he too could be driven to such an infantile act? Or, worse yet, somehow the target himself was the one who provoked the act. So in the end every victim of the Shitter thought of himself as the guilty one, the true Shitter. As Fuss again read between the censored lines of Marvin's letter, he understood his brother's frustration. As long as the Shitter hadn't personally struck Marvin he was still clean, guiltless; in a world full of Shitters he was still ahead of the game.

Hi Guy!

Well, another day another doughnut. Did I tell you a big movie star was on board? Henry Fonda. Oh, yah, I guess I did. That was a couple of months ago, time goes so slow you forget what was what when, and even that you're not sure of. You civvies think you got it bad being rationed only two pounds of meat a week, a few eggs, and half a cup of sugar. Well, let me tell you, there's nothing worse than being a swab jockey floating around on ten million square miles of flat blue ocean with every Jap sub and Zero in the world hunting you. I tell you, I'd rather be some island-bound gob any day than a swab jockey. At least the gobs only have to worry about getting it from the air, us out here, we get the shaft from both directions, above and below. I'm going so crazy, every time I go to the head I think I see Jap subs coming up in the toilet. I'm afraid to even look in the damn thing without seeing a periscope come up out of it. There's no peace in this man's Navy, what with the Japs to worry about and the Shitter saying I'm next. I haven't slept for weeks. Oh, I fake it like I am, in case the Shitter makes his move. Boy, something terrible happened last night. A guy I know, went through boot camp with him right after Pearl Harbor, just a great guy, really. He got one of the Shitter's threatening notes; he was under the gun. So he camped out on his bunk like me, refusing to go to chow, even to the head. Then pow, out of nowhere, he can't stand it anymore and goes to take a leak, then runs back and there it is, bigger than life, a whole hot brown pile of it on his bunk. What a stink! You won't believe this, but guys talking the other night said there was a Shitter last month on one of the tubs in the Atlantic. Nobody knew who it was for months, but when they figured it out he was thrown overboard. That's how they handle Shitters in the Atlantic. Last night a petty officer went overboard on the carrier. Now I know that happens all the time in wartime, thousand guys locked on a ship together. But this was strange. We had good weather last night, yet nobody saw him go over or heard screaming. The scuttlebutt is if there are no more hot piles then somebody got the real Shitter. But every guy on board still suspects every other guy. Me, I'm still going to stay awake all night. I'm scared as hell.

Take care guy,
Your brother, Marvin

P.S. Don't forget to save your Coke caps. Ten zillion make one aircraft carrier. Have you planted your V-garden yet? Vitamins for victory!

28

Flores Street was thick with people and howling with the sounds of Friday night. Fabulous color from neon signs cracked and jumped through the air over crowded sidewalks like freak summer lightning hopping over a cornfield. Radios blared a babble of Latin and American rhythms from open windows of apartments stacked four high above small shops. Irregular lines of Zoots in baggy suits slouched against shop windows, as if laying claim to all the merchandise displayed in mountains of enticement behind them. Tidepools of teenage girls in tight black skirts and sweaters, silver crosses swinging between the golden skin of their budding breasts, swirled around corner street lamps, the strong light outlining their rouged young faces. From the middle of the block the girls appeared to Fuss like flittering black moths in the moonlight, intoxicated by their blossoming youth. As Fuss passed the girls, they lowered their voices, the soft sounds of their Spanish words turning to swift whispers of anger, hissing like steam in Fuss's ears.

"Hey, macho!"

A gang of Zoots leaning against the Signal Gasoline Station pumps on the corner moved onto the sidewalk to block Fuss. He navigated through speeding and honking cars at the intersection. The Zoots laughed, shouted and spit their words in Spanish and English from all directions at Fuss. The words, more than the threatening stance of the Zoots, stopped Fuss cold.

"Hey, macho mon! Where you go, mon? You got the hot date with the loca girlfriend?"

"Hey, hombre, you copped her cherry yet? You getting mushy with her cookie?"

The Zoots moved around Fuss, screening out the wild laughter from their black-outfitted girlfriends beneath street lamps.

"You been making some hotcha ouchimagooga? Ahhhh-wiiieee!"

One of the Zoots leaned in front of Fuss, the leer on his face wide as the lapels on his chartreuse sport coat. "How you face yourself in the morning time, mon? Taking the advantage on a loca like her? Do you confess much to the padre, chico? Is that why you go to the confessions so much? You be telling the priest, 'Bless me, padre, for I have sinned. My poor little mucha-cha has a pair of maracas no bigger than pigeon's eggs!' "

The laughter of the Zoots came up like a net, stretched and pulled tightly over Fuss's red face.

"Hey, mon, you getting Cruz a job?"

The laughter stopped. The anger silently surrounded Fuss, real and powerful. Instead of an invisible net, it was like a knife at his throat. From behind the gas pumps a tall Zoot swaggered out, the bottom of his long red coat scraping the knees of his yellow slacks, his hand coolly swinging a length of gold watch chain looping from his vest pocket almost to the dirty sidewalk. Even in the shadow of the floppy brimmed hat Fuss recognized the Zoot leader immediately. He was Venegas Delgado, cousin to six of the Zoots about to stand trial for shooting the two FBI agents. The elaborate draping of Delgado's Zoot suit could not hide his pitifully thin body. He had the look of a starving animal. Delgado walked with the pained determination of a ninety-year-old man, not a twenty-two-year-old.

"Hey, big macho mon, you wanna buy a Zoot?" The sneer on Delgado's face left no doubt as to the vicious intentions in his voice. "We fix you up good. Hepcat alterations while you wait, all first-class duds, dynamite jive garments to make you look like us, kool, keen, kleen, and kee-rect." Delgado tugged at the arrowed tip of Fuss's tie. "How can you have no pride? You're in the Barrio, chico, not Westwood. You got to be tricking yourself out like the dude, get yourself up in some pants with stuff-cuffs, reet-pleats, look like a Zoot, walk like a Zoot, talk like a Zoot. Isn't that it, chico? You want to pass, look like a *native?*"

The knot of Fuss's tie tightened around his neck. Behind the gas pumps another Zoot casually spun a four-pronged tire iron on the blacktop like a child's giant jack, the iron bar wobbling and falling over with a clank.

"Look, Delgado." Fuss tried to talk normally, as if the tie wasn't choking him. "You were at the hearing. You heard my testimony. I said I didn't see who shot the FBI guys. I said I never saw a Zoot with a gun in his hand."

Delgado yanked the tie. "We hear you give secret testimony."

"I've given other testimony, sure. But I always say the same stuff. I didn't see your cousins, or anybody else that night, actually shoot the FBI agents."

"Chico, you think we don't know what you are up to in the Barrio?" Delgado jerked the tie, pulling Fuss against his bony chest. "Let me tell you! We know you, chico, and we want you to stay out of the Barrio. No talking to our people."

"I've still got business here, with the church, with the CYO boys." The stiffness of a billyclub beneath Delgado's pants zipper pressed insistently against Fuss's leg. Fuss knew most of the Zoots around him had a club hidden inside a special pocket sewn into their pants legs.

"I don't think you understand the deal here." Delgado's fist yanked Fuss's tie so hard it cut off his breath. "We don't want you here, that's the deal, get it? It's a straight black-and-blue deal, understand? You hang around asking more questions and we kick your keester. We are going to beat you black and blue from top to bottom till you won't know which end is up, till you talking from your ass and shitting from your mouth. Comprende?"

"Comprendo."

Delgado shoved Fuss away and walked back into the shadow of the gas pumps. The rest of the Zoots belligerently opened up a narrow path for Fuss, making him brush against their hidden billyclubs as he continued to the next corner and crossed the street quickly, afraid to look back. By the time he walked the remaining five blocks to Kathleen's apartment, his suit was soaked through with sweat. He rang the buzzer at her door and ran up the steps. She was way above him, at the top of the winding staircase, a candle in her hand, the flame playing around her red curls. He ran faster, afraid he wouldn't be able to reach her before something terrifying happened. She seemed so far above him.

"Oh, Oscar, you look a wreck!"

He stood before her, panting, wanting to take hold of her fragile body, press its softness against him, protect her. He gulped at the air like a floundering fish helpless on the bottom of a boat. He caught his breath and smiled weakly. "I'm sorry to be late."

She reached out her pale white hand, placing the coolness of her fingers affectionately on his hot cheek. "You look just a *wreck,* poor boy, come with me. Were you in an accident?"

He followed her obediently into the candlelit cavern of her living room, sinking heavily in one of the fat chairs. "No, no accident. I just couldn't find a cab. You know how it is, Friday night, all the sailors have liberty, impossible, really."

Kathleen set the candle carefully on the dining table. "You mean you walked all that way?"

"Ran all that way."

"Poor boy, you look so sad. Would you like a Coke?"

"Swell." Fuss followed Kathleen into the kitchen. She opened the icebox door and reached for two bottles of Coke, exposing on the metal rack her breathalator and the hypodermic needle next to vials of adrenalin. She uncapped the bottles and handed him one, placing the glass tip of her own to her lips, a slight brown foam from the cool liquid tracing down from the corner of her lips as she drank.

"Now." Kathleen took Fuss's arm and led him back into the living room. "We must talk about our experiment. Did you bring the plant?"

"Yes." Fuss settled back into the fat chair across from Kathleen, pulling a bulging paper sack from his coat pocket. "It's all here, nice and dried out."

"Oh, good." Kathleen pressed her knees together. "It should make a perfect tea."

"Perfect."

"I'm so excited, Oscar." She placed her hands carefully around the Coke bottle like it was a prayer book. "I've had the most terrible asthma attack today. I had to use the breathalator again. I used up all the medicine in it. I thought I'd die. Something is getting to me in this city, just choking me up. I feel like I have water in my lungs. Like I'm underwater, drowning. Just awful, this feeling of suffocation. I can't tell you"—she laid her cool hand on his knee—"how heavenly kind you are to come over here tonight just so I could try our witch's tea. I'm so desperate all the time. I must try everything. When I called you earlier I was just praying you wouldn't let me down. That you would come over and help me."

"Maybe it's the ragweed."

"You mean what is causing the congestion?"

"Yes, it's in the hills all around here, drying up and dying this time of year. Maybe the smell of it blows down into the city every day from the mountains."

"Yes, maybe that's it." Kathleen leaned back wearily in the chair. "That's why I want to leave this city, go to the Grand Canyon."

"Why don't you just do it? You're going to die of asthma if you don't."

Kathleen pushed herself upright, a slight arc in her back beneath her thin shoulders. "Oscar, you know I couldn't possibly do that. You know I have my mission to accomplish."

"Yes, of course, I forgot."

"I could never leave now. Things are going so well for my Latin Bureau, never been better." She looked at him affectionately, like a mother promising a small boy his birthday present. "Next week the Voice is going to make an appearance here in the Barrio."

"That soon?"

"That soon, Oscar. He's been promising for months. Can you believe how exciting? You're finally going to meet him. I've promised that for so long. I've told him all about you. We don't have too many Catholic converts, you know." Kathleen winked mischievously, a clear animal light in her eye.

"Kathleen, I don't believe I'm much of a catch for you. I've never been much of a strict Catholic." Fuss winked back. "I'm afraid you could convert me to the Hitler Youth. You're the most persuasive woman I've ever met. Persuasive and," he rolled the empty Coke bottle between his palms; all he wanted to do was reach out and touch her "beautiful."

Kathleen's bright red lips shaped into a sly smile. "I'm too skinny to be beautiful, Oscar. I've been sick ever since I was a little girl with rheumatic fever and asthma. You can flatter me, but I know the truth of the matter. Most men want a woman who has lots of curves and dimpled cheeks, like Betty Grable or Barbara Marr."

"I'm not most men, Kathleen."

"No, you most certainly are not." She rose quietly. The candlelight made her look even thinner, more refined. The flickering light traced an expression of strength on her lips, the strength of one who has accepted gracefully the absolute vulnerability of her position in the universe. "You are always so heavenly kind to me."

"I'll make the tea." Fuss stood up before her. Everything in his nature surrendered to her. Her slightness dominated him, holding him off; he was afraid to touch her.

"You make the tea, Oscar." She rested a hand on her heart. "I'll go into the bedroom and lie down for a few moments. After my attack this morning I feel like a truck has run over my chest."

"Do you need some help?" Fuss took her arm to steady her.

"No, thank you. You just make your magic witch's tea, maybe that will be the big help I need." She disappeared down the hall through the murky light into the bedroom.

"Swell." Fuss spoke the word aloud to himself as much as to Kathleen, who could no longer hear him. "I'll whip up the magic brew." He clapped his hands together in preparation and went into the kitchen, striking a match and exploding a puff of gas from the stove pilot into a high flame beneath a pan of water. He shook the dried twigs carefully out onto the table, making two little neat piles. "I don't know whether I should put the twigs into the cups, then let them steep in water for twenty minutes, or dump all the twigs into the boiling water in the pan. What do you think?" Fuss shouted over his shoulder out of the kitchen doorway. Kathleen did not answer. She either couldn't hear him or had fallen asleep. "What I'll do," he mumbled to himself, scooping together the two neat piles and dumping them into the water boiling up to the top of the pan, "is just let the whole thing simmer for twenty minutes, then pour it out." He covered the pan and turned down the heat, guarding the situation closely so the water wouldn't become too hot and boil out onto the stove. A yellowish steam hissed from beneath the lid of the pan, puffing like a small angry geyser, filling the room with an odd and overpowering aroma, sickly sweet, reminiscent of the last breath of ether taken anxiously in before a patient on an operating table blacks out into a swirling, heady pool and drowns. Fuss bent over the brackish steam and took a deep breath; it made him cough. He turned off the flame and meticulously poured two cups of the dark, almost purplish brew, carrying them back through the dimly lit hall to Kathleen's bedroom. He stood outside her door; it was closed. "Kathleen, would you like to come out now?" The water was so hot in the cups that the heat coming down through the china saucers began to burn his hands. "Kathleen, it's ready. The witch's magic tea." She still did not answer. He knocked softly, thinking she was asleep. Not a sound came from the other side of the door. He pushed it quietly open with his foot. He had never seen the inside of her bedroom before. A bright candle on top of a dresser reflected its faltering light against a high mirror, like a torch held at the mouth of a vast cave. He pushed the door further. Next to the dark dresser the flutter of a curtain moved silently from fingers of a soft breeze prodding from the open window behind. The lacy edge of the curtain barely touched the back of a chair, not disturbing the fluffy orange ball of a curled cat, its eyes two giant rubies in the candlelight, watching Fuss impassively from the chair.

"Oh, my God!" Fuss dropped the teacups, knocking the door all the way open. The cat jumped without a sound through the window. Kathleen was sprawled across the bed, one leg bent beneath the length of her dress, a hand draped from her forehead across her eyes as if she had fallen back in a dead faint. Fuss pushed her hand back. Her eyes were clamped closed, her face gone totally white, drained of all blood. "Kathleen! Talk to me! Wake up!" He slapped her face. "Kathleen!" He locked his hand around her wrist, feeling for a pulse, but only the wild beat of his own excited blood echoed at him. He put his arms around her, pulling her limp body roughly to him, attempting madly to squeeze life back into her, trying to will her back into the real world. He let her fall back on the bed. He knew what he had to do. He jumped up and ran down the hall, tripping over the fat chairs in the living room, throwing the door of the icebox open in the kitchen. He saw the hypodermic needle, its glass-vial plunger filled with clear liquid. He grabbed the syringe and ran back to the bedroom, slamming shut the window in case the cat tried to slip back in. He knelt over Kathleen, the syringe of adrenalin clutched in his hand like a knife. There was not the slightest sign of life on her lips. She looked dead.

For a moment he was completely stunned, gazing at her spread across the bed, her face whiter than the sheet beneath her. He ripped her dress open, pulling it down over one shoulder and grabbing the soft flesh above the elbow of her limp arm, sticking the needle into her. His thumb drove the plunger down, the adrenalin screaming in his own body as adrenalin in the vial leaped out of the needle into the throbbing bulge of blue vein. Kathleen's eyes opened, rolling backward, bulging with terror, her lips barely parting, wordless, breathless. Fuss jerked the needle out, throwing the empty syringe across the room. A sudden burst of blood oozed from the needle puncture in Kathleen's arm, spreading quickly, rolling down the sheet. Fuss bent the arm into itself, locked up like a folded bird's wing, stopping the bleeding. He slapped at Kathleen's face, trying to get her eyes to open again, trying to get her to breathe. He tried to think, tried to recall what he had read in a Civil Defense manual about what to do for a shocked bomb victim. He thought maybe the adrenalin wasn't in her, maybe he had made a mistake, maybe he would have to shoot her with another dose in the heart. Suddenly he saw the page of the Defense manual in his mind clear as day. He knew what to do. When someone can't breathe, when someone is dying, *massage* the heart, press on it, knead it, pound it, anything, get it pumping. He cupped his hand over the stiff white cloth of her brassiere, pressing down on the soft cone of her small breast, trying to get rhythm, trying to sense the life in her. He felt a slight beat coming up beneath the pressure of his hand. He leaned the full weight of his body against his hand over her heart, pressing up and down, again and again, feeling the beat coming stronger, then fading, then surging back, pounding, faster and faster. A cry escaped from her lips, drew them back in agony, followed by a rush of air, softening her mouth, almost as if she had gone beyond pain to pleasure. Her eyes were on him, no longer terrified, filled with a strange and powerful wonder, like a newborn child looking at its mother for the first time. It was a gaze devoid of all desire and envy, a plea of pure vulnerability.

Fuss's heart banged blood up to his temples, surging a strange heat of desire between his thighs, frightening and inexplicable, dazzling him with a sensation of dizziness, flooding him with such a momentary rush of passion for the simple flame of life he had just saved that he was left totally robbed of all reason. What he did next was quick and crazy, involuntary and extraordinary. He leaned over and kissed the bright red lipstick softness of Kathleen's lips like she was a helpless child. She coughed and gasped, sucking up his breath like a starved baby at a mother's breast, her tongue coming into his mouth, fleshy and insistent, not hard and desperate, but soft and searching. He found himself sucking back. Sucking frantically on her, his hand spreading over her entire breast, feeling the wild beating of her heart beneath the hardening of her nipple. Her tongue struggled from his mouth. She shook her head wildly, red curls flying up from the white sheet, scattering around her face like flaming snakes. Her heaving breasts had worked free of the brassiere, the tight nipples almost touching his lips. He ripped her dress down between her legs, exposing the whiteness of her thighs. She did not take her eyes from him. He felt totally trapped in their bright blue circles, like they were pulling him on top of her, compelling him to spread her legs, unbuckle his belt, probing with a gasp her openness. His gasping was like a drowning man, a man sucked into a current beyond his control.

29

WAR PRODUCTION BOARD PROHIBITS ZOOT
SUITS

The headline roared across the top of the morning paper.
It seemed to Fuss there were getting to be more stories about
Zoots every day, more than the war itself: sensational stories
about knife stickups, steel-chain, brass-knuckle, and tire-iron
fights between rival Zoot gangs, slugfests between Zoots and
sailors, sailors giving Zoots "white man's haircuts" to cheering
crowds. Maybe the stories took people's minds off the real terror
in their daily lives. He read the article quickly. It left no doubt
the prohibition was aimed at breaking up Zoot gangs in the
Barrio. But for the War Production Board to step in meant the

desperate situation of unemployment and uncontrolled violence in the Barrio was becoming a national issue. The board issued a decree making it illegal for any Zoot suit to be sold, claiming the suits were counterproductive to the war effort, since scientific study proved Zoot suits required fifty percent more material to make than a normal suit. The coat alone was thirty-six inches from collar to hem, using sixty-five dollars' worth of precious wool and cotton that could go into making badly needed uniforms. The mayor of Los Angeles applauded the prohibition and asked the City Council to make it a crime for anyone to wear a Zoot suit within city limits. The mayor insisted his actions involved no discrimination against any of Los Angeles' quarter million Mexican-Americans, as ninety percent were born north of the Mexican border and were full-fledged citizens. When Fuss finished the article he was convinced the logic of the War Production Board and the mayor was more complex than it first appeared. Stories were going around the Barrio that U.S. sailors were roaming the streets down south in San Diego, beating Zoots, even chasing them into stores and theaters. It was like a civil war. If it became illegal to wear a Zoot suit, then the sailors would have no one left to beat up, and the problem would end. But Fuss knew the problem wouldn't end, an article buried behind want-ads left no doubt to that:

LATINS WATCHING FOR YANKEE IMPERIALISM

The explosive implications of the article could not be hidden. Mexico lodged a protest over reports of brutalities against those of Mexican descent in Southern California. Mexico asked for an investigation of charges, made by America's War Manpower Commission, that discrimination and segregation against Latin people were responsible for the rise of the Zoots, idled and restless because they were not allowed work in the war industries.

Fuss let the paper drop from his hands. There was nothing in it but bad news. The Japs were counterattacking in the Pacific, Hitler had completed his iron wall around Western Europe, the Stars dropped a doubleheader to the San Diego Padres. It was all rotten, and the silence from Marvin didn't sweeten the pot. Outside, rain from a summer storm that had swept up from Mexico was beginning to come down in the fading dusk. Fuss picked up the telephone and dialed God; the line was busy. That must be the trick, he thought, gazing through a milky film building up on the inside of the window as rain bounced off the brittle green skirts of palms like ricocheting glass bullets. The trick was to advertise for people to call a certain number; the more they called, and the more there was no answer, the more curious they became. He called Kathleen. Her phone rang and rang as hard rain needled the windowpane, glass bullets rapping like distant machine-gun fire. Fuss hung the phone up and thought about the article. If America was at war for the equality and brotherhood of man, why were its Latin citizens treated with such disrespect? Why not give them jobs in war industries? What was the real reason? Fuss thought he knew. It had taken him a long time to fit the pieces into a clear picture. He knew the answer had nothing to do with segregation and discrimination. It was simpler than that, more basic. But he did not know how he could change it. Only the end of the war could change it, and by then it would be too late to explain. That's why what he did now was so important, why he risked his life. He was a good soldier, a good American.

The ringing of the phone startled him. Jumping up, he knocked the receiver off the hook. He heard a voice shouting at him from the other end of the line. He grabbed the receiver and pressed it to his ear.

"What's going on there?" Cruz's voice was strong and commanding in Fuss's ear.

"Nothing. Where are you? Why didn't you call earlier? I've been worried."

"I've been clean for two weeks. No hot Horse. Only cold turkey."

"Swell! Do you need help?"

"How come you weren't at Hollywoodland?"

"I was there! I swear I was there, Cruz!"

"Not at seven."

"I had trouble finding it."

"You know where it is now, mon, Hollywoodland?"

"Yes."

"Bueno, because you only have fifteen minutes to be there."

"I can't make it in fifteen minutes, impossible! Cruz, don't hang up! Cruz! It's raining. I have to find a cab!"

"Make it, Fussy!"

The empty streets were running rain. Water a foot deep raced down steep roads. Through slapping windshield wipers the shiny black pavement snaked endlessly into night, curling, twisting, and coiling higher and higher into the hills above Hollywood, making Fuss sick to his stomach in the backseat of the cab. When the road ended and he got out to walk, his legs felt shaky under him, his feet sliding in mud as he scrambled quickly along the steep trail leading to the giant sign. All he made out through dense rain was the incessant, rhythmic blur of the radio tower light on the ridge top. Mud sucked up into his shoes, caking around his socks as the trail softened, rising quickly toward the looming letters leaning awkwardly from the hillside:

HOLLYWOOD

The huge letters were bone white, rain washing them free of dust. The maze of iron and wooden struts supporting them from behind dripped with water like a forbidding rain forest.

"Cruz!"

Fuss's call disappeared into wet wind driving around him, dying beneath the rush of water carving irregular quick rivers in every direction on the mountainside, spouting sudden waterfalls, tumbling with a roar into the echoes of distant deep canyons. The metal of the gun tucked underneath his shirt was cold and clammy. Fuss slipped the gun out carefully; it was dripping wet. He didn't know if it could still fire.

"Cruz!"

Fuss leaned against the giant *H* of the sign for protection from raindrops growing colder and harder, turning to hail, beating on the high arms of the letter *H* above his head, hammering the wood loudly like bony knuckles beating into a face. The hail forced Fuss behind the *H* to protect his own face. Through the long line of the sign's support struts it was impossible to see farther than the letter *L*. There could be someone at the end of the sign, all the way down to the *D*.

"Cruz!"

The name tangled in the dripping struts, tore to pieces in the wild wind drumming the hail. Fuss wound his way cautiously through the protruding struts, holding a hand before him so one of the splintered boards or iron pipes couldn't bang him in the forehead. He had to reach the other end of the sign. Someone might be there and not be able to hear him. He stopped, trying to quiet his breath. Someone was calling in the wind, so thin and distant, like a lost child. His ears picked up the full sound; it was not human. The sound against the wind whistled through the chinks and cracks of the giant letters, the sound of a coyote, moaning and lamenting, an inconsolable spurned lover.

"Fuss?"

The word slid down the muddy incline of the steep hill-side above Fuss.

"Yes! Cruz! I'm down here!"

"Where? I can't see you."

"In back of the second *L!*"

The three gunshots came so fast for a split second Fuss thought they were part of the hammering hail; the bullets tearing and splintering through the thick wood of the letter above his head came, not from the sky but straight out of the barrel of a .38. Fuss slipped in the mud, sliding around to the downhill side of the *L.* He lay flat on the ground, directly in line with the letter. The only sound was wind and hail mixed with his frightened breath against the back of his cold hand clutching the gun. The rip of another gunshot stopped his breathing totally. He held his breath to hear how close the bullet would strike to him, or in him. No sound. The bullet must have completely missed the letter shielding him. He slithered silently, his chin scraping through mud until he was sprawled along the length of the *W* for protection. Then he heard it, the heavy sound of someone coming down the steep hill toward the sign, someone coming fast, trampling over wet brush, running, threatening to crash right into the sign. Fuss was afraid to expose his position, but he couldn't wait until he was at pointblank distance from Cruz. He knew he had to get up and shoot, he had to get up and fire. Fuss jumped up. On the other side of the sign the bulk of a shadow hurtled toward him. He lifted his gun and fired. The shadow kept coming, low to the ground. Fuss fired again and again into driving hail. The shadow kept coming; it couldn't be stopped. Fuss emptied his gun into the shadow, the gun hammer clicking futilely. He was defenseless. Out of the hail the shadow came into his vision, a body, rolling and tumbling. Fuss could tell, even in the dense rain, it was Cruz. He must have hit Cruz, shot him, killed him. The dead weight of Cruz's body couldn't be stopped, the momentum hurtling him at the sign, rolling him down through the crisscrossed support struts of the giant letters, bumping, banging, slamming him against Fuss and the wooden *W*, tearing the *W* away from its supports, ripping it from the line of letters on the mountainside.

"Cruz?" Fuss tried to stand, pushing the mud and hair caked over his face away from his eyes. "Cruz? Where are you?" Fuss focused his eyes. Above him the entire letter *W* was knocked out from the sign, the jackknifed hump of Cruz's body directly below a giant *O*. Fuss started toward the body. Maybe Cruz wasn't dead, maybe he was still alive, maybe the bullets only maimed him. Fuss struggled uphill against tearing sheets of hail, desperately trying to reach Cruz. Straight above him, through the empty space of the *W*, Fuss saw it, unexpected as a quick coal-bright glare from a dangerous animal's eye. The sudden flash of a gun being fired. Fuss dropped to the ground, squirming into mud for protection, clawing at the wet earth like a beached crab trying to sink from sight into sand. There had been *two* of them. The gun fired again, the smack of lead making the mud jump around Fuss's body. More gunshots whizzed over his head, but they weren't coming from the hole in the sign; they were coming from behind Fuss. There were even more than two men. Suddenly the gunfire stopped. The sound of hail beat tirelessly on the slick letters. Fuss turned his head slightly, toward the sucking sound of shoes coming clumsily from the deep mud as two men worked their way up the hill below him. He clutched his hands over the back of his head, as if he could stop the bullets he knew the men were going to pump into him. He waited, trembling.

"Oscar Fuss?"

Fuss turned his face slowly into the bright beam of a flashlight aimed down at him by the two men. "Yes. I'm, ah, I've heard of him. Who are you?"

"Are you Oscar Fuss?" One of the men clicked the hammer back on his gun, the barrel sticking into the flashlight beam. "Are you or aren't you Oscar Fuss?"

"Yah, sure." Fuss turned his eyes away from the bright beam. "I guess so."

"Goddamn!" The man with the cocked gun reached down and pulled Fuss up from the mud. "Christ Almighty, buddy, we thought we might have gunned the wrong guy! It was damn confusing in this rain to tell who was who! We couldn't tell if we were nailing the right guy, lead was flying so fast!"

"Who are you?"

The man flipped open his coat and shined the light on the bright metal of a badge. "FBI."

"Look." Fuss started across the slippery mud, toward the body beneath the big *O*. "We've got to get to the kid. We've got to see if Cruz is hurt!"

The FBI agents followed Fuss, shining the light on Cruz as Fuss rolled him over, brushing the mud out of the boy's face.

"He's dead, Fuss." The FBI agent with the flashlight flicked the beam off Cruz's motionless face and trained it through the hole in the sign above him, tracking the beam around on the dark slope. "Let's get up there and make sure the other one's in the same condition."

"I killed him." Fuss let Cruz's head sink back into mud. "He was coming straight at me and I shot him. He was only a kid."

"He was a spic, buddy." The agent with the gun pulled Fuss to his feet. "And that means he was probably a Fascist to boot."

"He wasn't a Fascist. He was a kid."

"Tell it to the Hitler Youth." The agent turned away and followed the trail up the slope his partner lighted with the flashlight.

Fuss stood alone, looking down at the dead boy in a stupor. The hail softened to a slow rain, the drops splattering noisily against the floppy coat and pants of Cruz's Zoot suit, washing mud from his handsome face, slicking back the black hair. For an odd moment he looked like a teenager shined up for his first date.

"Hey, buddy! You comin' up?" The agent with the gun shouted down through the empty space in the sign where the *W* had been. "I think you're going to be interested in this!"

Fuss struggled up the slippery hill, trying to steady his wobbling legs. The FBI agent held a flashlight to the face of a man snagged behind the sign in the struts, his body dangling like a wet noodle from the prongs of a fork.

"Recognize him?" The agent with the gun rested its metal barrel against the dead man's cheek, pushing the face into the center of the harsh flashlight beam.

"Yes, I recognize him."

"Friend of yours?"

The bright stab of light in the dead man's face hurt Fuss's eyes. He turned away. Over the giant letters clouds were suddenly torn away from the mountainside, exposing the crystal-clear lights of Hollywood far below. "He was a friend all right, a real close friend." Fuss started walking toward the beckoning light. "That's Chiquito Banana you've got there."

30

The Hollywood Stars were burning up. Angel had thrown so many rocket pitches it looked like his arm was going to fall off. The crowd was hysterical with the scent of blood. The stadium was a great open wooden mouth, roaring, whistling, screaming as each San Francisco Seal swung hard at Angel's pitches, striking out in a splutter of curses, spitting madly toward the high pitcher's mound. Angel's loose arm twitched with inspired life of its own. It wound and fired the ball like a bat out of hell going straight for the batter's throat, then unexpectedly screeching straight through the strike zone into the surprised catcher's mitt.

"There's no way they can stop Angel now." Kinney leaned forward on the edge of his seat, resting his arms on the iron-bar railing separating him and Fuss from the action on the playing field. "The Seals can't stand up to him. Angel's broken them. Only two more innings to go and the Stars will clinch the pennant."

"Why didn't you tell me the FBI had been trailing me?"

"Just relax and watch the game." Kinney's words came out of the side of his mouth as his body tensed, waiting for Angel's next strike to sail across the plate.

"Relax! Senator, I must know what is going on!"

"Keep your voice down, Fuss. We don't want anybody recognizing us."

"Keep my voice down! FBI has been secretly trailing me for months, and—"

"Just two months."

"My life has been threatened in the Barrio, and I've shot a teenage kid, and all you can say is relax and watch the ball game!"

"You didn't kill the kid."

Fuss spit his gum angrily over the railing with his words. "What? Don't play with me anymore, Senator! What do you mean by that?"

"Just what I said. It wasn't you that shot the kid."

"You don't mean to tell me the FBI shot him?"

"Don't be ridiculous. I talked to the morgue just a half-hour before leaving to come over here. Cruz was shot in the back. This Chiquito Banana guy kept Cruz alive just long enough to smoke you out, then he nailed him, put the gun right up against him and *pow.*"

"That's reliable information?"

"Gospel."

Fuss peeled the foil slowly off another stick of Juicy Fruit. "That still doesn't let me off the hook. It's the same thing as me having shot him. I was the one who made him go there."

"You didn't make him go there; he was a dead man already."

"What do you mean?"

Kinney reached inside his coat pocket and handed Fuss a round tin can with a key opener attached to the top.

"What's this? Looks like a . . ."

"Like a can of tuna, doesn't it? Open it."

Fuss slipped the key onto the tin tag of the lid and twisted it back, exposing a neatly packed plastic bag filled with fine brown powder.

"That's what it is, all right." Kinney spoke without looking at the contents of the can. Behind his dark glasses he followed another of Angel's perfect strikes across home plate. "Five ounces of pure Mexican brown. They found four cans of it in Chiquito Banana's pockets. You see, Cruz was a dead man all along."

"My God, Senator, how can you sit there? You know what this means? Wino Boy's tip on the Horse was right. Sea Biscuit was bringing the Horse in all the time. These are tuna cans; the Admiral's been canning heroin!"

"The FBI knows that, Fuss, just calm down. They raided the Admiral's place last night. Remember, we're all on the same team. I told you the FBI was on the job."

"How come there wasn't anything about it in the morning papers? Nothing about that, nothing about Chiquito Banana or Cruz."

"Fuss, this is still a national security issue. Do you think we want it printed that a retired admiral was smuggling heroin to support the Fascist cause in America? Do you think we want to tip our hand before we clear up the issue in the Barrio?"

"Where's the Admiral?"

"Under armed guard on a slow boat headed north for Alcatraz Island."

"And the yacht?"

"There was more than one—payoffs for heroin, cleaner than money. After the tuna fleet brought in enough catches of heroin a yacht was tucked away in a grain ship and sent to the Mexican official who was supplying the heroin. It was easy to get the heroin through. It's wartime, we need food. Coast Guard isn't about to inspect tuna boats the way they would in peacetime. In wartime you can get away with almost anything, *anything.*"

"How long have you known about this?"

"He struck him out, did you see that? Angel struck him out. That leaves only one more inning. One more inning to glory."

"How long have you known about this heroin thing? How it was channeled into the Barrio? How long have you and the FBI been using me as bait?"

"I haven't had the *whole* story till now." Kinney turned the hard glare of his sunglasses at Fuss, the green lenses reflecting Fuss's angry face. "The FBI knew the Admiral was funneling heroin into the Barrio, but once it got there they couldn't track down who controlled it. They found out it wasn't the Zoots early on. The Sinarquistas knew using heroin to gain power over the gangs would backfire on them; that's why they got rid of Chiquito Banana. Banana was nothing but a gangster, using the Sinarquistas and the Admiral to push heroin. But what made it tough was the Zoots would die before exposing him; their street code wouldn't allow it. That's how the FBI lost those two agents on the Barbara Carr deal."

"What do the Zoot-suit murders have to do with it?"

"Everything." Kinney leaned forward on the rail again. "That's it! The Stars are taking the field again. This is the last inning. Is that Angel a wonder? I tell you, he just gets word of another of his brothers dying and he walks out on the mound and murders the Seals."

"What do you mean, everything?"

"Carr was a junkie, Fuss. Didn't you figure it out? I thought you covered all the angles in the Barrio. Carr was there because since the war broke out the Barrio's the only place she's been able to get a ride on her favorite Horse, pure Mexican brown. The FBI set her up, posing as dealers, figured she'd tip them to the main man. FBI logic was if they trapped Carr in the Barrio she'd spill all to keep her public from knowing she was a Horse jockey. Strike three. Angel's got the first man down."

"So what happened?"

"Someone tipped Carr about the agents."

"But she came into the Barrio anyway? She walked into the trap?"

"Carr was hungry for Horse. She took a chance. When she realized there was no way out she ran, screaming she was being kidnapped."

"Then the Zoots shot the agents to protect Banana?"

"That's what the FBI thought at first, but now we know better." Kinney slapped his hand on the iron rail excitedly. "Strike one. Five more strikes and this game is history."

"Know what better?"

"The Zoots were set up. Whoever tipped Carr to the FBI agents was also the one who killed them."

"Who'd want to set the Zoots up?" Fuss couldn't help watching Angel intently, as if somehow the answer was out there on the pitcher's mound. "The Sinarquistas can't survive in the Barrio without the Zoots protecting them."

"Right, that's why someone wanted the Zoots destroyed, discredited with their people, talked about in the press as mad murderers. Destroy the Zoots and you destroy the last chance for the Sinarquistas to establish a political beachhead in America."

Fuss didn't even blink as Angel threw another perfect strike. "The FBI wouldn't kill two of its own men just to discredit the Zoots."

"No."

"Then who, Senator?"

"Who hates Fascists more than us?"

"The Communists." Fuss spoke the word as the third strike flashed before the baffled Seal at home plate.

"That's it, Fuss. Two Seals down, one Seal to go."

"How could Communists have shot the agents? The shots were fired from the gang of Zoots."

"Fired by a Communist undercover agent."

"But there wasn't anyone else with the Zoots except La Rue."

"And no fingerprints on the gun found lying on the ground. Remember, Fuss, that always bothered you?"

Fuss placed his hand over Kinney's and squeezed it against the iron rail. "You can't be serious?"

"We think she's a Fellow Traveler. We think the whole damn Mankind Incorporated thing is a stinking Commie front, rotten from top to bottom. FBI has tried to move in on the Voice, but he's dropped out of sight. The *DIALGOD* number they have is for passing coded messages back and forth between different Communist cells."

"So that's why, when I first started seeing La Rue, Cruz called me a Commie. The Zoots knew." Fuss dug his fingernails into the back of Kinney's hand. "You knew she was a Pinko all this time and let me play the game!"

Kinney pulled his hand from under Fuss's maniacal grip. "Get hold of yourself, man! She's a Fellow Traveler—did you hear me, Fuss? She's a Red. And the one in the best position of getting the truth is you."

"It's not safe for me in the Barrio anymore; that's one of the things I had to report. La Rue doesn't know who I am, but now with this Cruz thing last night . . ." Fuss felt a dryness in the back of his throat as he spoke Cruz's name, a hard dryness like a fist had punched his throat, making it painful for him to speak.

"What about the Cruz thing last night?"

Fuss continued, swallowing hard. "The Zoots are on to me; it's not safe."

"You're a soldier, Fuss. We all are. It's going to get more dangerous for you now, but the issue here is national security.

These are the biggest un-American activities of all we're talking about here. You've got to get all the truth from La Rue."

Fuss pressed against the iron rail so his words were close to the Senator's ear. "If she really is a Pinko, I have a way to find out. I hate to do it, but I will if I have to."

"It's not a question of whether or not the girl's Pink." Kinney's hot breath was on Fuss's cheek, his words like tiny knives jabbing into the skin. "I suppose it never occurred to you, when La Rue and the Voice were at the Shrine Auditorium, that they condemned every national leader from Roosevelt to Hitler, every leader except one: Joe Stalin. She's Red as the blood that would come out of Uncle Joe Stalin's veins if he slashed his wrists today."

Fuss looked at the Seal stepping to the plate. He felt as nervous as the ball player, his sweaty palms gripping the iron rail before him like it was a bat. The game was up. Fuss could no longer put off the confrontation with Kathleen. He knew that by doing his job, staying loyal to his country, he was going to kill the one bright moment of his life, the woman he had seduced himself into believing was above the mean corruption of mere mortals. An angel in a world gone to hell, who gave him the belief he could be born again in his love for her as a better man. Fuss heard his words come out clear and even, spoken from some deep source of strength in his gut. "She's a Red, Senator. I know how to handle Reds."

The Seal swung his bat furiously at empty air, the fans in the stands thundering their approval. Fuss leaned wearily back in his seat. All around him people were going crazy. Photographers charged onto the field like an invading army, popping the flashbulbs of their cameras off before them in a barrage of blinding light. Everyone was trying to get to Angel, slap him on the back, shake his hand. Fuss saw Angel running through the mob. But Angel was not headed for the dugout; he was coming straight at Fuss. The photographers tried to head Angel off with their flashing line of fire; it was impossible.

Angel stopped in front of Fuss's box seat, panting, sweat pouring from beneath the gold cap over his handsome face. Without a word, a wad of spit flew from Angel's mouth, a wild spray striking Fuss full in the face. The madness of the moment caught the mob off guard, and they started screaming in a frenzy as Angel tried to leap over the iron-bar railing, lunging for Fuss's throat. The hysterical cry of Angel's voice was drowned out by fanatical fans as they took him captive, lifting him to their shoulders in jubilant victory, racing back onto the field. Only Fuss heard the cry of Angel's words clearly.

"Thanks for getting my brother a job you bastard!"

31

You seem so nervous, Oscar. Would you like another Coke?"

"No, Kathleen." Fuss looked out the window, not mentioning the orange cat pawing around nervously on the fire-escape ramp behind her. The sunset caught the fluffy fur of the cat, dazzling the animal's presence until it looked more like a burning spirit than a harmless house pet. Fuss ran the back of his hand across his eyes, trying to block out the odd vision of the cat. "I'm just tired, I guess. The war, not hearing from Marvin in so long, the usual. I'm like you. I'm ready for a vacation up to the top of your Bright Angel Rim on the Grand Canyon. Far away from people; nothing but the desert far as the eye can see, nothing but the lazy Colorado River winding its way through the bottom of the endless canyon. Simple, all so simple."

Kathleen smoothed a hand back through her wild curls, as if she could tame them all into a nice soft halo of red around her head. "Is Marvin still being terrified by that awful man on board his ship?"

"The Shitter?"

"Yes." Kathleen's gaze fell to the floor in embarrassment. "Yes, he's the one I mean."

"I suppose so. It's a shame a boy has to fight a war and worry about a thing like that as well."

"It's a shame young boys have to fight any war." Kathleen's solemn face brightened. "But soon all this devastation will end. Mankind will triumph and we can get on with the work of rebuilding the planet, and the armies of the world will be dismantled and sent into fields to plant crops, not sow devastation and disgrace."

Fuss watched the cat tapping the window behind Kathleen's earnest face. "You really believe that?"

Kathleen slipped off the chair and knelt beside him, taking his hand in both of hers. "I believe that with all my heart."

"Maybe it will happen one day." Fuss was distracted by the cat's soundless scratching on the other side of the glass pane.

"It can happen, Oscar, and it *will.*" Kathleen lifted his hand to her face, her lips almost touching his fingertips as she spoke. "I promise you will live to witness that day of perfect brotherhood."

Fuss let his fingertips rest in the curved hollowness of her cheek. "And you Kathleen, will you live to see that day with me?"

"It makes no difference if one day you don't know me as I am now. Don't you see? I've explained to you so many times before." She pressed Fuss's hand desperately closer to her cheek. "We all have three bodies: physical, astral, and cosmic. I know I will soon die. But I am God-conscious. I must trust my ultrahigh vibrations to free me from this physical body. No one can exist on the spiritual plane and animal plane simultaneously. Don't you see? I must free myself from this wretched, hacking, wheezing body." She brought his fingertips to her lips so he could feel the excited breath of her words. "And you, dear Oscar, must cure your skeptical mind. Think only thoughts harmonizing with the greater universal law. Then you will be born again, and we . . . we can be together always, in mind as well as spirit."

"Jesus!" Fuss pulled his hand from Kathleen's lips and jumped up from the fat chair, stalking back and forth before the long bookcase. "Don't talk like that! It's so macabre. I want to be with you now, just like you are, sick body and all. I don't care about the rest of it. I don't care about meeting you out on some godforsaken astral plane. I don't want to rendezvous in a millennium on some distant planet. I want you, now. Just as you are."

Kathleen put her hand to her heart and sank against the arm of the chair, gasping for breath. "Oscar, how can you shout at me like this? What's wrong with you? You've never talked to me like this before. And I thought you had learned so much, cared so much for ultimate liberation from our temporal selves. That's what I have been talking about all these past months. I thought that's what we were progressing toward, what this has been all about—spiritual freedom."

"What it's really been about is *us,* Kathleen." Fuss knelt next to her, putting his arms around her thin body, cradling her against him. "I didn't want to scare you." He placed his cool hand gently across her hot forehead. "But all this stuff happening to us is crazy. It doesn't make any sense. We have to be honest with each other if we are both to survive this. I can't bear to think of you dying. I can't bear to think of losing you to some higher unseen vibration that will translevitate you away from me. It's just that I've only suddenly come to realize," He slowly reached above his head, slipping a heavy book from the bookcase and flinging it across the room so it crashed loudly against the wall next to the window, the frightened cat nearly leaping over backward, flashing up the fire escape. "I've come to realize I love you too much to lose you over any differences in our beliefs. If we can't believe in our feeling for each other, our love for each other, then what good is all the rest of it? What possible good? If we are more dedicated to our ideals than to the faith of our love for each other, then we are doomed." He watched the tears in Kathleen's eyes come swiftly, without hesitation, her cheeks glistening as she uttered her words in short, almost painful gasps.

"How much I know what you are truly saying. How much I have longed to say it myself but have been too afraid to even think it, to even speak it."

Fuss felt himself trembling, shaking like a frightened child on a department store Santa Claus's knee. It was odd, the closeness of Kathleen in his arms. Her physical vulnerability made him feel afraid, out of control. "Look, Kathleen." He pulled her to her feet. "We can't sit around feeling sorry for ourselves. We're young, vital. There's a war going on and thank God right now we're two people not out there in it. I have a swell idea." He gently pushed her back and wiped the streaks of tears away from her cheeks with his thumb. "Let's go have some fun. Let's forget everything and go to a movie."

"A movie? You want to go to a movie, now?" Kathleen looked at him suspiciously. "I'm so upset, and it's so—it's so late."

"There's a new Barbara Carr picture downtown at the Orpheum. It premiered at Grauman's Chinese in Hollywood just last month. It starts at eight tonight. We can catch the streetcar and be there in plenty of time." Fuss watched her face intently, trying to divine the flickering expression of surprise in her eyes, hanging on her words as if their consequence might promise some final truth.

"I don't know if I can do that. Not a Barbara Carr movie. I've been trying so hard to forget that awful night last summer and those horrible days of preliminary hearings afterward, all those questions, those poor frightened boys being held without bail for a murder trial. Every time I see Barbara Carr's face on a movie ad I just think of the whole ugly nightmare."

"That's just why you should go, to prove to yourself the nightmare is over. Everything is normal now." Fuss couldn't control the tone of his voice. His words came back to him in the room with too much urgency, too much insistence. He tried to soften their effect, but what he said still sounded like a challenge. "We *must* go. It's Barbara Carr's first picture since she was involved in the Zoot-suit murders; she's spent eight months making it. She's such a good actress. We can't blame Barbara Carr for what happened."

Kathleen said nothing. A strange light in her eyes made her seem distant even though she was close to him, so close Fuss felt the heat from her frail body. There was some other part of her far away, and from that place, slowly, her words finally came. "If you say we should, Oscar, I'll go. I'll go anywhere you say."

"How come there are so many sailors out tonight?" Kathleen watched the busy sidewalk outside the window of the packed streetcar. Everywhere in the bright lights of busy department stores there were sailors. Sailors by twos and threes, fives and eights, hundreds of sailors walking quickly in their dark blue uniforms, white caps cocked back on their shaved heads as they roved nervously in packs, alert, as if searching for some mysterious and illusive game, expecting some ultimate danger. Elbowing their way through the sailors, clubs swinging at the sides of their white pants legs, squads of Shore Patrolmen roamed easily, aloof but alert, sensing potential violence, riding herd on the thickening packs of sailors growing more numerous as the streetcar rolled along the widening streets, block by long block, farther into the deepening canyon of towering downtown buildings.

"It's Friday night, Kathleen, no more sailors than usual. They're all out hunting for girls. It's like this every weekend. You don't get out of the Barrio enough. Usually you're spending all your off moments going from door to door preaching."

"Well, what's wrong with that?" Kathleen turned quickly from her reflection in the window, her body stiffening next to him.

"Nothing." Fuss laughed, tightening his arm around her shoulders. "Nothing in the world wrong with it. But you must have some fun, relax. We can't be so serious all the time."

Kathleen turned and looked back out the broad window. "Just so *many* sailors. It doesn't seem right, so many like this."

"Maybe the fleet's in." Fuss leaned across her to get a better view of the crowding sailors clogging sidewalks. "Maybe they're all looking for a girl pretty as you." He kissed Kathleen unexpectedly on the cheek and laughed. "A pretty redhead with lots of curls and great legs."

"Oscar!" Kathleen jabbed him in the ribs with her long fingernails. "Be quiet." She looked around the streetcar self-consciously. "People may be listening. That's not the kind of thing to joke about in public."

"Here we are." Fuss yanked the buzzer cord to stop the streetcar. "The Orpheum Theater, where we get off."

The gold-red-and-blue neon of the theater sign fell from three stories high in a sparkling waterfall over heads of people lined at the ticket booth. The giant painted face of Barbara Carr loomed behind sheets of glass over display windows. She swooned in the arms of a dark romantic man with his shirt torn open, her glazed-over eyes fixed in a stupor on the man's bare chest, the wild blond cascade of her hair flung in a careless tangle of knots behind her.

"Hey, this really looks swell! These are the kinds of pictures Barbara Carr is best in, jungle pictures." Fuss studied the slack expression on Carr's face behind the smudged glass. "Aren't you glad we came, Kathleen?"

"I'm glad." She took Fuss's arm as the line moved slowly toward the ticket booth and into the gold-pillared lobby. The slightly mildewed and smoky odor of hot popcorn wafted to far recesses of the balcony's ceiling, its false baroque angels flittering about in brash coats of bronze paint.

Fuss fumbled along the dark aisles inside the crowded theater, finally finding two vacant seats. Before him the United States Army was marching triumphantly across the movie screen through the bombed and shattered city of Naples, the announcer of the newsreel shouting excitedly:

> *The men of General Mark Clark's Fifth Army have scored their greatest victory of the twenty-two-day Italian campaign! Tough American troops and hard-fighting British Tommies who just five days ago fought and won the ferocious battle of Salerno have quickly smashed through to capture Naples! These men have defeated the best of the German war machine can offer! Today a jubilant communiqué from General Eisenhower's headquarters in England announced . . .*

"Down in front!"

"Get down! Down in front!"

"I can't see what's going on. Who's doing the shouting?" Kathleen rose in her seat, trying to see over the sea of heads before her stretching to the foot of the movie screen. "Can you see what is going on up there, Oscar?"

"No, I can't see either."

"Get down! Hey, what's going on?"

"Somebody call the police!"

Kathleen grabbed Fuss's arm. "Let's go. Something terrible is happening up there."

From the back of the theater the swinging doors on all six aisles banged open, men running down the aisles with flashlights, stabbing bright beams out into the audience. Beams of blinding light shot into Fuss's face. He jumped up with his arm around Kathleen. People were pushing and shoving, screaming to get out, trapping themselves in their own panic.

"Oh, my God!"

"Stop them! *Stop them!*"

The newsreel died on the screen, pitching the entire theater into darkness. The shadows of the men with the flashlights leaped into the audience.

"My God! They're killing people! They're killing people!"

The men with the flashlights waded into the screaming audience, knocking people down, grabbing others.

Fuss pushed Kathleen into her seat as he tried to shove back the hysterical people stampeding in all directions around him.

"They're going to kill us all! We're all going to die!"

Brilliant showers of light shattered the vast darkness from tiered chandeliers that dangled from the high ceiling of the theater, exposing the panicked crowd, exposing the men with flashlights. Fuss was shocked. The men with flashlights were sailors. More sailors kept pouring through the swinging doors, searching out anyone dressed in a Zoot suit. Three aisles before Fuss two teenage Zoot-suiters crouched down, trying to hide from six sailors pushing their way to them through the terrified crowd.

"No nos matan! No nos molestan! Don't let them get us! Don't let them kill us!" The two Zoots screamed, caught in the trap of the crushing crowd. The sailors surrounded the Zoots, knocking their slouched hats off, grabbing them by their long black hair, dragging them kicking and shouting up to the stage in front of the blank movie screen, where more sailors stood with their young captives, tearing off their Zoot suits, ripping off their underclothes. Sharp metal of scissors flashed in the sailors' hands as they cut the hair from struggling Zoot boys crying out in Spanish for mercy, pleading not to be murdered. Everywhere in the audience sailors found more Zoot-suiters, beating them to the ground, quickly stripping them naked and shearing their hair off, shaming them before the eyes of the horrified crowd.

Fuss pushed and knocked his way from the theater, pulling Kathleen along with him, people smashing against her frail body from all sides in their panic to escape. The streets were filled with screams of running people and the wail of police sirens. Sailors chased Zoots into stores. Two streetcars were barricaded in the center of the street, sailors shouting and pulling people from them, trying to get to Zoots cowering under the backseats. With a terrifying scream and crash of glass, a Zoot jumped from the display window of a drugstore on the corner, three sailors jumping through right behind him. The Zoot saw two Shore Patrolmen watching from the opposite side of the street. He ran to them, shouting for protection. When he got to them the clubs at their sides came up quickly, cracking into his head. He fell stunned and bloody to the ground as the three sailors came up behind him kicking. Kathleen fell to her knees on the sidewalk, a stream of vomit pouring from her mouth. Fuss put his arm around her for support, half pulling, half dragging her gasping body through the terror of the street, around the corner onto the next block. He pushed Kathleen against a storefront and stood before her, trying to hide her. He wished he had stayed on the other street. In the chaos of the screaming crowd before them, sailors were hurting and clubbing not only Zoots but anyone who looked Mexican. A struggling pregnant woman slipped from the grasp of a sailor, darting through the crowd as he lunged at her flying coat. She shouted at Fuss, her terrified eyes screaming for mercy. She reached toward him just as the sailor caught hold of her coat, whipping her around and knocking her across the face before his knee knifed into her stomach. The woman fell with a gasp, her dead weight crumpling on the hard pavement. Kathleen pulled at Fuss's coat, trying to hold him back, screaming at him it was too dangerous to get involved. Fuss shook Kathleen loose, lunging at the young sailor, grabbing him around the neck and choking him. The sailor's hollow breath came out of his mouth in a hoarse whistle as he turned his darkening face toward Fuss. Fuss's hands went limp, losing all their strength, releasing the fury of his grasp. The young sailor looked just like his brother.

32

Please stay with me tonight." Kathleen stood in the open doorway of her apartment, her whole body shaking and shivering. She took Fuss's hand and pulled him into the dark hallway. "I'm afraid, Oscar. Please stay with me tonight. I'm so frightened some of those sailors might break into my apartment in the middle of the night."

Fuss flicked on the light switch and pressed Kathleen's quivering hand firmly between his own. "They won't come here. They're all downtown. All that is far away."

She cocked an ear to the wail of sirens in the distance, her eyes wide with fear. "You must stay." She led him down the hall. "Promise to stay with me all night or I'll have nightmares. I'll never be able to sleep."

Fuss wearily eyed the fat chair in the living room. "All

right." He slumped heavily into the chair. "I'll spend the night; this is as good a place as any."

"No." Kathleen reached her shaking hands down and pulled him back up. "I'm so terrified, I want you to sleep with me."

"With you?" Fuss couldn't keep the smile of surprise from his face. "Kathleen, are you certain that's what you want? I mean, I can stay out here. Anyone breaking into the house has to pass right by me to get to you."

"I know what I want, Oscar." She dropped his hand. There was a solid tone in her voice he did not question. "Now you don't stay out here too long because I want you with *me.*" She turned and disappeared into the bedroom, leaving him standing alone.

Fuss went into the kitchen and flipped the light on. He sat at the table, rubbing his eyes, trying to erase the screams of the night from his mind, thinking if maybe what he had seen downtown was a dream, a crazy, bizarre dream. He just couldn't believe it happened. He still felt the sickness in his stomach, as if he was the one who had been kicked and beaten. He just couldn't believe he would ever witness such a thing in America. It disgusted him. But he knew the reason for it, he understood fully, and he knew it would get worse.

A sharp rapping wove its way through Fuss's thoughts, like an ice pick scraping on an ice block. The strange sound brought him back to where he was, reminded him of how late it was. He looked up from the table, his gaze going around the kitchen, trying to locate the sound. Then he saw it. Outside the window on the fire escape the cat was framed against the distant glare of a street lamp. Reared up on its hind legs, its front paws clawing at the clear glass pane, the animal's wide liquid eyes peered straight at Fuss. He knew what he had to do. There was no way he could put it off any longer. The time had come, and the sickness deep in the pit of his stomach spread quickly through his body as he rose from the table.

"Oscar?" Kathleen called his name, watching the dark shadow of reflection in the high mirror of the bedroom dresser. Her shaking hand clutching a hairbrush swept swiftly through her hair, spreading red curls over sleek satin shoulders of her white robe. "Oscar, is that you?" She peered closely at the reflection moving in the mirror. "You're so quiet." She set the brush on the dresser and turned slowly around. "Oscar, I'm so glad you decided to—" The words went numb on her bright red lips. She quickly put out her hand on the dresser to stop herself from collapsing. "Sweet Lord, Oscar, what on earth are you do—"

Fuss watched her from the doorway, the purring cat securely tucked under one arm, the needled syringe of adrenalin held firmly between his fingers. "Don't move." He pointed the needle at Kathleen. "Sit down in that chair, next to the dresser." He walked toward her, dropping the cat on the bed's soft quilt cover. The cat watched him as he placed the needle carefully on the dresser, looking down at Kathleen. "Move and I'll kill you." The muscles of her throat constricted with fear, hardening into protruding lines along her slender neck as she turned away from the cat. He stood before her and slipped off his belt. He knelt down, tying her hands quickly to the back of the chair. She didn't move, her heavy breathing close to his ear. He placed his hands on the sleek shoulders of her satin robe, then shoved the robe back over her thin shoulders, pinning her arms close to her body so she couldn't suddenly free herself. He picked up the syringe and stepped back from her, sitting down on the bed next to the cat, his hand going over the animal's arched back in quick familiar strokes.

"Talk."

□ 215

"Talk?" Kathleen swallowed hard. "Talk about what?" She looked at the purring cat. "Have you lost your senses?"

"I want to know the real name of the Voice. I want to know where he is. *You* are going to tell me."

"I don't know his real name, I swear to you, Oscar. Darling, I swear to you I don't know where he is."

Fuss ran his fingers through the thick orange fur of the cat. "It's over, the whole stinking charade is over. You're a Communist. I know it, the FBI knows it. Now where is he? Where is the leader of your cell?"

Kathleen's eyes widened in fright as she watched the cat. She tried to push herself farther away from the animal's strong scent, but the chair was already backed against the wall. Tears came up in her eyes, rolling down her face, splashing on her bare breasts. "Oh, my dear God, Oscar, you are making a terrible mistake."

"How long is it, before this cat is going to give you an attack? Two minutes? Three? Half a minute?"

"I beg of you." Kathleen's slender fingers stretched and scraped frantically at the belt binding her to the chair. "Let me free before it's too late. I know absolutely nothing."

"Are you a Communist?"

"No!"

"I know the truth. The FBI knows your whole phony setup from top to bottom."

"I swear to you! This is absurd!" Kathleen's nostrils flared, her eyes bulging at the cat, her breasts heaving as her stomach pressed violently in and out as she gasped for breath. "I'm innocent! Oh, Lord, don't do this to me!"

Fuss's hand fastened on the back of the purring cat's neck. He wanted to squeeze it, kill it. "Tell me where the Voice is!"

Kathleen's lips pulled away from her gums as she threw her head back, gulping for air like a drowning person. She suddenly doubled forward, trying to break the hold the belt had on her, her small breasts swinging free of the robe, the nipples hard as brown stones. She flung her head back up, eyes terrified, trying to speak, the air barking from her lungs, the high pitch of her wheezing stabbing into Fuss's ears like the ice pick of the cat scratching on glass. "Osc—I can—n't! I'm—not!"

Fuss jerked the cat up by its neck, squeezing it with all his strength, hating it, hating himself as the cat clawed at his arms. He held the creature menacingly before Kathleen, rubbing its struggling body slowly across her breasts up to her chin, pressing the hairy belly to her nose and mouth as she tried desperately to avoid the smothering fur, shaking her head frantically back and forth, the painful wheezing bellowing from her lungs. She looked at Fuss, pleading, the whites of her eyes suddenly turning up into her head as she slumped forward, toppling the chair over. She lay on the floor perfectly still.

Fuss hurled the cat disgustedly against the wall. "Tell me! Tell me and I'll give you the shot!"

Her eyes were closed. She did not move. Her mouth was open but there was no breathing. Fuss knelt next to her and pushed back the skin covering her eyes. All he could see was white. "Kathleen!" He slapped her face, his hand striking hard again and again beneath the hollow bones of her cheeks. "Speak to me!" She did not move. He grabbed the syringe and plunged the needle into her arm. "For Christ's sake, say something!" He pulled the needle from her arm. The quick sight of blood bubbling up from the puncture in her pale skin brought a rush of blurring tears to his eyes. "You must forgive me! I know the truth. You're not a Communist! You've been duped. Forgive me, oh, God, forgive me! I had to do it!" He cradled her in his arms, the tears blinding his eyes. He couldn't see anymore. "I had to do it! I'm an undercover agent! I work for the government. It's all been a lie! I'm not even a Catholic! Oh, please talk to me!" He pressed her entire body hard against his own, his loud sobbing filling the room as he rocked her back and forth, screaming, "I'm not even a goddamn Catholic!"

33

The Santa Ana came in unseasonably from the
desert, its hot dry wind blowing through the empty streets of
the Barrio. Fuss quickly walked down the deserted sidewalks,
the brim of his hat tipped forward to hide his face. Saturday
morning was strangely quiet. No one was out. The wind rushed
along the sidewalk before Fuss as he hurried toward the
church, clattering the short skirts of palm fronds above his
head. Fuss didn't glance at the hills of early morning newspapers stacked on the corners. He had already memorized the
bold headlines jumping in black ink from the front pages:

*POLICE ROUND UP 300 MEX-AMS IN AFTERMATH OF ZOOT
WAR!*

□ 218

NATIONS 5TH LARGEST CITY PARALYZED BY
ZOOT-SUIT RIOTS!

SERVICEMEN BY TRUCKLOAD TAKE OVER DOWNTOWN
LOS ANGELES!

PACHUCO HUNT! BARS, THEATERS, CAFES, CLUBS
INVADED!

POLICE CHIEF SAYS ZOOT CLEANUP BY SAILORS
NOT RACIAL ISSUE!

LA DECLARED OUT OF BOUNDS TO ALL NAVAL
PERSONNEL!

ZOOT GANG LEADERS VOW TO FIGHT BACK!!!

Sun struck down bright and clear through the arched bell tower of the old church across from the fading green of Olivera Park, its strong light exposing fresh slashes of red paint on the old adobe walls:

VIVA SINARQUISTAS! VIVA LA RAZA! VIVA LA CAUSA!

Fuss walked quickly up the church steps, pushing through thick doors into fragments of colored light streaking from high stained-glass windows. The sweet scent of incense hung in the air over veiled gray heads of old ladies dressed in black scattered about the pews, their wrinkled lips whispering intimately, expectant eyes dimly gazing heavenward as if expecting to be united with a long-lost lover.

"You're early."

"I have much to confess, padre." Fuss knelt before the priest lighting a bank of candles before the Virgin of Guadalupe, flames from the candles almost reaching beyond the confines of their red glass chimneys to touch the Virgin's flowing green robe.

□ 219

"It's been a long time since you have confessed, my son."
The priest glanced over the shoulder of his black cassock at
Fuss, flickering flames erasing the deep lines crisscrossing his
face, giving his skin the same unearthly glow as the smooth
plaster face of the Virgin he tended.

"It's been a long time since I have had anything to confess." Fuss looked anxiously behind the priest, along the aisle
leading to the side altar. Next to the small, regally robed statue
of a smiling Infant of Prague, the light above the confessional
door was off; no one was inside.

The priest knelt next to Fuss, his knees cracking, a candle
held before him as he gazed upon the Virgin. "You have heard
of the wars in our own streets?"

"Yes, I've heard." Fuss shifted his weight uneasily.

"It is terrible this thing. I was once, as a young novitiate
in Oaxaca, a medical volunteer for Villa's revolutionary army.
I have seen this horror before. When soldiers are attacked by
citizens in their own towns, it means only one thing: the enemy
is within. Some of these children in the Barrio are doing the
work of the enemy. The Fascists tell them not to fight for their
country, and they do not. These Zoot suits are part of a fifth
column and must be stopped."

"You can't believe that, padre. You know the truth. You
know better."

"I believe that." The priest lifted his eyes higher to the
Virgin's serene face. "And the Church believes that."

"That's not how it is! Damn it, you of all people should
know it isn't true!"

"Do not speak profanely in our Lord's house." The priest
held a finger to his lips and smiled over his shoulder at the old
ladies who stopped their whispering prayers, rosary beads
swinging silently in clasped hands as they glared at Fuss. The
priest turned back to Fuss, speaking low under his breath as if
he were addressing a demon. "Why do you think I have allowed
you these meetings in a house of God? To fight Fascists and

Communists. To fight the anti-Christ." He nodded toward a sudden blinking light above the confessional. "It is time."

Fuss mumbled angrily, piercing his tongue with his teeth, trying to remain silent as he stood to go.

"My son," the priest called softly, "ask God for His forgiveness. You have many sins to confess."

Inside the dark confessional Fuss closed the door securely behind him and knelt down. The bare shadow of a face was on the other side of the sliding screen. "Listen Senator, I know damn well what the game is now. There's no way the government wasn't behind last night's attack on the Zoots, on innocent women and children. That attack was as well planned as the Japs' strike on Pearl Harbor. The police and Shore Patrolmen stood by the whole time and watched, the only ones being arrested were the very people who were being beaten. I know there's a war on. I know there are some Fascists in the Barrio, but there's everything in the Barrio. You can't condemn a single person there; you can't go on persecuting them, denying them their right to jobs in the war industries just because you think one or two are saboteurs, spies, or part of some mythical fifth column. Most of those people are good Americans, not what the newspapers make them out to be. Most of those people are fighting this war every bit as much as you are." Fuss stopped talking. He realized the anger of his words was almost making him shout. He waited for Kinney to say something, but there was only silence. He continued, trying to control the frustration in his voice. "Something's got to be done; this madness has to be stopped. It's not like the problem with the American Japs. There weren't many of them. You could just truck all the Japs off to prison camps, but you can't keep a quarter of a million people living in terror in the Barrio, make all of east Los Angeles a concentration camp. You can't set the Navy, Army, and Marines on good Americans like a pack of rabid dogs. I know it's confusing with the Zoots, but my job was to learn about them, and what I learned is everybody's been using them—the Fascists, the Communists, even us. It's got to stop, because when this war ends those people in the Barrio are going to go on hating us, never understanding the truth. Those people have rights just like every other American, and if we destroy those rights what the hell is the whole goddamn war for anyway?"

A lightbulb flicked on over the shadow behind the screen. The screen rolled back, a black revolver held right at the level of Fuss's eyes, the tip of the barrel almost touching his forehead. "Shut your mouth." Fuss recognized the man with the gun; it was the FBI agent who shot Chiquito Banana. The agent flicked the light back off, the cold metal of the barrel touching the skin of Fuss's forehead. "Keep your mouth shut, get up slowly, walk out of the church. I'll be right behind. Walk across the street to the bandstand in the park. I want you to do that very carefully, or you'll be damn sorry you didn't use your last moments here today to make a real confession."

Fuss walked out into bright sunlight. He did not turn to look behind; he knew the agent was following. He recognized immediately the other agent in the battered brown hat waiting for him next to the wood lattice circle of the bandstand; it was the other agent who had been on the mountain the night Cruz was shot. Beneath the broad brim of his hat the other agent was smiling as Fuss approached, but when Fuss reached the bandstand the agent's smile dropped off like a paper mask.

"Where is the Voice, Mr. Fuss?"

"I don't know."

The agent put his hand to his chest, but it wasn't his heart he was feeling. It was the bulge of a gun in a shoulder holster beneath his overcoat. "You were requested several days ago to bring in that information. You were informed the matter was urgent."

"I tried everything I could. Every lead. The girl was a deadend street."

"The girl is a Communist, Mr. Fuss."

"You're crazy. She's not." Fuss looked over his shoulder. The other agent leaned against the fat trunk of a date palm, fingering a gun beneath his coat. "Look." Fuss turned around. "The girl is innocent. She knows nothing. She's a physically sick person who has been duped."

"She is a dangerous Red, Mr. Fuss. We know now she killed our two men in the Barrio. The Zoots are innocent."

"She couldn't kill anyone, I'm telling you! I almost killed *her* to make her talk. If she was a Communist she would have said so to save her life. She wouldn't die like that, suffering that way. She's just a sick, poor, pathetic dupe."

"She's a Red. We don't want to scare her off. We need her information. We need her alive. We want you to bring her in. All of these people involved with the Voice are threatening national security."

"I won't do it. She's innocent, she's not a killer." Fuss turned to walk away, but the agent in the shade of the date palm blocked his way. Fuss knocked him in the chest and shouted, "I don't care what you do anymore! Go get yourself another boy! Tell Kinney that too. I quit. Finito. I'm going down to the Army recruiting office and upping to fight a real war, not this stinking game you're playing!"

"Wait a second." The agent reached inside his coat pocket and pulled out a telegram.

"What's this?" Something made Fuss grab the telegram. He unfolded it; it was from the office of the President of the United States.

"Your brother is a dead war hero."

Fuss read the telegram in his shaking hand as the agent continued to talk.

"They say the big carrier took one of those kamikaze hits. Once the ammunition hold started to blow that was all she wrote, a regular inferno. Everyone on board is listed as missing in action, but there's no way anyone could have survived. Eye-witnesses on other ships in the fleet say when she went down the melting steel hull was hissing like a steam kettle."

Fuss dropped the telegram; he didn't hear the last of the agent's words. He looked back past the bandstand in the cool green of the park, a cold sweat breaking out on the hot flush of his face. He felt himself falling and grabbed hold of the agent and bent over.

"Hey, buddy, you're not going to puke, are you?" The agent held Fuss's coat to keep him from falling. "What the hell, go ahead and puke if you want to." He slapped Fuss on the back. "You earned it."

Fuss forced himself to stand straight. He watched as the wind flipped up the thin yellow telegram, twisting it into a crazy flight high through the air, out across the browning park grass. He did not go after the telegram. His anguished face stared up at the agent. "The girl is innocent, I'm telling you, *innocent*. But some way or another, I'll get the Voice for you."

"Not some way or another, Mr. Fuss. Do it." The agent's words were flat and simple.

Fuss turned back to the telegram. It was way out over the lawn, beneath the feet of small running boys cheering a snaking kite into the powerful wind that blew in from the desert. It was hard for Fuss to see the boys through his tears. "I'll get him."

34

The phone was ringing in his apartment as Fuss jammed the key into the lock of the door, twisting it frantically, pushing the door open and grabbing the ringing phone off the hook.

"Hello!"

"Oscar?" Kathleen's voice came across to him distant and weak, as if she were calling down to him from some very high place.

"Where are you? Kathleen, are you all right?"

"Fine. I have a monstrous headache, but that's not important."

"Where are you calling from?"

"Home. I'm safe at home. But someone has been calling

for you here all morning. Someone named Ignacio Gasset. Do you know him?"

"Wino Boy."

"Well, he sounded very drunk. He said he had to talk to you. He has information. He said it was a life-or-death matter and you must go to him."

"Where?"

"He said it wouldn't be safe for you, to be very careful."

"Where?"

"In the Barrio. On Flores Street in a boardinghouse above Butch Mendoza's poolhall. Do you know the place? It sounds like a flophouse."

"I know the place."

"Oscar?"

"I've got to go."

"Please be careful. If something happens to you, I'll never forgive myself for giving you this man's message."

"You did the right thing, Kathleen. And I'm always careful." Fuss hung up the phone, pulled his suitcase from beneath the bed, snapped it open, and took out the gun, tucking it under his belt as he ran from the room. He didn't stop outside to get a cab; he kept running, sprinting up long blocks and across to deserted Flores Street. All the stores were closed; there were no people to be seen anywhere. Even Mendoza's poolhall was closed, the shades pulled down over the green windows. Fuss tried the door next to the poolhall. It swung open before him. A sleepy-looking woman with huge looped plastic earrings dangling from her ears sat behind a battered counter.

"Ignacio Gasset! Does he live here? What room is he in?"

The woman quietly set her movie magazine on the countertop and smiled shyly at Fuss. "Yo no se."

"El viejo. El borracho."

"Ahh, si. Señor Ignacio." She pointed up the staircase behind her. "Numero cinquenta tres."

Fuss ran up the stairs, checking the numbers on the doors

down the length of a narrow hallway. He found the number. He slipped the gun from beneath his belt and pulled back the hammer, then placed his hand carefully on the doorknob, pushing the door back slowly until he saw the trail of blood glistening across the floor. He shoved the door all the way open. "Wino Boy?"

Wino Boy's eyes stared straight up and dead at Fuss from the floor alongside the bed, a broken wine bottle next to him, its jagged glass covered with blood. Wino Boy had not brutally slashed his own throat from ear to ear with the jagged bottle. The word scrawled clumsily across the wall in Wino Boy's blood gave testimony to that:

DIALGOD.

Fuss ran back down the stairs, shouting at the woman, "El teléfono! El teléfono!"

The woman reached beneath the counter and brought out a telephone. Fuss grabbed it from her and dialed frantically. He dialed God. The line was not busy; it clicked in Fuss's ear. Fuss heard steady breathing, then a voice familiar and unmistakable, the words measured and lilting, sweet and pure as if pouring from the heavens themselves.

"Is that you?" Fuss shouted into the phone. "Answer me! Is that *you?*"

The words of the Voice were so intimate, so close, his very breath was in Fuss's ear. "We are waiting for you, Mr. Fuss. Don't be too long in coming."

"Where are you? I'll come right over. I'll be right there!"

"We cannot wait forever, Mr. Fuss."

"Tell me!"

"At Miss La Rue's."

Fuss threw the receiver down and ran out the door. As the taxi he flagged down sped through empty streets, he knew why the Voice had tricked him into going to Wino Boy's. The reason had to be Kathleen. Fuss knew she was in love with him and the Voice just discovered it. She could no longer be trusted; she was too dangerous. The Voice had to have time to kill Kathleen, and then kill him. Fuss jumped from the cab as it screeched to a stop outside Kathleen's apartment. He couldn't think of anything but getting to Kathleen before the Voice did. He had to save her.

The orange cat darted down the stairs past Fuss, meowing loudly like an obsessed spirit. Fuss ran to the top of the steps, the gun out and ready to fire. Kathleen's door was open. He saw her down the narrow hallway, content and serene, calmly sitting in one of the fat chairs, a small blue Mankind Incorporated book open on her lap. Fuss walked down the hall, carefully, expecting at any moment that someone would jump out at him. He stepped into the living room. In the other fat chair he saw the Voice.

The Voice smiled up at Fuss, his words gliding, as if borne on a silver platter. "Ah, dear Mr. Fuss. We were beginning to lose hope. We thought your journey would never end."

Fuss was astonished, standing so close to the Voice; the man was far older than the vigor of his voice implied, old enough to be Kathleen's father. The wrinkles of his face were smoothed over evenly by a deep tan. Stamped across his lips was the indulgent expression of one patiently awaiting the world to serve his superior motivations.

Fuss aimed the gun above the slender bridge of the Voice's nose, between the gaze of his piercing eyes.

"That's not the appropriate action to take, Mr. Fuss. A very un-American activity, shooting an unarmed man, a defenseless man."

"A man who just killed Ignacio Gasset."

"Comrade." The Voice's benign gaze did not leave Fuss for a moment as he spoke to Kathleen. "I want you to shoot Mr. Fuss."

Fuss was afraid to take the gun off the Voice. He turned

his head slightly toward Kathleen. He saw her lift the book off her lap, a gun held steadily in her hand as she raised it before her, pointing it straight at Fuss.

"Comrade, I want you to send a telegram to our American patriot who thinks he's going to win this war."

Fuss felt the sweat in his hand around the gun. Outside in the distance a siren wailed. He couldn't distinguish if it was an air-raid siren or a police siren.

The gun wavered in Kathleen's hand, as if she had it pointed at the wrong person. She brought her other hand up to support it, then shifted the direction of the barrel slightly so it was trained on the Voice.

"Do your duty, comrade. Shoot him *now.*"

Fuss pulled the trigger, the explosion kicking his hand back, the force of the bullet ripping open the Voice's forehead in a shattering sound of bone and metal. The gun was heavy in Fuss's hand, an awesome weight with a fearful gravity of its own, as he turned it on Kathleen. Outside the wail of the siren grew louder.

Around the red rims of Kathleen's eyes a watery film glistened, like heavy moisture on a windowpane, threatening to break and streak down sheer glass. She held her gun in trembling hands, pointed straight at him. "Don't make me shoot you, Oscar. Don't make me choose again. Leave!"

Fuss took a hesitant step toward her. "I'm sick of the ideologies. What good are they if they destroy people? Both sides have made us killers. Now we're going to kill each other. We can't let them kill us, Kathleen." He started to kneel down before her and she fired into his heart.

Kathleen was above him. Way above him. He couldn't reach her. The sun was behind her red hair. A brilliant desert sun. She was like a bright angel on the rim of a canyon. So far away. She kept calling and calling, but he was so deep in the canyon with the river running cold next to him he couldn't hear her. He felt like his heart was broken in two. The hurt boiled up and out of his chest and stung his throat. He thought he heard her words, her white face against the hot breath of the snarling sun, a bright angel, her words coming cool as she leaned over the edge of the canyon in the hazy distance, a tear falling from her eye, a bright diamond spinning brilliantly down, trapping all light from the kindly heavens before going black. He felt the cool breath on his face, lips on his lips, robbing the last breath going out of him. He felt as if he was being born again.

THOMAS BERGER
Neighbors

Earl Keese, a middle-aged gentleman with a tendency towards a thickening midriff, lives quietly with his wife in their home at the end of a country lane.

And then a young couple move into the vacant house next door . . .

Within hours the Keese's world is turned upside down and what starts as merely a nightmare develops into a lunatic confrontation between Earl and his neighbors, Harry and Ramona. As the horrible hours move on, Earl finds his benevolent, peaceful life has turned hostile, unpredictable and dangerous.

'It could happen to anybody,' says Ramona . . .

'Berger is insanely plausible. He writes like the demented son of Lewis Carroll or Edward Lear. He has stirred up the most engaging crock of lunatics in many a moon'

New York Magazine

ANN REDMON
Emily Stone

Emaciated Sasha Courtnay lies dying from an unknown disease. But her life-long and supportive
friend, Emily Stone, refuses to see her, even ul-
timately to attend her funeral.

What could have given root to the jealousy that
slowly but assiduously eroded their consuming
friendship? Sasha's histrionics? Her enveloping
passions? Her encroaching friendship on Peter,
Emily's husband? Or her reckless liaison with
Boris, the Russian emigré?

All or any of these conflicts could be the key to
the acerbic parting of ways, which brings this sensitive study of friendship, to its tragically
inevitable close.

'The book has a solidity and reality which only
true talent could evoke.'

The Sunday Times

More top fiction from Magnum Books

David Creed
417 05540 4 Death Watch £1.35

Philip K. Dick
417 04290 6 Confessions of a Crap Artist £1.25

George Duncan
417 05950 7 The Bloody Legionnaires £1.50

Jonathan Fast
417 04790 8 The Inner Circle £1.25

Penelope Fitzgerald
417 06010 6 Offshore £1.10

Anthony Fowles
417 06210 9 Rough Trade £1.25

Colin Free
417 02090 2 Vinegar Hill £1.25

Nicholas Guild
417 04350 3 The Summer Soldier £1.25

James Hallums
417 06430 6 Coup D'Etat £1.50

Michael Harner &
Alfred Meyer
417 05990 6 Cannibal £1.50

Ruth Harris
417 06300 8 The Last Romantics £1.75
417 03890 9 The Rich and the Beautiful £1.50
417 03860 7 Decades £1.50

John Harvey
417 05320 9 Blind £1.25
417 03940 9 Frame 95p

Ursula Holden
417 04210 8 The Cloud Catchers £1.35
417 04110 1 String Horses 95p

Christopher Isherwood
417 02850 4 A Single Man 80p
417 02720 6 Down There on a Visit £1.25
417 02710 9 Lions and Shadows 95p
417 06390 3 All the Conspirators £1.10

Ronald S. Joseph
417 05310 X The Kingdom £1.75
417 05320 7 The Power £1.95

John Jost
417 05710 5 Kangaroo Court £1.50

Howard Kaplan
417 05440 8 The Chopin Express £1.40

Robert Katz
417 03120 3 Ziggurat £1.10

Ken Kesey
417 04590 5 Sometimes a Great Notion £1.75

J. I. M. Stewart

413 36770 3	The Gaudy	£1.25
413 36780 0	Young Pattullo	85p
417 01890 8	A Memorial Service	85p
417 02190 9	The Madonna of the Astrolabe	£1.25
417 03780 5	Full Term	£1.25

Irving Stone

417 05390 8	Lust For Life	£1.50

Rowland Summerscales

417 05280 4	The Ballot	£1.25

Elliot Tokson

417 04860 2	Cavender's Balkan Quest	£1.40
417 04850 5	Appointment in Calcutta	£1.50

Harriet Waugh

417 03660 4	Mother's Footsteps	£1.00

Peter Way

417 05160 3	Sunrise	£1.25
417 06290 7	Icarus	£1.50

Ken Welsh

417 05570 6	Fear for the Hero	£1.50

Edward Whittemore

417 03410 5	Jerusalem Poker	£1.50

David Williams

417 04140 3	Second Sight	£1.25

Barbara Wood

417 03900 X	Curse This House	£1.25
417 03530 6	Hounds and Jackals	£1.25
417 03180 7	The Magdalene Scrolls	£1.25
417 04780 0	Night Trains	£1.40

Mickey Ziffren

417 06030 0	A Political Affair	£1.50

These and other Magnum Books are available at your bookshop or newsagent. In case of difficulties orders may be sent to:

Magnum Books
Cash Sales Department
P.O. Box 11
Falmouth
Cornwall TR10 109EN

Please send cheque or postal order, no currency, for purchase price quoted and allow the following for postage and packing:

U.K. 40p for first book plus 18p for second book and 13p for each additional book ordered to a maximum charge of £1.49.

B.F.P.O. & Eire 40p for the first book plus 18p for the second book and 13p per copy for the next 7 books, thereafter 7p per book.

Overseas Customers 60p for the first book plus 18p per copy for each additional book.

While every effort is made to keep prices low, it is sometimes necessary to increase prices at short notice. Magnum Books reserves the right to show new retail prices on covers which may differ from those previously advertised in the text or elsewhere.